DATE DUE			

POWER OF THREE

Also by Diana Wynne Jones

Archer's Goon

Aunt Maria

Believing is Seeing: *Seven Stories*

Castle in the Air

Dark Lord of Derkholm

Dogsbody

Eight Days of Luke

Fire and Hemlock

Hexwood

Hidden Turnings:
A Collection of Stories Through Time and Space

The Homeward Bounders

Howl's Moving Castle

The Merlin Conspiracy

The Ogre Downstairs

Stopping for a Spell

A Tale of Time City

The Time of the Ghost

Warlock at the Wheel and Other Stories

Wild Robert

Witch's Business

Year of the Griffin

Yes, Dear

THE WORLDS OF CHRESTOMANCI

Book 1: Charmed Life

Book 2: The Lives of Christopher Chant

Book 3: The Magicians of Caprona

Book 4: Witch Week

Mixed Magics: *Four Tales of Chrestomanci*

The Chronicles of Chrestomanci, Volume 1
(Contains books 1 and 2)

The Chronicles of Chrestomanci, Volume 2
(Contains books 3 and 4)

THE DALEMARK QUARTET

Book 1: Cart and Cwidder

Book 2: Drowned Ammet

Book 3: The Spellcoats

Book 4: The Crown of Dalemark

Diana Wynne Jones

POWER OF THREE

Greenwillow Books
An Imprint of HarperCollins*Publishers*

Library of Congress Cataloging-in-Publication Data
Jones, Diana Wynne.
Power of Three.
Summary: The curse on Orban spreads bad luck to the rest of the Otmounders,
the Giants, and the Dorig until three Otmounder children are born with Gifts.
[1. Fantasy.] I. Title. PZ7.J684Po3 [Fic] 77-3028 ISBN 0-688-80106-4

New Greenwillow Edition, 2003: ISBN 0-06-623743-2

FOR KIT AND JANNIE

Chapter

1

THIS IS THE STORY OF THE CHILDREN OF ADARA—of Ayna and Ceri who both had Gifts, and of Gair, who thought he was ordinary. But, as all the things which later happened on the Moor go back to something Adara's brother Orban did one summer day when Adara herself was only seven years old, this is the first thing to be told.

The Moor was never quite free of mist. Even at bright noon that bright summer day there was a smokiness to the trees and the very corn, so that it could have been a green landscape reflected in one of its own sluggish, peaty dikes. The reason was that the Moor was a sunken plain, almost entirely surrounded by low green hills. Much of it was still marsh, and the Sun drew vapors from it constantly.

Orban was swaggering along a straight green track, away from Otmound, which stood low and turfy behind him, slightly in advance of the ring of hills round the Moor. Beyond it, away to his left, was its companion, the Haunted Mound, which had a huge boulder planted crookedly on top of it, no one knew why. Orban could see it when he turned to warn his sister, loftily over his shoulder, not to go near marsh or standing water. He was annoyed with her for following him, but he did not want to get into trouble for not taking care of her.

It was one of those times when the Giants were at war among themselves. From time to time, from beyond the mists at the edge of the Moor, came the blank thump and rumble of their weapons. Orban took no notice. Giants did not interest him. The track he was on was an old Giants' road. If he looked down through the turf, he could see the great stones of it, too heavy for men to lift, and he thought he might kill a few Giants some day. But his mind was mostly taken up with Orban, who was twelve years old and going to be Chief. Orban had a fine new sword. He swished it importantly and fingered the thick gold collar round his neck that marked him as the son of a Chief.

"Hurry up, or the Dorig will get you!" he called back to Adara.

Adara, being only seven, was nervous of the Giants and their noise. It was mixed up in her mind with the sound of thunder, when, it always seemed to her, even bigger Giants rolled wooden balls around in the sky. But she did not want Orban to think she was afraid, so she hurried beside him down the green track and pretended not to hear the noise.

Orban had come out to be alone with his new sword and his own glory, but, since Adara had followed him out, he decided to unveil his glory to her a little. "I know ten times as much as you do," he told her.

"I know you do," Adara answered humbly.

Orban scowled. One does not want glory accepted as a matter of course. One wants to shock and astonish people with it. "I bet you didn't know the Haunted Mound is stuffed with the ghosts of dead Dorig," he said. "The Otmounders killed them all, hundreds of years ago. The only good Dorig is a dead Dorig."

This was common knowledge. But, since Adara really thought Orban was the cleverest person she knew, she politely said nothing.

"Dorig are just vermin," Orban continued, displeased by her silence. "Cold-blooded vermin. They can't sing, or weave, or fight, or work gold. They just lie underwater and wait to pull you under. Did you know half the hills round the Moor used to be full of people, until the Dorig killed them all off?"

"I thought that was the Plague," Adara said timidly.

"You're stupid," said Orban. Adara, seeing it had been a mistake to correct him, said humbly that she knew she was. This did not please Orban either. He sought about for some method of startling Adara into a true sense of his superiority.

The prospect was not promising. The track led among tufts of rushes, straight into misty distance. There was a hedge and a dike half a field away. A band of mist lay over a dip in the old road and a spindly blackbird was watching them from it. The blackbird would have to do. "You see that blackbird?" said Orban.

A blunt volley of noise from the Giants made Adara jump. She looked round and discovered that Otmound was already misty with distance. "Let's go home," she said.

"This is one thing you don't know. Go home if you want," said Orban. "But if that blackbird is really a Dorig, I can make it shift to its proper shape. I know the words. Shall I say them?"

"No. Let's go home," Adara said, shivering.

"Baby!" said Orban. "You watch." And he marched toward the bird, saying the words and swishing his sword in time to them.

Nothing happened, because Orban got the words wrong. Nothing whatsoever would have happened, had not Adara, who hated Orban to look a fool, obligingly said the words right for him.

A wave of cold air swept out of the hollow, making both children shiver. They were too horrified to move. The blackbird, after a frantic flutter of protest, dissolved into mist thicker and grayer than the haze around it. The mist swirled, and solidified into a shape much larger. It was the pale, scaly figure of a Dorig, right enough. It was crouched on one knee in the dip, staring toward them in horror, and holding in both hands a twisted green-gold collar not unlike Orban's or Adara's.

"Now look what you've done!" Orban snarled at Adara. But, as he said it, he realized that the Dorig was not really very large. He had been told that Dorig usually stood head and shoulders above a grown man, but this one was probably only as high as his chin. It had a weak and spindly look, too. It did not seem to have a weapon and, better still, Orban knew that those words, once spoken, would prevent the creature shifting shape until Sundown. There was no chance of it turning into an adder or a wolf.

Feeling very much better, Orban marched toward the dip, swinging his sword menacingly. The Dorig stood up, trembling, and backed away a few steps. It was rather smaller than Orban had thought. Orban began to feel brave. He scanned the thing contemptuously, and the collar flashing between its pale fingers caught his attention. It was a very fine one. Though it was the same horseshoe shape as Orban's and made of the same green gold, it was twice the width and woven into delicate filigree patterns. Orban glimpsed words, animals and flowers in the pattern. And the knobs at either end, which in Orban's collar were just plain bosses, seemed to be in the shape of owls' heads on this one. Now Orban, only the day before, had been severely slapped for fooling about with a collar rather less fine. He knew the art of making this kind had been lost long ago. No wonder the Dorig was so frightened. He had caught it red-handed with a valuable antique.

"What are you doing with that collar?" he demanded.

The Dorig looked tremulously up at Orban's face. Orban found its strange yellow eyes disgusting. "Only sunning it," it said apologetically. "You have to sun gold, or it turns back to earth again."

"Nonsense," said Orban. "I've never sunned mine in my life."

"You live more in the air than we do," the Dorig pointed out.

Orban shuddered, thinking of the way the Dorig skulked out their lives under stinking marsh water. And they were cold-blooded, too, so of course they would have to sun any gold they stole. Ugh! "Where did you get that collar?" he said sternly.

The Dorig seemed surprised that he should ask. "From my father, of course! Didn't your father give you yours?"

"Yes," said Orban. "But my father's Chief Og of Otmound."

"I expect he's a very great man," the Dorig said politely.

Orban was almost too angry to speak. It was clear

that this miserable, tremulous Dorig had never even heard of Og of Otmound. "My father," he said, "is the senior Chief on the Moor. And your father's a thief. He stole that collar from somewhere."

"He didn't—he had it made!" the Dorig said indignantly. "And he's not a thief! He's the King."

Orban stared. The Giants interrupted with another distant thump and a rumble, but Orban's mind took that in no more than it would take in what the Dorig had just said. If it was true, it meant that this wretched, skinny, scaly creature was more important than he was. And he knew that must be nonsense. "All Dorig are liars," he explained to Adara.

"I'm not!" the Dorig protested.

Adara was in dread that Orban was going to make a fool of himself, as he so often did. "I'm sure he's telling the truth, Orban," she said. "Let's go home now."

"He's lying," Orban insisted. "Dorig can't work gold, so it must all be lies."

"No, you're wrong. We have some very good goldsmiths," said the Dorig. Seeing Adara was ready to believe this, it turned eagerly to her. "I watched them make this collar. They wove words in for Power, Riches and Truth. Is yours the same?"

Adara, much impressed, fingered her own narrower, plainer collar. "Mine only has Safety. So does Orban's."

Orban could not bear Adara to be impressed by anyone

but himself. He refused to believe a word of it. "Don't listen," he said. "It's just trying to make you believe it hasn't stolen that collar." Adara looked from Orban to the Dorig, troubled and undecided. Orban saw he had not impressed her. Very well. She must be made to see who was right. He held out his hand imperiously to the Dorig. "Come on. Hand it over."

The Dorig did not understand straightaway. Then its yellow eyes widened and it backed away a step, clutching the collar to its thin chest. "But it's mine! I told you!"

"Orban, leave him be," Adara said uncomfortably.

By this time, Orban was beginning to see he might be making a fool of himself. It made him furiously angry, and all the more determined to impress Adara in spite of it. "Give me that collar," he said to the Dorig. "Or I'll kill you." To prove that he could, he swung his new sword so that the air whistled. The Dorig flinched.

"Run away," Adara advised it urgently.

Finding Adara now definitely on the side of the Dorig was the last straw to Orban. "Do, and I'll catch you in two steps!" he told it. "Then I'll kill you and take the collar anyway. So hand it over."

The Dorig knew its shorter legs were no match for Orban's. It stood where it was, clutching the collar and shaking. "I haven't even got a knife," it said. "And you stopped me shifting shape till this evening."

"That was my fault. I'm sorry," said Adara.

"Shut up!" Orban snarled at her. He made a swift left-handed snatch at the collar. "Give me that!"

The Dorig dodged. "I can't!" it said desperately. "Tell him I can't," it said to Adara.

"Orban, you know he can't," said Adara. "If it was yours, it could only be taken off your dead body."

This only made it clear to Orban that he would have to kill the creature. He had gone too far to turn back with dignity, and the knowledge maddened him further. Anyway, what business had the Dorig to imitate the customs of men? "I told you to shut up," he said to Adara. "Besides, it's only a stolen collar, and that's not the same. Give it!" He advanced on the Dorig.

It backed away from him, looking quite desperate. "Be careful! I'll put a curse on the collar if you try. It won't do you any good if you do get it."

Orban's reply was to snatch at the collar again. The Dorig side-stepped, though only just in time. But it managed, in spite of its shaking fingers, to get the collar round its neck, making it much more difficult for Orban to grab. Then it began to curse. Adara marveled, and even Orban was daunted, at the power and fluency of that curse. They had no idea Dorig knew words that way. In a shrill hasty voice, the creature laid it on the collar that the words woven in it should in future work against the owner, that Power should bring pain, Riches loss, Truth disaster, and ill luck of all kinds follow the feet and cloud the mind of the possessor. Then it ran its pale fingers along the intricate twists and pattern of the design, bringing each part it touched to bear on the curse: fish for loss by water, animals for loss by land, flowers for death of hope, knots for death of friendship, fruit for failure and barrenness, and each, as they were joined in the workmanship, to be joined in the life of the owner. At last, touching the owl's head at either end, it laid on them to be guardians and cause the collar's owner to cling to it and keep it as if it were the most precious thing he knew. When this was said, the Dorig paused. It was panting and palely flushed. "Well? Do you still want it?"

Adara was appalled to hear so much beauty spoiled and such careful workmanship turned against itself. "No!" she said. "And do get them to make you another one when you get home."

But Orban listened, feeling rather cunning. He noticed that not once had the Dorig invoked any higher Power than that of the collar itself. Without the Sun, the Moon or the Earth, even such a curse as this could only bring mild bad luck. The creature must take him for a fool. The Giants began thumping away again beyond the horizon, as if they were applauding Orban's acuteness. Determined not to be outwitted, Orban flung himself on the Dorig and got his hand hooked round the collar before it could move. "Now give it!"

"No!" The Dorig kept both hands on the collar and

pulled away. Orban swung his new sword and brought it down on the creature's head. It bowed and staggered. Adara flung herself on Orban and tried to pull him away. Orban pushed her over with an easy shove of his right elbow and raised his sword again. Beyond the horizon, the Giants thundered like rocks raining from heaven.

"All right!" cried the Dorig. "I call on the Old Power, the Middle and the New to hold this curse to my collar. May it never loose until the Three are placated."

Orban was furious at this duplicity. He brought his sword down hard. The Dorig gave a weak cry and crumpled up. Orban wrenched the collar from its neck and stood up, shaking with triumph and disgust. The Giants' noise stopped, leaving a thick silence.

"Orban, how could you!" said Adara, kneeling on the turf of the old road.

Orban looked contemptuously from her to his victim. He was a little surprised to see that the blood coming out of the pale corpse was bright red and steamed a little in the cold air. But he remembered that fish sometimes come netted with blood quite as red, and that things on a muck heap steam as they decay. "Get up," he said to Adara. "The only good Dorig is a dead Dorig. Come on."

He set off for home, with Adara pattering miserably behind. Her face was pale and stiff, and her teeth were chattering. "Throw the collar away, Orban," she implored him. "It's got a dreadful strong curse on it."

Orban had, in fact, been uneasily wondering whether to get rid of the collar. But Adara's timidity at once made him obstinate. "Don't be a fool," he said. "He didn't invoke any proper Powers. If you ask me, he made a complete mess of it."

"But it was a dying curse," Adara pointed out.

Orban pretended not to hear. He put the collar into the front of his jacket and firmly buttoned it. Then he made a great to-do over cleaning his sword, whistling, and pretending to himself that he felt much better about the Dorig than he did. He told himself he had just acquired a valuable piece of treasure; that the Dorig had certainly told a pack of lies; and that if it had told the truth, then he had just struck a real blow at the enemy, and the only good Dorig were dead ones.

"We'd better ask Father about those Powers," Adara said miserably.

"Oh no we won't!" said Orban. "Don't you dare say a word to anyone. If you do, I'll put the strongest words I know on *you*. Go on — swear you won't say a word."

His ferocity so appalled Adara that she swore by the Sun and the Moon never to tell a living soul. Orban was satisfied. He did not bother to consider why he was so anxious that no one should know about the collar. His mind conveniently sheered off from what Og would say if he knew his son had killed an unarmed and defenseless creature for the sake of a collar which was cursed.

No. Once Adara had sworn not to tell, Orban began to feel pleased with the morning's work.

It was otherwise with Adara. She was wretched. She kept remembering the look of pleasure in the Dorig's yellow eyes when it saw she was ready to believe it, and their look of despair when it invoked the Powers. She knew it was her fault. If she had not said the words right, Orban would not have killed the Dorig and brought home a curse. She could have gone on thinking the world of Orban instead of knowing he was just a cruel bully.

For Adara, almost the worst part was her disillusionment with Orban. It spread to everyone in Otmound. She looked at them all and listened to them talk, and it seemed to her that they would all have done just the same as Orban. She told herself that when she grew up she would never marry—never—unless she could find someone quite different. But quite the worst part was not being able to tell anyone. Adara longed to confess. She had never felt so guilty in her life. But she had sworn the strongest oath and she dared not say a word. Whenever she thought of the Dorig she wanted to cry, but her guilt and terror stopped her doing even that. First she dared not cry, then she found she could not. Before a month passed she was pale and ill and could not eat.

They put her to bed, and Og was very concerned. "What's on your mind, Adara?" he said, stroking her head. "Tell me."

Adara dared not say a word. It was the first time she had kept a secret from her father, and it made her feel worse than ever. She rolled away and covered her head with the blanket. If only I could cry! she thought. But I can't, because the Dorig's curse is working.

Og was afraid someone had put a curse on Adara. He was very worried, because Adara was far and away his favorite child. He had lamps lit and the right words said, to be on the safe side. Orban was terrified. He thought Adara had told Og about the Dorig. He stormed in on Adara where she lay staring up at the thatch and longing to confess and cry.

"Have you said anything?" Orban demanded.

"No," Adara said wretchedly.

"Not even to the walls or the hearthstone?" Orban asked suspiciously, since he knew this was how secrets often got out.

"No," said Adara. "Not to anything."

"Thank the Powers!" said Orban and, greatly relieved, he went off to put the collar in a safer hiding place.

Adara sat up as he went. He had put a blessed, splendid idea into her head. She might not be able to tell Og or even the hearthstone, but what was to prevent her confessing to the stones of the old Giants' road? They had watched it all anyway from under the turf. They had received the Dorig's blood. She could go and remind them of the whole story, and maybe then she could cry and feel better.

Og was pleased to see how much better Adara was that same evening. She ate a natural supper and slept properly all night. He allowed her to get up the next morning, and the next day he allowed her to go out.

This was what Adara had been waiting for. Outside Otmound she stayed for a while among the sheep, until she was sure no one was anxiously watching her. Then she ran her hardest to the old road.

It was a hot day. The gray mists of the Moor hung heavily and the trees were dark. When Adara, panting and sweating, reached the dip in the track, all she found was a column of midges circling in the air above it. There was not a trace of the Dorig—not so much as a drop of blood on a blade of grass—yet her memory of it was so keen that she could almost see the scaly body lying there.

"He looked so small!" she exclaimed, without meaning to. "And so thin! And he did bleed so!"

Her voice rang in the thick silence. Adara jumped. She looked hurriedly round, afraid that someone might have heard. But nothing moved in the rushes by the track, no birds flew, and the distant hedge was silent. Even the Giants made no sound. High above Adara's head was the little white circle of the full Moon, up in broad daylight. She knew that was a good omen. She went down on her knees in the grass and, looking through to the old stones, began her confession.

"Oh stones," she said. "I have such a terrible thing to remind you of." And she told it all, what she had said, what Orban had said and what the poor frightened Dorig had said, until she came to herself saying, "Off your dead body." Then she cried. She cried and cried, rocking on her knees with her hands to her face, quite unable to stop, buried in the relief of being able to cry at last.

A little mottled grass snake, which had been coiled all this while in the middle of the nearest clump of rushes, now poured itself down onto the warm turf and waited, bent into an S-shape, beside Adara. When she did nothing but rock and cry, it reared up with its yellow eyes very bright and wet, and uttered a soft *Hʃʃt!* Adara never heard. She was too buried in sorrow.

The snake hesitated. Then it seemed to shrug. Adara, as she wept, thought she felt a chill and a rising shadow beside her, but she was not aware of anything more until a small voice at her shoulder said imperiously, "Well, go on, can't you! What did my brother say next?"

Adara's head whipped round. She found herself face to face with a small Dorig—a very small Dorig, no bigger than she was—who was kneeling beside her on the track. His eyes were browner than the dead Dorig's, and he had a stouter, fiercer look, but she could see a family likeness between them. This one was obviously much younger. He did not seem to have grown scales yet. His pale body was clothed in a silvery sort of robe, and the gold collar on his neck was a plain, simple band, suitable for somebody very young. Adara knew he could not possibly harm her, but she was still horrified to see him.

"Go on!" commanded the small Dorig, and his yellow-brown eyes filled with angry tears. "I want to know what happened next."

"But I can't!" Adara protested, also in tears again. "I swore to Orban by the Sun and the Moon not to tell a soul, and if you heard me I've broken it. The most dreadful things will happen."

"No, they won't," said the little Dorig impatiently. "You were telling it to the stones, not to me, and I happened to overhear. What's to stop you telling the stones the rest?"

"I daren't," said Adara.

"Don't be stupid," said the Dorig. "I've been coming here and coming here for nearly a month now, and I've got into trouble every time I got home, because I wanted to find out what happened. And now you go and stop at the important part. Look." His long pale finger pointed first to the ground, then up at the white disk of the Moon, and then moved on to point to the Sun, high in the South. "Three Powers present. You were *meant* to tell, don't you see? But if you're too scared, it doesn't matter. I know it must have been your brother Orban who killed my brother and stole his collar."

"Oh, all right then," Adara said drearily. "Stones, it was my brother. I tried to stop him but he pushed me over."

"Didn't my brother say anything else?" prompted the Dorig boy.

"Yes, he put a curse on his collar," said Adara. "Stones."

"Ah!" said the Dorig boy. "I thought he must have done *something*. He wasn't much of a fighter, but he was very clever. What was the curse?"

"Stones," said Adara, and hesitated. She dared not repeat the words of the curse, well though she remembered them, for fear of bringing it on herself. She had to pick her way, telling it haltingly in her own words, through the pattern of the collar and the pattern of disaster woven into it, until she reached the owls' heads at either end. "Then he said the birds' faces were to—er—watch and make sure the one who has the collar will—not be able to let it go even though—er—it costs him the—everything he's got. Stones," she concluded, thankful to have got it over.

The small Dorig beside her frowned. "But didn't he name any Powers? I thought—"

"Oh yes. Stones," said Adara. "But not ones I know, and not until Orban tried to take the collar off him."

"What Powers? Sun, Moon—?"

"No, no. Stones," said Adara. There seemed to be no

way of mentioning the Powers without naming them. Adara dropped her voice and crossed the fingers of both hands, with her thumbs under that for added protection. "The Old Power, the Middle and the New," she whispered.

"Oh." The Dorig boy looked very awed and also very satisfied. "That's all right then. Nothing will stop the curse working now."

"Unless the Powers are appeased," Adara said. "Can't I try and appease them? It was my fault."

"I don't think so. Not all Three."

"Well, I swear to try," said Adara.

The Dorig boy seemed a little troubled by her decision. "But I don't want you to." He thought a moment. "What's your name?" he asked.

Adara simply looked at him. She knew well enough that you did not trust strangers with your name. And the worst of it was that she had already made him a present of Orban's.

"It's all right," he said irritably. "I quite like you. And I only asked so that I shouldn't swear to kill you by mistake. Mine's Hathil—truly. Now what's yours?"

Adara looked into his yellow-brown eyes and thought he was telling the truth. Having glanced at his hands, in case his fingers were crossed, and found them straight, she said, "Adara."

"Thanks," said Hathil. "Now I can swear. You can

swear to lift the curse if you want. I swear to revenge my brother by helping the curse in every way I can. I shall spill every drop of Orban's blood, except Adara's, and dedicate it to the Powers. I call on them not to be placated until none of Orban's people are left alive on the Moor. May the hidden stones bear witness, and the Sun, Moon and Earth."

Adara listened dejectedly. She did not deny Hathil had the right to swear, but it did not seem fair on all the other people who had done him no harm. When he finished, she said, "Don't you think you're rather young to swear all that?"

"Blame your brother," Hathil said stiffly. "He's a murdering brute." Adara sighed. "And I liked H—my brother," Hathil explained. "He was clever, and he told me all sorts of things. I was going to go exploring when I grew up, and now I can't, because they're going to make me King instead. They won't let me out of their sight most of the time now. But the one good thing I can see about being King is that I can order everyone to fight Orban. And I'm *not* too young to swear. Do you see those stones?" He jabbed his pale finger down at the old road. Adara looked through at the cracked old stones in some perplexity. Though they had figured largely in the conversation, she could not see quite what bearing they had on Hathil's age. "The Giants who made this road," said Hathil, "were almost destroyed by a Giant who swore to stamp them out when he was not much older than I am."

Adara was impressed. "How do you know that?"

"I learned it," said Hathil. "It pays to learn things."

Adara, in spite of her dejection, felt Hathil was right. Perhaps, if she learned and learned, she might find a way of lifting that curse before it destroyed Orban, and before Hathil was old enough to carry out his oath. "I think," she said, "you'll make an awfully good King."

Hathil looked at her suspiciously. "You seem to know so well what you're going to do," Adara explained.

"Oh, that," said Hathil. "Yes, I do."

After that Adara went home greatly comforted and worked hard to learn as much as she could. She grew up famous for her wisdom. Orban, on the other hand, grew steadily more unlucky. He broke his leg twice. When he was fourteen, he accidentally killed his best friend. When he was eighteen and had grown into a sulky young man with scraggly red hair, he fell in love with the most unpleasant woman on the Moor. Her name was Kasta. Many people thought it was the greatest misfortune yet, when Kasta married Orban. They had several children, but none lived to be a year old.

The bad luck spread from Orban to the rest of Otmound. Sheep died, hunting was bad and other food scarce. Otmound got steadily poorer. Outside, Dorig roamed in increasing numbers, and grew bolder and bolder. Otmounders soon dared not go out alone for fear of being pulled underwater.

The bad luck spread from Otmound to the other mounds. There was fire in Beckhill and flooding in Islaw. And, as Adara, for all her learning, could not learn how to lift the curse, it went on spreading, so that long before Ayna, Ceri and Gair were born, even the Giants were affected.

Chapter

2

AYNA, GAIR AND CERI WERE BORN IN GARHOLT. Their father was Gest, who was a hero. This is how Gest became famous.

Garholt was on the south of the Moor, not far from the other end of the old Giants' road. It was the largest of all the mounds and by far the most prosperous. While Chanters and Wise Women all over the Moor were shaking their heads and wondering what could be causing the growing bad luck, for many years the curse seemed to pass Garholt by.

Garholters—rather unwisely—prided themselves on their luck. They had gold, wool and hides in plenty; salt, fuel and wine. Their sheep were more numerous and in better shape than any on the Moor. Their honey was famous. Indoors, the houses were roofed with stone, and the five wells, round and stone-roofed like the houses, had been made safe from Dorig and from every other danger. The walls of the mound, below the big windows, were hung with tapestries embroidered in dark, bright colors. And Garholt could, in a quarter of an hour, muster more than a hundred of the fiercest and best-armed fighting men on the Moor—not to speak of equally warlike women and children.

But this took a good, careful Chief to maintain it. Gart, the old Chief, was just such a one. But he died quite suddenly, and his two sons were killed the same night. Hearing their father had been taken ill, Gart's two sons were hurrying home from hunting, using one of the new Giants' roads for speed. This was unwise of them. As the curse had affected the Giants too, they had grown fewer, but those few had become very violent and untrustworthy. While Gart's sons were hurrying along the road, a Giant caught and crushed them. So, as Miri the Beekeeper's wife, who was a Wise Woman, pointed out, the bad luck came to Garholt after all and left it without a Chief.

That was how Gest came to be Chief in Garholt. He was old Gart's nephew and lived in the much smaller mound of Islaw. Messages were sent to Gest at once, but the Garholters were very much afraid he would not be the good, careful Chief they were used to. Islaw people had a name for being queer and shifty—though, of course, no one in Garholt would have dreamed of calling them half-Dorig the way the Otmounders did. Still, Islaw people were known to be different. And Gest's Islaw father had been a Chanter, who were odd people at the best of times. Then it was learned that Gest was bringing his own Chanter, a man called Banot, with him. From being dubious, the Garholters became indignant. Weren't the Garholt Chanters good enough for Gest? Or what?

When Gest arrived, everyone was relieved to find him fair, handsome, jolly, and not at all peculiar. He was a big man, as a Chief should be, and obviously a seasoned fighter. Nor did he seem particularly clever. The Chanter, Banot, though his thin face had the dreamy look of his profession, seemed to have no harm in him either. It soon became clear that Gest had brought him simply because he and Banot were bosom friends. The Garholters all heaved sighs of relief and began to maneuver Gest into marrying Tille, the granddaughter of old Gart. Nothing came of that. Gest was nice to Tille—as he was to everyone—but it was Banot who fell in love with Tille and married her.

Gest had not been a month in Garholt when a messenger arrived from Og of Otmound. Og greeted the new Chief and wanted a band of fighting men from Garholt at once to help him fight the Dorig. Hearing this, Gest smiled a wide, jolly smile. Banot, who knew that smile, looked apprehensive. But the older and more responsible Garholters, who did not know it, took Gest aside and gave him the benefit of their advice. They did not know then that Gest was a hero.

"See here," said the oldest Chanter, "Og has no right to take that tone with you. He may be the senior Chief, but we've made no treaty with him. Send me back to say no."

"He's giving you orders because he can't afford to pay for our help," said the goldsmith. "But we Garholters have our pride." He looked round, with satisfaction, at the gold glimmering on people's necks and wrists.

"I'll say no very tactfully," said the Chanter.

"Why is he so set on fighting the Dorig?" Gest asked.

"It's the natural order of things," Miri, the Beekeeper's wife, told him. "Men against Dorig, Giants against men."

"They say the only good Dorig is a dead Dorig," added the oldest smith.

The Beekeeper, who always had news, said, "The Dorig have been pulling their people and sheep underwater for years. A while back, they took to waiting outside Otmound in their own shapes and attacking anyone they met. Og warned everyone who went outside to carry a thornbush against them, but Dorig don't seem to be afraid of thorns the way they used to be. Their latest trick is to pretend to be game when the Otmounders are out hunting: let a man chase them, then shift to their true shape and kill him. You know their crafty ways."

"Well, no," Gest said apologetically. "I've only met a Dorig once and it ran away before I could speak to it."

"Then you have a lot to learn," said the smith.

Gest smiled again. "I know I have. That's why I think I'd better go over the Moor and talk to Og."

To the consternation of all Garholt, this is just what Gest did. He sent Og's messenger back to say he was coming, and then prepared to set out himself with only Banot for company. Everyone implored him to consider. They reminded him there was no one left to be Chief after him. They said, if he must go, he should take twenty good men with him to protect him from Dorig. They told him fearsome tales about the way the Dorig sacrificed their victims and hung them up to the Sun.

Gest attended to none of it. He was quite pleasant, but completely firm. The Garholters discovered that their new Chief was the most obstinate man on the Moor. They respected him greatly for that, but it made them all the more anxious to have him back safe again. They took Banot aside and made him promise to see Gest was safe.

"I'll do what I can," said Banot. "But you don't know Gest."

They had to be content with that. Everyone anxiously watched the two set off along the line of the old road. The early Sun glinting on the gold collar of each was the only bright thing about them. Their clothes and weapons were dull and serviceable. Banot's harp was shut in a dingy traveling case, so that it would not catch the attention of Giants. When the two had disappeared into the mists, the Garholters retired to the mound and spoke words for their safety. Then they waited.

Two days later, to their dismay, Banot came back alone. He was vague-eyed and abstracted, and Tille was the only one who was wholeheartedly glad to see him. The rest crowded round him, demanding to know where Gest was.

"In Otmound, I suppose," Banot said vaguely. "He sent me home."

Though they were all relieved to hear Gest was still alive, they wanted to know what Og had said, why Banot had been sent back and what Gest was doing.

Banot seemed tired. "Gest always does things his own way," was all he would say. "Someone bring me a drink."

Miri, the Beekeeper's wife, hurried up with beer, hoping it would loosen Banot's tongue. Tille helped him take the harp off his back. The case came open as she did so, and she noticed that one of the harpstrings had broken. It had been replaced by a queer pale length of gut, which gave off a strong smell of glue.

"Where did you come by that peculiar string?" she said.

"Oh that—I had to take what I could get," said Banot. He drank some beer, seemed to recover and began to laugh a little. "I've been singing and playing and talking for hours," he said. "I've no voice left and I ache all over."

"Was this in Otmound?" said Tille, glad to hear things were so merry there.

Banot shook his head. "No. By the roadside. We met some friends, Gest and I, while we were on our way—no one you know, but great fellows—and I stopped over with them on the way back." He laughed. "The best of friends."

"But when is Gest coming?" everyone wanted to know.

"In a day or so," said Banot, yawning. "If he comes at all. And he may be in a hurry." With that, he laughed and yawned and staggered off to sleep, leaving no one much the wiser. Nor would he say any more the next day.

Gest arrived in the middle of the following night. The first anyone knew of it was when Gest turned and shouted the words that sealed the main door against enemies. Startled by the shout and the thump of the door, people scrambled from their beds. Someone had the sense to raise the light, whereupon everyone stared in amazement. Gest had brought with him a beautiful young woman, tall and pale, with hair as black as peat. Both of them were splashed with mud to the eyebrows and almost too much out of breath to speak. Gest no longer wore his golden collar. The woman, on the other hand, wore a collar richer and more intricate than any-one in Garholt had seen before in their lives.

"Speak the rest of the doors shut!" Gest panted to the first person to arrive.

The boy scampered to do as he was told. The rest crowded up, shouting, "Why? Is it Dorig?"

Gest had used up all his breath and could only shake his head. The young woman shyly answered instead. "It's my brother, Orban. I'm Og's daughter, Adara."

This caused gasps and murmurs. It was well known that Og loved his daughter more than he loved himself. Adara was said to be the most beautiful woman on the Moor, and the wisest who ever lived. And it looked as if Gest had carried her off.

"War," said the Beekeeper gloomily. "This means war."

"Doesn't," said Gest, still very short of breath. "Did three tasks for her. Marry her tomorrow. Got to rest now. Get a feast ready."

"Just like that!" Miri said indignantly, as she and Tille led Adara off to Tille's house to rest. "Does he think we can have a feast ready in five minutes?"

"Of course you can't," said Adara. "I don't suppose he thought. I'll go back and tell him to put it off, shall I?"

This of course put both Tille and Miri on their mettle. "You'll do no such thing!" said Tille. "We'll manage."

"Besides, if he's carried you off, it's not proper to wait," said Miri.

"He didn't carry me off. I came of my own accord," Adara protested.

"What you thought of it doesn't count," Miri said severely. "Now you get to bed and get some rest. We'll see to it."

By the time she and Tille had put Adara to bed, they

had both lost their hearts to her. Neither of them blamed Gest for losing his. "Or his head into the bargain," Miri said sourly. Adara was gentle and sympathetic and not in the least proud. But the greatest point in her favor, Miri and Tille agreed, was that though she was supposed to be the Wisest Woman ever, you would never have known it from the way she talked. "I can't abide Wise Women who are always letting you know what a fool you are," said Miri, from bitter experience, being a Wise Woman herself. "I wish she'd told us what happened though. Now we'll have to wait for brother Orban to tell us."

Orban arrived as she spoke. Garholt quivered with the noise. From the shouts and thumps at the main door, it sounded as if half the men of Otmound had come with Orban.

Gest, refreshed with a long drink of beer, took all the men of Garholt out of the side doors. The two bands confronted one another under a full Moon, and everyone inside the mound waited for the battle to begin.

Orban, who had grown into a lumpish, sulky man, stepped out in front of the massed Otmounders and scowled at Gest. "I want to speak to you alone," he said.

The Garholters were beginning to get used to Gest. They were not surprised when he agreed. The Otmounders, however, were clearly very surprised. They stared uneasily after Orban and Gest as the two climbed to the top of the mound together. But Orban made no attempt to hit Gest. Instead, he spoke to him in an undertone, savagely and urgently. Nobody heard what he said. Once Gest, who had been shaking his head at Orban every so often, put both hands up to his neck, with the gesture of a man about to remove his collar. Then he seemed to remember his collar was gone, and took his hands away.

"No, the *other* one, you fool!" Orban was heard to say. "The one Kasta—" But then he realized other people could hear and lowered his voice again.

"Who's Kasta?" the younger smith whispered to Banot.

"Orban's wife," whispered Banot. "Awful woman. She—"

He was interrupted by a roar from Orban. "GIANTS! *You*—!"

Gest said something loudly at the same time. Orban seemed to calm down. He stood under the Moon with his arms folded, growling sullenly at Gest, and Gest seemed to be watching him warily. One thing at least was clear: Orban did not like Gest and Gest did not much care for Orban. Gest said something. Then, to everyone's surprise, the two of them shook hands. Orban turned and came jauntily down the mound, looking as if a weight was off his mind. He smiled, and waved airily to the seventy Otmounders waiting below Garholt.

"Right, everyone," he said. "That's it. We're going."

"Going? Without Adara?" one of them asked blankly.

"Yes. I've told Gest she can stay. He did three tasks for her after all," Orban said gaily. He shepherded them back along the roadline. They went reluctantly, and it was plain they were very puzzled indeed.

So that was how Gest came to marry Adara. As to quite how he had managed it, the Garholters were mystified. But from what they had heard so far, it was clear to them that Gest was a hero and a Chief straight out of the old stories. Three tasks! They were agog with pride and curiosity. Though some people took the reasonable line that this kind of thing was well enough in the days of King Ban, but what was needed nowadays was a careful, steady Chief, nobody could wait to find out exactly what Gest had done to win Adara.

But neither Gest nor Adara would talk about it, and, if Banot knew, he was not saying either. People kept their eyes and ears open for hints all through the bustle of preparing the wedding feast, working a new gold collar for Gest, making clothes for Adara, and the hundred other things necessary, but no one learned anything until the wedding feast was in full swing. Then Miri happened to come up with wine for Banot, just as Adara approached him from the other side.

Adara looked more beautiful than ever in her wedding dress, but she also looked troubled. "Banot," she said. "What do you know of the Old Power, the

Middle and the New?"

Banot, like all the Chanters, was working hard, playing for the dancing and singing. His face had been flushed and shiny. But Miri saw, when he looked up at Adara, his face was pale. "Those are Dorig things," he said. "You shouldn't talk of them at a time like this."

"Just tell me if you know how to appease them," Adara said coaxingly.

Banot would not look at her. He stared straight ahead, with his fingers ready on a chord. "I only know one way," he said. "And that's by sacrifice. And if I told you what kind and how made, we'd have to stop the feast and chant for luck until the new Moon." Then he struck the chord and began playing to prevent Adara saying any more.

Adara turned away, looking appalled. It was some time before she seemed happy again. And Miri was equally upset. It was well known how the Dorig sacrificed. Sometimes hunting parties would come upon the corpses of their sacrifices hanging in the Sun to rot. If you had the bad luck to find one, the only thing to do was to stop and use the very strongest of the strong words, or the Dorig Powers would fasten on you. Giants sometimes sacrificed in the same way, but they only used moles, weasels and other small animals, whereas the Dorig used men, women and Dorig. Miri, not knowing why Adara should ask otherwise, began to have a suspicion that Gest or Adara had invoked the Dorig Powers to help Gest perform his three tasks. She became more anxious than anyone to know just what had happened in Otmound.

The story came out gradually, piece by piece — nobody really knew how. It seemed that Gest and Adara had fallen in love as soon as they set eyes on one another. Gest promptly asked Og if he could marry Adara. Now Og was hoping Gest would bring him the men of Garholt to fight the Dorig, so he did not want to offend him. But neither could he bear to have his beloved Adara go right away to the other side of the Moor. He had been in great distress. "The silly old woman!" Miri said contemptuously. No one in Garholt thought much of Og.

During a sleepless night, Og hit on the notion of making Gest do three tasks to win Adara's hand. He had an idea this would appeal to Gest's adventurous spirit. But he would make the tasks totally impossible. When Gest failed to do them, Og would be very sorry and very kind, keep Adara to himself and still keep Gest friendly enough to help him fight the Dorig. As Og hoped, Gest was delighted to perform three tasks for Adara, but, since he saw Og was going to refuse to let him have Adara if he could, Gest sent Banot home, so that no one could say he had used a Chanter's help.

Og thought he had chosen cunningly. He announced that the first task was to answer riddles. He could see Gest was a man of action, not a thinker. Anyone in

Garholt or Islaw could have told him that, too. Gest could not answer riddles to save his life. Yet Gest had stood in front of Og for a whole day steadily answering all the riddles Og and his Chanters could devise, and getting them right. Perhaps love had sharpened his wits. But no one in Garholt thought it was natural.

Og was forced to concede Gest had done the first task. He took care to make the second as difficult as he could. Gest was to fetch him a gold collar off the neck of a Dorig. Orban and a number of other Otmounders had protested, saying Dorig did not have gold collars. And Adara had made matters more impossible by calling out to Gest, "I shall never marry you if you kill a Dorig! Never!" Yet Gest had simply smiled and gone out on to the Moor to try his luck. In the early evening, he returned with a magnificent collar.

At this, Og took fright and made the third task truly monstrous. Even Gest had despaired at first. Adara had been so upset that Og gave her the magnificent Dorig collar to console her. Og said Gest was to move the great boulder from the top of the Haunted Mound, drag it a quarter of a mile and put it on top of Otmound. The boulder was as big as a house and locked in place with words. Ten men — twenty — could hardly have shifted it. But Gest had done it. Around midnight, he had come in and invited Og out to look. And there was the great stone, perched on top of Otmound, and the marks of it all the way across the field from the Haunted Mound.

Og nearly went mad. By then, he was so frightened of Gest that he wanted nothing more to do with him. He refused utterly to let him marry Adara and ran away inside Otmound. This made Gest angry. He went after Og and found Adara coming out. The two of them ran most of the way across the Moor with Orban in pursuit.

Miri wondered very much about some parts of this story. It was queer enough that Gest had been able to answer riddles. But then he had apparently killed a Dorig for its collar, and Adara had not only still married him, but wore the collar every day. It was beautifully and intricately worked, in a filigree of twisted signs and symbols around a pattern of Power, Riches and Truth, all flowing like a song into the exquisitely modeled birds' heads of the bossed ends. Miri knew it could not have come from any Dorig. It was a collar from the Old Days, such as a King might have worn. Miri thought Gest must have traded his own missing collar for it.

But then there was the matter of the stone from the Haunted Mound. Miri, remembering Gest's father had been a Chanter, had some hopes that it was an illusion which would not last. But, after the wedding, Og graciously forgave Gest and Adara, and there was more coming and going between Garholt and Otmound. Miri went and saw the stone on top of Otmound for herself. It was really there. The marks where it had been dragged from the Haunted Mound had not yet grown over. Miri was shaken, because she knew it could not have been done without the aid of some mighty Power.

"Well, I wish Og joy of it, that's all," she said. "I wouldn't like a great thing like that on top of my mound. Whatever words I said, I'd be afraid of it coming through and squashing me."

Og might have forgiven Gest, but Gest was clearly still angry with Og. He refused outright to help Og against the Dorig. Og and Orban were forced to help themselves. In the autumn, having carefully armed and drilled the Otmounders, they attacked a huge body of Dorig who were moving east across the Moor. The Dorig were taken by surprise. Since words had stopped them shifting shape, they fled frantically south and west. Islaw saw them coming and hurriedly sealed its gates. But the Dorig did not attack. They went into the river near Islaw, and that was the last of them for some time. The Moor became much more peaceful.

Luck seemed to return to Otmound after that. The people there grew richer. Orban's wife Kasta at last had a baby which did not die. She called him Ondo. He was a fine, healthy child, but Kasta nevertheless fussed over him as if he was the most delicate baby alive.

"She makes me *ill*!" Miri said, after a particularly tiresome visit.

"She had four babies before, and they all died," Adara reminded her.

"So she did!" said Miri. "Which makes this one *so* unusually gifted, *particularly* intelligent"—she mimicked Kasta's harsh voice—"*so exactly* cut out to be a Chief! How can she tell? Just let her wait till *your* son's born, that's all. *I'll* have the nursing of him, and *I'll* show her!" Though she was the Beekeeper's wife and a Wise Woman, Miri was determined to nurse Adara's son. There was quite a struggle for that honor, since everyone expected that son to be special, but Miri won the struggle because she was a Wise Woman.

But when Adara's baby was born, it was a girl. Miri was speechless. She could think of nothing to say for a whole hour. Then she said, "Don't you dare let her marry that Ondo!"

"No fear!" said Gest. He was enchanted with his daughter. He called her Ayna and walked about holding her proudly. She was fair and rosy and very like him.

Miri swallowed her disappointment, looked after Ayna carefully and waited for the next baby.

He came the following year. Adara called him Gair. "Ah!" said Miri proudly. "Just look at him, Gest."

Gest looked and was rather startled. Gair was dark and pale, like Adara, and stared solemnly up at Gest with big gray eyes. "Why doesn't he smile?" said Gest.

"They don't at first," said Adara. "Even Ayna didn't."

"I expect you're right," said Gest. All the same, he remained a little awed by the strange, solemn baby, even when Gair was old enough to smile.

Two years later, Adara had another son. Gest, looking resigned, took Ayna in to have a look at him. Miri, chuckling with pride, unwrapped a baby with huge blue eyes and hair as dark as Gair's. "Ceri," she said. "Isn't he a fine one?"

"Isn't he a bit pretty for a boy?" Gest said doubtfully. He would have preferred another girl. Miri scolded him. She was delighted. Whatever Ondo's nurse, Fandi, said, Miri knew they had done three times as well as Kasta.

The children grew up with all the other children, tumbling and quarreling in the Sun that streamed into Garholt. It was a good time to grow up in. In spite of being the hero of three tasks, Gest proved the careful Chief everyone had hoped for. Garholt prospered, and there was plenty to eat. Adara taught the children. Miri spoiled all three, particularly Ceri. In the evenings, Miri told them the stories from the tapestries round the walls. Their favorite was the newest: How Gest Performed Three Tasks to Win Adara. Miri always told it to them as it was generally told. She never hinted at her doubts, but she felt a little guilty at the way they drank it up and asked for it again and again.

Chapter

3

ONE DAY, WHEN GAIR WAS FIVE AND AYNA SIX, Gair said wistfully, "When shall I be allowed to go hunting?"

"Next full Moon, of course," said Ayna.

Gair looked at her incredulously. She was standing very straight and her face was grave and serious. He could see she meant it. Without bothering to ask how she knew, he trotted off to Gest and told him he was coming on the next hunt.

Gest looked up from lashing a spearhead and laughed. "Whatever put that into your head?"

Gair did not like being laughed at. His mouth trembled. "Ayna says I'm going. She told me."

Ayna had followed Gair out of interest. Gest asked her angrily what she meant by putting such nonsense into Gair's head. "It's not nonsense. It's true," Ayna said. She was quite certain.

Gest opened his mouth to tell her what happened to children who made up stories. Before he could speak,

Miri dashed forward. "Ask her something else!" she said excitedly. "Go on!"

Gest was annoyed. Miri was far too fond of bobbing up and preventing him scolding his children. "Ask her yourself," he said crossly.

"All right," said Miri. "Ayna, who's going to be the next person to come into Garholt?"

Ayna again stood straight and grave. "Uncle Orban. He's hurt himself."

"Of all the — !" Gest began.

Before he could say more, Orban tottered through the doorway above them with a broken arm. "Met a Giant," he said miserably. "Your place was nearest." Seeing the way Gest was staring, he said irritably, "I'm not a ghost!"

Gest pulled himself together and welcomed Orban properly. He helped Orban to Adara to have the arm set. Miri bustled round in the greatest excitement. It was clear to her that Ayna had the Gift of Sight, which had not been known in Garholt for two generations. Better still, since Orban was here, she knew Kasta would hear of it at once. Gest and Adara both took a little more convincing. But, after careful questioning, they agreed that Ayna really did seem to have Sight. Gest went to the goldsmith to order the double-twisted collar Ayna was now entitled to.

The news caused great excitement. People crowded

round Ayna to ask her things. One or two people, knowing that the Gifts often went by families, hopefully asked Gair questions, too. Gair was unable to answer. He was ashamed. He tried saying the first thing that came into his head, but they soon saw through that and lost interest in him. Gair began to see that he was just ordinary.

Adara caught sight of him standing to one side of the excited group round Ayna, looking humble and sad. She pointed him out to Gest.

"I'll take him out hunting to make it up to him," Gest said without thinking.

So Ayna's first prophecy was fulfilled. To his huge delight, Gair was taken on a real hunt. He thought he enjoyed it enormously. He toiled in the rear, his calves aching with the effort, bitten by midges and shivering in the night mist. The marsh underfoot made his boots three times their usual weight and his feet were numb. But he still thought he was enjoying it.

No one else on the hunt enjoyed it at all. It seemed to them that they were continually going back for Gair, waiting for Gair, telling Gair to be quiet, explaining things to Gair or finding Gair in the way when they wanted to shoot. Twice they lost him completely in the tall marsh grass. It grew as high as a man's head, and to Gair it was like a bamboo forest. Thoroughly exasperated, Gest told one of the girls to look after Gair. She did her best, but Gair was too proud to be carried and would not hold her hand. He kept asking questions, too, and he was too young to understand the answers.

The full Moon set. Gest, by this time, had sworn never to bring Gair on a hunt again. He would have gone straight home, except that because of Gair, they had caught next to nothing. They had to go on. At dawn, they had caught sufficient, but they were far out in the marshes. Gair did not think he was enjoying himself any more. He was tired out and slower than ever. Gest debated waiting for night and decided it would be too much for Gair. He trusted to the long white grasses to hide them and they turned back.

In the middle of the morning, they met a party of Giants.

Gair could not think what was going on. The ground seemed to be quivering. Agitated birds went whirling up all around him, but he was suddenly quite alone. There was not a soul, not a dog, in sight. All he could see was grass.

Gest looked between the grasses and saw Gair standing in full view, directly in the path of the Giants. Cursing, he leaped up, threw himself on Gair and rolled with him into the damp bushes beside the nearest dike.

"What—?" Gair said loudly. Gest pushed his face into the ground.

The booming voice of a Giant said, "What was that? It looked like an animal." It sounded alarmed.

"Rabbit," suggested another thunderous voice.

"Too big," rumbled another. "More like a badger. Let's see if we can catch it."

Three or four of the Giants rushed trampling along the edge of the dike. They had thick sticks, and they jabbed about with them, shouting. The bushes whipped about. The ground shook. Gair lay with most of Gest on top of him, most uncomfortable and utterly terrified. If he moved his face round in the peaty earth, he could see pieces of the bank falling off into the dike. If he screwed round the other way and squinted, he saw twigs wildly shaking. Once, an enormous blurred foot came heavily down beyond the twigs. Gair winced. The size of the body above that foot must have been horrendous.

Luckily, the Giants had mistaken the place where Gest and Gair were lying. After crashing about for five minutes or so, they became bored and took themselves off, laughing and rumbling, away along the dike. Eventually, the bank ceased to quake. Gest moved cautiously. Gair bobbed up from underneath, red and indignant with terror.

"Those were Giants! Why didn't you kill them?"

Gest wondered how to explain that the only thing to do with Giants was to leave them alone. "There are far more Giants than people," he said. "If we harmed a Giant, they'd kill everybody on the Moor. Get up."

Gair realized he had said something stupid. That, and

the thought of hundreds of huge Giants, so depressed him that tears began to trickle down his face.

Gest picked him up and carried him the rest of the way home. As they went, he went on trying to explain about Giants. "They're stronger than we are, Gair, and they have a great deal of magic, which makes them very dangerous. And they steal children. If they'd seen you standing there, they'd have taken you away with them. I know. They stole a little girl from Islaw."

"Why?" said Gair. He was growing sleepy and demanding with jerking about in his father's warm arms.

"They seem to think they can bring children up better," Gest explained.

"Tell them they can't," Gair suggested.

Gest sighed and explained, several times, that one had nothing to do with Giants. Nothing. "And certainly not with the Giants near here," he said. "You see—well—they're under a curse. It makes them even more dangerous."

"Why?" said Gair, and fell asleep before Gest answered. He slept the rest of the way back and did not wake until Gest dumped him into Miri's arms. Gest wondered if Gair would remember anything he had said. He rather thought not. But he was wrong. Gair, though he did not talk about them, thought about Giants often. What puzzled him particularly was the uneasy, almost guilty, way his father had talked about a curse. But he did not ask to go hunting again.

In fact, there was more than enough to do in and around Garholt. Children picked fruit, helped with the Feasts and played. They were given lessons by Wise Women and Chanters. Adara taught them to read. Gest himself saw to it that Ayna, Gair and Ceri learned to handle weapons. They learned how to drop out of sight if Giants were near. "Keep still and rely on your clothes to hide you," Miri impressed on them. "Giants don't see much. Your coats are the color of the marsh and Moor, so drop and lie. Don't stir a finger and you're safe." Before long, Gair could do this without needing to think. He was ashamed of the way he had behaved on the hunt.

The other early lessons were about Dorig. They were warned, over and over, never to go near standing water unless it had been made safe. They were warned to watch for the thorn trees that showed water was safe from Dorig. The first words of power they learned were those which made water safe. They were made to say them till they could say them in their sleep. They were told, almost as often, that Dorig were shape-shifters and never to trust any animal they did not know. But they were not taught the words to shift a Dorig to its true shape. Adara forbade it.

Meanwhile, it was discovered that Ayna's Sight was very clear indeed. She could foretell the future as far on as anyone could test. She was consulted frequently. She often talked to Gair about it, usually at night, sitting up very straight in bed because the responsibility weighed on her. For the Gift was quite as mysterious to Ayna as it was to anyone else.

"You see, I don't *know* the future," she would explain. "You have to ask me a question. And then I know the answer, without knowing I knew. And I don't know any more until someone asks me something else."

Gair listened humbly and nodded. When Ayna talked like this, he knew how ordinary he was.

"The worst of it is," Ayna said, "they can ask me the wrong question. I won't know they have. Suppose I'm asked if food will be plentiful, and I say yes. And it turns out that there's plenty of food because the Giants have killed most of us. It worries me. Do you see?"

Gair nodded and tried to feel sympathetic, as far as an ordinary person could. But it was hard not to feel saddened, too. And it was worse when Ceri's Gift was discovered.

Ayna and Gair had known about Ceri's Gift for nearly a year before Miri discovered it. It was very useful to be able to say, "Ceri, where's our ball?" and be told it had stuck between the second and third stones of the fourth well. But they kept it to themselves. Ayna said, "Don't tell a soul. The little beast will get more spoiled than ever if they find out he's useful."

Ceri was certainly spoiled. He had big blue eyes, clustering black curls and an enchanting smile. He made shameless use of all three. He could get exactly what he wanted from anyone, from Gest to the stupid young man who worked the bellows in the forge. But Ceri was no fool. He very soon grasped that no one else could find things as he could. Unknown to Ayna and Gair, he began to make shameless use of that, too. One day, Miri found him in a ring of older children. Ceri was saying, "Tops and balls are a handful of nuts—a *real* handful, Lanti, not just a few—but I need a honeycake to find your knife, Brad."

Miri's sister had had Finding Sight. It was not as uncommon as Ayna's Gift. She tumbled at once to what was going on. She broke up the group and led Ceri by one ear to where Gest was. "Do you know what this child of yours has been up to?" she said.

Gest looked down into Ceri's blue eyes. "What was it?" he said, doing his best to sound stern. No one but Ayna and Gair found it easy to be angry with Ceri. But Gest pretended fairly well. Ceri's knees knocked.

"I caught him asking a whole honeycake to find a knife!" said Miri. "And for all I know he may not have Finding Sight at all. Ask him where that spearhead you lost is. Go on."

Gest had to try hard not to laugh at Ceri's enterprise, but he asked, pretty sternly. Ceri quaked and wondered if he dared lie. But all Sight forces you to be truthful—unless you hold your tongue, and Ceri dared not hold his. "Gair's got it," he quavered. "He's using it to dig with, by the beehives."

Gest strode to the hive-gate, snapped out the words and stormed outside. Sure enough, there was Gair, using the head of a prime hunting-spear as a trowel to make mud pies with. The bees came out of their clay tunnels to defend Gair, saw it was Gest and went in again. The upshot was that Gair was in dire trouble, and Ceri was given a double-twisted collar like Ayna's.

"I couldn't help it! Really!" Ceri protested when Gair came to hand some of his punishment on to Ceri.

"He probably couldn't," said Ayna. "A Gift makes you tell when you're asked. Just hit him once to stop him getting spoiled."

Gair was forbearing. He hit Ceri twice. He was fairly sure nothing would stop Ceri getting even more spoiled anyway. And certainly the presents Ceri got to find things after that would have corrupted Ban the Good himself.

"He'll be as odious as Ondo if this goes on," Ayna said gloomily.

"No one could be," said Gair.

In fact, Ceri stayed much the same. He had had all the attention he could wish for before his Gift was discovered, and he was perfectly happy. It was Gair who changed. He was now convinced to the core of his being that he was unspeakably ordinary. He suspected that his parents, Gest particularly, were secretly disappointed in him. He took to spending long hours on his favorite windowsill, one hand hooked into his plain gold collar, brooding over what he could do about it.

It was a splendid windowsill. Gair had been going there ever since he was large enough to make the climb. It looked out above the beehives to a wide view across the Moor. Even before Ceri's Gift was discovered, Gair had liked sitting there alone, watching the Giants' flat fields, the woods and the ever-waving marsh grasses change with the changing weather. From it, you could watch a rainstorm march clear across the Moor, in a sky-tall column of gray and white. The bees buzzed beneath the window on the outside. On the inside, the looms clacked steadily and the people at them talked and laughed. You had the advantage of smelling the Moor under rain and Sun and, at the same time, all the homely smells of Garholt: wool, cooking, smoke, leather, people. But now Gair spent so much time there that everyone came to think of that windowsill as his place. Few people would have climbed up there unless he let them.

After some weeks of brooding, it occurred to Gair that one way to stop being ordinary was to have wisdom, like his mother. People came from all over the Moor to consult Adara. And she was only too willing to teach him. Gair was so fired by this notion that, for one wild moment, he had impossible dreams of becoming a Chanter. But he knew that was out of the question. He was not very musical, and he would be Chief after Gest. Chiefs were never Chanters. But anyone could have wisdom, if they were willing to learn.

Gair threw himself into learning. Much of it was words. Gair already knew the simplest and most practical words, which many people never got beyond: words for fastening and unfastening, entering and leaving, invoking and dismissing, blessing and cursing. Now he learned new words and the rules for combining them in new ways. Before long, he had overtaken even Banot's son, Brad, and knew how to fix the green gold so that it could be worked; how to make food grow and herbs heal; how to give cloth the power of concealment; and how to divine weather. Then, to his delight, Adara began to show him something of the rules behind all this, the more hidden knowledge of the dangerous, narrow path between Sun, Moon and planets, without which the stronger words were useless. Gair began dimly to see that one could call on the power in everything, provided one knew when and how to do it.

Adara was often very pleased with him. Whenever he saw she was pleased, Gair tried to coax his mother to tell him something he and Ayna had always longed to know: the story of Gest's three tasks from her point of view.

But Adara never would tell him. She simply laughed and changed the subject.

What with Adara's teaching and Gest's instruction, Gair was said to be very accomplished. The time came when the children and young dogs were taken out on a training hunt, and Gair was expected to do well. It was very different from Gair's first hunt. They had the good luck to meet one of the rare herds of deer that sometimes strayed down into the Moor. Gair staggered home under a heavy hind he had killed himself. His parents were pleased. Banot praised him. Gair was proud and pleased himself. But it made no real difference. He still knew he was ordinary.

No one else thought he was. The opinion in Garholt was that Gair was the most extraordinary of Gest's three children. People said confidently that when Gair had done all the thinking he needed and left his windowsill, you would not find a better Chief. They would not have believed Gair if he told them he was ordinary. And he was much too reserved to do that.

Gest found Gair extraordinary, too. He had never got over his first awe of Gair as a solemn baby. Then Gair, instead of behaving like other children, chose to spend hours sitting on that windowsill of his. "What's the *matter* with the boy?" Gest kept asking Adara.

"Nothing," Adara always answered. "He just likes to be alone."

Gest could not understand it. He liked to live surrounded by other people. Things he did not understand always irritated him. He tried to be fair, but he could not manage to show as much affection to Gair as he did to Ayna and Ceri. Gair saw it. He knew his father was disappointed with him for turning out so ordinary. He went on to his windowsill all the more to avoid Gest. And the longer he spent there, the less Gest could understand him. By the time Gair was twelve, no two people in Garholt understood one another less than Gest and Gair.

Shortly after Gair's twelfth birthday, Ondo came to pay a visit in Garholt. With him came Kasta his mother, Fandi his nurse and his two friends Scodo and Pad.

"I wish Ondo were more likable," Ayna sighed. "We might get him to tell us about Father's three tasks."

But Ondo was not likable. All they ever got out of him on that subject was a knowing sneer, and sniggers from Scodo and Pad. Ondo detested his three cousins. In Ondo's opinion, no one was so fine a person as Ondo of Otmound, and he could not tolerate anyone who threatened to dim that fine person's glory. Ayna and Ceri dimmed it by being Gifted, so he hated them heartily. But it was Gair he hated most. Thanks to Miri's boasting, Ondo knew Gair was supposed to be the most extraordinary of the three, and that was reason enough to detest him. But it is probable that, even without Miri's boasting, Ondo would have concentrated his hatred on Gair. The Gifts set Ayna and Ceri apart—but what business had Gair, with no more Gifts than Ondo, to look at Ondo in that solemn, speculative way? It made big, strong Ondo feel small. It also gave him a hazy but certain knowledge that Gair was more easily hurt than the other two. That, and the fact that Gair was more than a year younger and half a head shorter than Ondo, made him the ideal cousin to pick on.

This visit, with Scodo and Pad to support him— "Those two horrid toadies," Ayna called them—Ondo picked on Gair all the time. He gave Gair no peace. It was not only sly arm-twisting and slyer kicks. It was a stream of hints, jeers and abuse: hints that Gair was not quite right in the head, jeers at the way he liked to sit on his windowsill and reminders that Gest had come from poor, queer Islaw. "You get your bad blood from Islaw," Ondo said. "Are you quite sure you can't shift shape?" Ondo took care never to be far away from his burly friends, or from Kasta or Fandi, so that Gair never had a chance to hit him. He just had to endure it. He was miserable. Ayna and Ceri were furious on his behalf, but there was nothing they could do either. They all counted the days until Ondo went home.

There were only three days left when Ondo came into the house with Fandi, looking for Ceri, because Fandi had lost a good gold thimble. Ayna, Gair and Ceri were all there, trying to keep out of Ondo's way. All three sighed when they saw Ondo.

"Your thimble's in your pocket," Ceri said coldly to Fandi. Gest had forbidden him actually to ask for presents, but he thought Fandi might have offered him something. Everyone else did.

Ondo said patronizingly to Gair, "Of course, you haven't any Gifts, have you?"

That hit Gair so much on the raw he could not answer. Ayna said quickly, "Neither have you!"

Ondo saw he had hurt Gair. He was far too pleased to bother with Ayna. He looked at his fingernails and polished them carelessly on his coat. "Oh," he said, "a man in my position doesn't need Gifts."

Gair thought of himself taking Ondo by his gold collar, rushing out of the house and upstairs with him and plunging him face-foremost into the nearest beehive. If Fandi had not been there, he would have tried to do it. Fandi was nodding and smiling as if they were all the greatest of friends, but Gair well knew that she would bawl for Kasta at the slightest sign of trouble. He had to content himself with advancing grimly on Ondo. Ondo glanced round for Scodo and Pad and remembered they were not there. He went pale, and his sneering grin wavered. Gair pushed contemptuously past him and stalked through Garholt to his windowsill. He wished he had realized before what a coward Ondo was. It made him easier to bear.

In the house, Fandi or no Fandi, Ayna and Ceri were determined to revenge Gair.

"I don't advise you to talk to Gair like that," Ayna said. "We'd put words on you, if we didn't think you were just too stupid to know better."

Ceri, relying on Fandi to stop any violence, went one better. "It isn't only that you're stupid, Ondo," he explained pityingly. "You're ugly. Your ears stick out."

As he said this, Ceri went red with pleasure and delight at his own daring. He had longed to say it for years. Ondo's ears sprang from his head like a sheep's. Unfortunately, Fandi was quite as insulted as Ondo. She had tried every way she knew to make those ears lie flat, and they had defeated her every time. So she made no attempt to stop Ondo when he advanced angrily on Ceri.

"Just you wait!" said Ondo.

Ceri backed away, feeling sick. Ondo towered above him and Ceri knew from painful experience Ondo was an expert at hurting smaller children. He knew he was in for it, if Fandi was simply going to stand by. "Ayna!" he said hopelessly.

Ayna, in spite of being very much afraid of Ondo, dashed to Ceri's side. Fandi caught her arm as she passed. Fandi was strong. "Really, Ayna," she said. "Be a lady."

Ondo pounced for Ceri and Ceri scudded for the

door. Fandi pushed Ayna aside and got in his way. Ceri was terrified. He was also furiously angry, on his own account, on Ayna's and most of all on Gair's. He turned on the pair of them and used a Gift which, up to that moment, he had no idea he possessed.

He did not say anything. He did not seem to do anything. But Fandi screamed. She clutched her head and her face went yellowish. As for Ondo, he gave a queer squawk and stuck, just as he was, with his arms crookedly outstretched to grab Ceri. "He looked exactly like a crayfish!" Ayna told Gair afterward.

Paralyzed and panic-stricken, Ondo shrieked the worst insult he knew. "You—you little *Dorig*!"

Ceri looked at them for a moment, with his own face rather a queer color. Then he ran out of the house and hid behind the tapestries.

Chapter

4

GAIR HAD NEVER HEARD ANYTHING LIKE THE bawling of Fandi and Ondo and the yells of Kasta, Scodo and Pad on their behalf. He came down from his windowsill to investigate. By then, the whole mound was in an uproar. Gair learned from Ayna and Miri that his brother had put a Thought on Ondo and Fandi, and, from Miri, that it was going to take the next three days to get it off them. There was great excitement, because the Gift of Thought was an extremely rare Gift. The last person to have it had died over a hundred years before.

None of this mattered to Kasta. She just wanted Ceri punished for damaging her Ondo. In intervals of wringing her hands over the stuck, crooked Ondo, she searched for Ceri and made everyone else search, too. Ayna and Gair did their best for him by suggesting all sorts of places where Ceri could not possibly be. But Kasta found him in the end—"She would!" said Ayna— and dragged him to Gest. Gest took his shoe to Ceri.

After that, Gest went to order the making of the

triple gold collar Ceri was now entitled to. Adara caught his arm and stopped him. "Why?" Gest said crossly. "Kasta can shout all she likes, but I'd bet half the gold in Garholt it was all Ondo's fault."

"I'm sure it was," said Adara. "But Ceri's far too conceited already. Give him the collar when he's old enough to have earned it. For the moment, I think this Gift is best forgotten."

Gest thought she was right, on reflection. Thought was a very dangerous thing in the hands of someone like Ceri. So Adara called Ceri aside and talked to him. She explained that the Gift of Thought was a serious responsibility: it could do a great deal of harm. Ceri was neither old enough nor sensible enough to use it. Therefore, he was not being given a triple collar yet, until he could prove he knew how to use the Gift responsibly. In the meantime, he was utterly forbidden to put Thoughts on people and was to do his best to forget he had the Gift. Adara talked for a long time, and Ceri cried.

When Adara had finished, he crept miserably away among the clacking looms to Gair's windowsill and asked Gair if he could come up. Gair agreed. He did not blame Ceri for wanting to be private, too. But Ceri did not want to be private. He wanted to consult Gair. Gair, to his great astonishment, discovered that his habit of sitting apart on the windowsill had given him a reputation for wisdom among all the children in Garholt. Gair was ashamed. He wanted to explain to Ceri that he only sat there because he was ordinary, but he had not the heart to. Ceri was sniffing and sobbing and trusted Gair to help him.

"I don't mind about the collar," he said. "Or the things Mother said. Or Father's shoe—much. But I don't know what I *did*, Gair. I don't know how to stop doing it again. I'm afraid of killing someone! What shall I *do*?"

Since Ceri thought he was wise, Gair did not like to disappoint him. He thought about it. "Perhaps," he said dubiously, "you'd better find out how you did it and practice using it on something that doesn't matter." This sounded very feeble to him. "Then you wouldn't do it by accident," he said.

Ceri seemed to think this was perfectly good advice. "Yes. But I don't know what I did," he said dolefully.

Gair could not tell him that. All he could say was, "Well, try and remember what you did. Go on. Think."

"All right." Ceri sat beside Gair on the sill, with his knees drawn up beside his ears and his hands between his feet, and thought until Gair was bored. At last he said doubtfully, "I *think* I sort of pointed a piece of the inside of my head at them."

"Then try and do it again now," said Gair.

"What on? I'm not supposed to use you," said Ceri.

Gair had worn the windowsill smooth. There was nothing there Ceri could use. Gair looked out at the bees—but you did not meddle with bees for a number of good reasons—and thought over the things in his pockets. He had nothing in them that he was willing to let Ceri spoil. He could think of only one thing that might do. "Here you are." He took the gold collar off his neck, careful to keep hold of either end so that it would not start turning to black ore again, and held it out toward Ceri. "Try and break this in two." Ceri looked awed by Gair's daring. "Go on," said Gair. "Plain collars are easy to mend, if *you* can't."

"All right." Ceri clasped his arms round his knees and stared at Gair's collar. Nothing happened. Gair was just about to give up and put the collar back on again when Ceri's eyes widened. Gair found his hands moving apart from one another, each holding half of the collar. "I did it!" said Ceri. Both of them burst out laughing.

"Now mend it," said Gair.

"Ooh!" said Ceri. "Suppose I can't?"

"I'll get into trouble. Not you. Go on. Try."

Gair held out the two halves. Ceri tried. The effect was immediate, but unexpected. The collar leaped together, dragging Gair's hands with it. One piece slid on top of the other and, the next second, Gair was holding one half of a collar twice as thick. He was forced to laugh again at the frantic bewilderment on Ceri's face.

"Oh dear!" said Ceri.

"Try again," said Gair. "We'll both get into trouble

if it stays like this."

Ceri knelt up and tried earnestly. The collar grew between Gair's hands, and grew, and went on growing, until Gair was holding both ends of a gold wire. The wire tied itself into a bow. The bow compressed into a little gold bar. It took Ceri half an hour to work Gair's collar back to its proper shape, and by that time they were both weak with laughing. Gair put the collar back on.

"Use something else next time," he said.

Ceri went away and fetched some marbles. Then for the next three days, while from among the houses below came the monotonous chanting of the words which would eventually take the Thought off Ondo and Fandi, Ceri sat on Gair's windowsill and exercised his Gift. He chopped marbles in two, turned them egg-shaped and rolled them this way and that. Gair grew heartily bored and longed to have his windowsill to himself again. But he saw Ceri felt safest there. He thought Gair was wise enough to protect him from the consequences of his new Gift. Gair felt like a fraud, but he had not the heart to turn Ceri out.

Gest saw Ceri sitting up there and began to feel that both his sons were turning out peculiar. "I think they'd both better come on the next hunt," he told Adara. Adara agreed, thinking it would help Ceri to forget about his latest Gift.

Ondo and Fandi were themselves again on the third

day. Orban arrived with an escort to take them home again, and they left. Kasta gave Ceri—and Gair, too—very baleful looks before she went. She was convinced Gair had egged Ceri on.

That same evening, Ceri put his marbles in his pocket, smiled happily and told Gair he knew how to manage Thoughts now. Gair was relieved. But the peace he was looking forward to was shattered when Gest told him he and Ceri were coming on the hunt. Gair enjoyed hunting, these days, but Ceri loathed it. So far, Ayna and Gair had prevented Gest finding out. Gest would have been furious to find any son of his did not love to hunt. Gair's heart sank, because he would be responsible for Ceri. They would be out two days, too, for the great midsummer Feast of the Sun was near and had to be provided for. Ayna had been consulted, and she had said there would be deer again, in the Northeast of the Moor. Gair thought he would be lucky to get Ceri all that way without some kind of trouble.

There was every kind of trouble. Ceri made every possible mistake and contrived to get left behind whenever he could. He hated every minute, and said so. By dawn on the second day, Gair was thinking that it was rather to his credit that he had only hit Ceri nine times in all: six times when he richly deserved it, and three times to stop him complaining in Gest's hearing. They trailed through a rushy meadow hung with mist. The coming dawn made the grass as white as the mist, and the chill struck through to their bones. They were behind as usual. Ceri was wailing that he needed a rest or he would die, and Gair, knowing everyone else was in the next meadow already, took Ceri's arm and dragged him along.

There was a pool of water in their way, edged with stiff rushes. Because of the whiteness of everything, Gair did not see it until he was in it. They splashed round one end of it and Ceri complained bitterly that his feet were wet now.

A dark shape about the size of Gair loomed at them through the mist. Ceri's whine stopped in a squeak. Gair jumped. But the shape was only a red stag, about to make off across the meadow.

"*Quick!*" Gair shouted to Ceri. In great excitement, he leveled his spear and ran through the whiteness to head the stag off. "Quick! Or I'll hit you again."

"That'll be ten times. And I'm cold," Ceri said sullenly. But when Gair glanced back to see, he found Ceri had stopped using his spear as a walking stick and was pointing it in the general direction of the stag. If Ceri stood firm—a thing not altogether to be relied on—they could pin the stag between them.

Gair circled quickly beside the pool, trying to drive the stag toward Ceri. But the beast circled with him, keeping its horns lowered. It seemed they had found a crafty one. Gair could not see it very well in the swirling whiteness, but it looked larger than he had thought. Some trick of the mist and the dawn light made its head look higher than his own. The antlers looked wicked. Gair advanced behind his spear, wondering why he felt so cold. And the stag grew again, until it towered over him.

"Gair!" said Ceri, in the squeaky voice of real terror. "Gair, that's standing water!"

So it was, Gair realized. He had made poor work of looking after Ceri. He thrust at the stag with all his strength, but the spearhead met nothing. The huge antlered shape wavered and swirled into mist, darker and grayer than the white mist around. There was a blast of cold air. Gair backed hurriedly round the pool toward Ceri, water squirting in sheets from under his feet, until they stood shoulder to shoulder. There they watched in fascinated horror the gray mist harden into a tall, tall shape covered in dim silvery scales like armor, a pointed head solidify, a pale face with queer yellow eyes, a round shield and a sharp, bent scimitar. Gair could have kicked himself. He had been told often enough that Dorig were shape-shifters. But he had had no idea they looked so dangerous. He hoped it would not notice how both their spearpoints were juddering.

It came toward them in a wafting, gliding way that had both of them sick with terror. "Keep back!" Gair said to it. It took no notice. Gair wondered if it spoke some other language.

Before he could speak again, Gest's voice barked, "Stop that, you!"

The Dorig jumped. Gair, feeling weak and bewildered, found that the entire hunt was back, and surrounding the pond in the mist. As soon as Gest spoke, the dogs began to paw and snarl to get at the Dorig. Those who were not holding dogs had their spears aimed at it. Slowly and haughtily, the Dorig looked round the hostile ring. It was a good head taller even than Gest. But it still said nothing.

"You're outnumbered," said Gest. "There's nothing you can do. Get out of here."

The Dorig did not say a word to this, either, but it plainly understood. It simply turned and dived into the pool. It made barely a splash. Smokily, it slid under the surface of the water and was gone, with not much more disturbance than if someone had thrown a small pebble into the pond. Indeed, Gair had the impression that the Dorig did become smaller—almost half the size—before it had quite reached the water.

Gest looked at the rippling white pool for a moment, as if something puzzled him. "Lucky for you two that we missed you," he said to Gair and Ceri. "Keep up with the rest in future." He had been pleased to find the two boys standing their ground against a full-grown Dorig warrior, but it never occurred to him to say so.

They felt they were in disgrace. As they moved on

again, Ceri burst into tears. He swore to Gair that he was crying out of annoyance. It had never occurred to him to put a Thought on the Dorig. Gair said sourly that it made a good story. He was quite as shaken as Ceri, but he hoped no one had noticed.

"You had a narrow escape," Brad said, coming up alongside Gair. "Why didn't you keep clear of the water? Didn't you notice the cold?"

"Yes. But I thought that was the mist," Gair admitted. He liked Brad best of all the boys in Garholt, or he would not have admitted it. "Why do they make it cold? Do you know?"

"Fishiness, I expect," said Brad. "They're cold-blooded, aren't they? Ask my father."

Gair left Ceri with Brad and trotted up beside Banot. Banot grinned. "You've got your mother's knack of asking the difficult questions, Gair. I don't think they *are* cold-blooded, but I couldn't say for sure. As for making it cold, they say the shape-shifting does it. It takes a good deal of heat to shift shapes, and they get it from the air. It's like—well, you may find it grows cold when Ceri puts a Thought on someone."

"Thanks," said Gair. Banot had given him a great deal to think about, but it did nothing to stop his growing feeling of shame. He had been so stupid! He had walked into standing water with Ceri, and it had taken the whole hunt to rescue them. No wonder Gest was disappointed in him. He longed to prove—to himself at least—that he was not quite that stupid and ordinary. He trotted back and asked Ceri to put a Thought on something.

Ceri, to Brad's keen amazement, obligingly broke his spear in two and joined it again. But, either this was only a very small Thought, or the dawn mists were still too chilly. Gair could not tell if the air round Ceri had gone any colder. Neither could Brad.

"I'll do something else when we get home," Ceri offered. Gair agreed that would be best. They turned for home soon after, and Gair thought about their narrow escape most of the way. He had been terrified, he had to admit that. The noisy, heavy Giants beating the bank of the dike for him had been nothing to the silent silver Dorig. It was the queerness of the Dorig that made it so frightening. Even Banot did not claim to understand or explain them; and Banot, Miri had told Gair, had made quite a study of the Dorig. Gair thought Banot must be a very brave man. He wished he was more like him. He was so ashamed of himself that he began to think he would like to find out more about Dorig, too, in spite of his horror at the mere idea. No one thought Banot stupid.

Gair never had a chance to find out if Ceri's Thoughts made the air cold. They arrived in Garholt that evening with a fair catch, ravenous for the good supper that was waiting. Gair and Ceri both tried not to fall asleep while they ate and told Ayna and Adara about the Dorig.

"It was tall," Ceri said, yawning, with his mouth full. "I couldn't believe even Dorig—"

There was a violent hammering at the main gate. A woman's voice screamed, *"Dorig!"*

All the chatter at the eating-squares stopped. Before anyone could move, the words had been spoken and the gate rumbled open.

"Dorig!" shrieked Kasta, towing a green-faced, terrified Ondo. "You have to help us, Gest!"

Streaming into the mound behind Kasta came a host of people from Otmound. All were white and frightened. Some were wet; some, Orban among them, were hacked and bloody. They had cooking pots, bundles, spindles, babies and all the gold they could wear. Sheep, dogs and cats came streaming into the mound among them.

For a time, there was desperate confusion. The Garholters had to leave their supper unfinished and find food, beds and medicine for the fugitives. And, as Kasta kept screaming that the Dorig had chased them the whole length of the old road, the Garholt sheep had to be got inside and the doors locked as quickly as possible. Gair found himself with Brad, both of them yawning till their ears cracked, guarding Ayna and the other girls, who were running about by Moonlight, shrieking the words to the sheep, which had scattered for the night nearly as far as the old road itself. They were relieved but puzzled not to see a single Dorig.

"Just as well," said Brad. "I think I'd snore in their faces. What do you think happened?"

Gair wanted to know that, too, but he had to wait until the sheep were in, the doors locked, watch posted and the fugitives all settled in somewhere. Orban, Kasta and Ondo were, of course, settled in Gest's house. Ayna, Gair and Ceri all gathered to watch Orban, with his wounds now bathed and bandaged, drink mug after mug of beer and explain what had happened. The long and short of it was that the Dorig had driven them from Otmound. That afternoon, the wells of Otmound had begun to overflow. While the Garholt hunt had been peacefully making its way home, Og's people had been struggling to hold back a flood which no words would stem. The water ran from the wells, filled the mound and went on rising. By Sundown, the flood had reached the rooftops and everyone was forced to go outside. And outside, the Dorig were waiting.

"Crafty swine!" said Orban. "It was just like smoking out bees. They hid in the Haunted Mound and waited for us to come out."

Orban and Og rallied those who could fight and attacked the Dorig, while the rest got away with their possessions. The fight had gone very badly. Og was killed. Orban had been forced to run for it with the rest of the fighting men, and the Dorig had pursued them. But the Dorig had not been anxious to go beyond the thorn trees along the first Giant road—Kasta, as usual, had overstated the case—and had turned back to Otmound. Orban had caught up with the rest and they had come on to Garholt as fast as they could.

"And you'd better watch that they don't try that trick with the wells here," Orban said, passing his mug to Miri for more beer.

"They can't," Gest said confidently. "All our wells are protected." He pointed to the nearest, with its rounded stone hood and the twig-shaped writing on the stonework, which was the indoor equivalent of a thorn tree.

"I hope you're right," Orban said glumly.

Gair looked from his uncle's weary face to the tears running down his mother's. In a shocked, distant way, he knew there had been a terrible disaster. War, he thought. But it did not feel like that. He could not imagine Otmound as an underground lake or think of more than one Dorig at a time. As for Og, it was a shame, but to Gair he was a fussy old grandfather whom Gair had not known very well, or to tell the truth, liked very much. He looked at Ayna and Ceri's sober faces and saw they felt the same. The important thing to all three was that here was Ondo back again after only two days, and the important question was when was he going?

Chapter
5

THAT NIGHT, ONDO HAD GAIR'S BED AGAIN AND he had to share with Ceri. Neither of them slept as well as they wanted. Gair woke feeling gloomy and apprehensive. He could hear the double flock of sheep bleating, the girls at the lookout posts calling to one another and Orban snoring. That in itself would have made anyone gloomy. But Gair felt uneasy too, in a way he could not explain. He forgot that he had intended to find out whether Ceri's Thoughts made the air cold, and hung about with most of the rest of Garholt, waiting for news.

Gest had sent Banot over to Otmound in the early hours of the morning. He came back, red-eyed and fagged, soon after midday. Gair and Ceri wriggled near enough to hear what he said. It was not cheering. Banot had gone right up to Otmound to find water running out of it and the fields beyond it turning into a marsh. He could see it was still flooded.

"Then the Dorig saw me," he said. "They came running out of the Haunted Mound—they seem to have made a camp there. And the captain—he was a long, tall one with a big opinion of himself—called out to know what I wanted."

"You were lucky they didn't kill you first and ask after," Orban said. Gair was chiefly surprised that Banot and the Dorig could understand one another.

Banot winked and tapped his harp. "Dorig love music," he said. "He waited till I'd finished playing, and then I asked what was going on. Told him I was making inquiries from Garholt. He didn't say too much, but he told me they were going to live in Otmound in the future. They want to keep it for themselves."

"Let them try!" Orban said angrily. "What then?"

"He went away for a bit and set a guard over me," said Banot. "I began to wonder whether I would come back. But he must have gone to ask advice, I think, because he came back and said two things. One was that they'd got their revenge for that battle the year Gest did those tasks. The other was that their King was not going to attack Gest. May I get some sleep now? I'm worn out."

"What did he mean by that?" Orban demanded.

"He didn't say," said Banot, who seemed to be falling asleep where he stood.

Gest smiled and signaled to Tille to get Banot away to bed. Then, still smiling, he turned to Orban. "This is a very sad business," he said. "But don't think you and your people have nowhere to go. You must make your home with us for as long as you need."

Ceri gave a small moan of dismay. Gair crossed his fingers and prayed to the Sun that Orban would refuse. There must be an empty mound somewhere where the Otmounders could live.

But Orban laughed and clapped Gest on the shoulder. "Thanks. I was hoping you'd say that, Gest. You're such a good fellow. We'll fight the Dorig together, then. Drive the brutes out of Otmound and then out of the Moor!"

Gair wondered how his father could smile like that. He wondered how he was going to bear having Ondo living in Garholt. He felt miserable, and also indefinably uneasy, worse than he had done when he woke up that morning. He tried to explain to Adara how he felt.

"Don't be stupid, Gair," said Adara. "What else could Gest have said?"

The next few days were very difficult. As there seemed no danger of a Dorig attack, the Otmounders settled in, and the Garholters began to resent them exceedingly. The mound was uncomfortably crowded. New houses had to be built—and it was the Garholters who did the building, the Otmounders being exhausted after their tribulations. The sheep got mixed up. The Otmound smiths set up their forge where they were most in the way of the Garholt smithies, and the Otmound ladies put up their looms where they cut off the light from the Garholt weavers. Adara protested about it to Kasta. "Really?"

said Kasta. "What a silly fuss about nothing!" And the looms stayed where they were, to Adara's fury. Much the same happened over the forges when Gest protested to Orban.

Orban was most genial. Defeated and homeless he might be, but now Og was dead, Orban was Chief of the Otmounders. Otmound was the oldest mound on the Moor and, therefore, even without a mound, Orban was the senior Chief and more important than Gest. He blandly refused to move the forge. He insisted that his new house should be larger than Gest's. And he wanted to lead out an army straightaway to kill as many Dorig as possible.

"Well, yes. But don't let's be too hasty about it," Gest said. "People could say the Dorig are quite justified, after the way you drove them into the water by Islaw."

"That was years ago!" said Orban. "This attack was quite unprovoked. You don't expect me to sit here and let them get away with it, do you?"

"Of course not," said Gest. "I just don't want to be rash. We're not prepared here. We ought to train the men."

"There's no training like real fighting," Orban said. "If we go quickly, we can catch them napping."

"I don't think we dare go that quickly, not with this many people in Garholt," Gest said. "We'd have to provision the mound first. It'll take at least one big hunt

before the Feast of the Sun, and that's only for meat."
This was true. There were now double the number of
people in Garholt, and the Otmounders had not brought
any food with them. The supplies from the last hunt were
eaten in two days. If the Feast was to be held in anything
like proper style, more meat had to be got and more drink
brewed. "Suppose we wait until after the Feast of the
Sun," said Gest, "and then consider attacking."

"We can send half out for food and the rest against
the Dorig," said Orban. "Dorig crumple if you hit them
hard. It doesn't take many men."

"But that means leaving Garholt without men or pro-
visions," Gest pointed out. "If the Dorig attacked it, it
would be completely defenseless."

"But you've had their word they wouldn't attack — and
I like their nerve!" Orban said, growing exasperated.
"What's the matter with you, Gest?"

"Nothing," said Gest. "I'd just prefer to wait at least
till Autumn, when we've got food in —"

"Autumn! You expect me to sit and let the Dorig lord
it in Otmound, and not do a thing about it till Autumn!"
Orban bellowed.

"Now don't think I don't see your point of view —"
Gest said.

"Nice of you! I don't see yours at all," said Orban.

The argument went on for days. Orban grew more
and more exasperated. Gest remained wonderfully polite

and steadily reasonable, and yet, as the days went by, it became clearer and clearer to Gair as he listened that his father had no intention of fighting the Dorig if he could avoid it. Gair could not understand it. Gest seemed so craven. He had given way to Orban about the forges, he had agreed to build Orban a very large house, but, on the one matter where it really seemed to Gair that Orban had right on his side, Gest politely refused to give in. This did not seem to be the Gest out of Miri's stories at all. The gloomy, foreboding feeling Gair had had the first morning came back to him whenever he heard Orban and Gest arguing. It did not seem quite to be connected with the argument, but it troubled him more and more every time they argued. He confided it to Ayna in the end, since Adara was not prepared to listen to him.

"I'm not surprised," said Ayna. "What with Father and Orban arguing, and Kasta saying catty things to Mother and boring everyone about Ondo, and Miri and Fandi looking daggers at one another, life's unbearable. And it's supposed to be forever! If Father doesn't agree to fight the Dorig, it *will* be forever. Gair, ask me if they're ever going, please!"

"Are the Otmounders going next month?" Gair asked.

The faraway look on Ayna's face was mixed with surprise and relief. "Yes. Thank the Sun!"

"Back to Otmound?" said Gair eagerly.

Ayna's face became even more surprised. "No. Far,

far away. Oh, what a relief!"

Gair was as relieved as Ayna. It made it easier to bear with Ondo. For Ondo, as soon as he had recovered from his fright, became more odious than ever. He dared not harm Ceri, and scorned Ayna as a mere girl, so all his dislike was now aimed at Gair. He wanted to revenge himself on Gair for Ceri's Thought, so he opened hostilities by reminding Gair that he had no Gifts. But that cut both ways. Ondo took up a new line. He came swaggering up with Scodo and Pad to where Gair was mixing mortar for Orban's new house.

"Kiss my hand, Gair," he said. "Come on."

"Whatever for?" said Gair.

"I'd have thought even an idiot like you would understand that," said Ondo, at which Scodo and Pad sniggered heartily. "Because I'm going to be High Chief, of course. You might as well kiss my hand now and admit it."

"Who says you're going to be High Chief?" Gair said scornfully. "You couldn't be High Caterpillar!"

"Don't you call names!" said Scodo. "And he is. So."

"Everyone says so," said Pad. "Like Orban."

"Orban's not High Chief," said Gair.

"He will be," said Ondo. "You should listen to what everyone's saying. They want to make my father High Chief because Gest is such a coward and daren't fight the Dorig."

"So kiss his hand," said Scodo.

Since Gair had been wondering for the last three days if Gest was a coward, this was more than he could bear. He growled with rage, and he would have gone for all three—a very unequal combat, as Scodo and Pad were both older and taller than Ondo—had not Brad strolled up, meaningly swinging a spade. Ondo, Scodo and Pad at once strolled away, laughing.

"Cowards!" said Brad. "Look, Gair, if you don't try and beat Ondo up, you'll have this for the rest of your life. You get Ondo. I'll see to the other two for you. All the Garholters are on your side."

Gair went back to his mortar, mixing it with stabs and punches, pretending it was Ondo. He knew Brad was right. Just let Ondo do one more thing—!

An hour later, he looked up to see Ondo, Scodo and Pad playing knucklebones up on his windowsill. It was deliberate. Ondo knew as well as anyone that the windowsill was Gair's. Gair stood up, so angry that everything in Garholt was blurred and faint except for those three figures on the sill. He did not see the way all the Garholters, old and young, were watching eagerly, ready for a general fight once Gair attacked Ondo.

Adara did see, and she hurried to prevent it. "Gair, can you help me fold these blankets?" Gair looked at her, muddled and fuzzy-eyed with rage. "But you'd better wash your hands before you do," Adara added. Without thinking, Gair went to the nearest bucket and put his hands in it. As soon as he touched the water, it dawned on him how she had tricked him.

"You made me wash my hands of him! It's not fair!"

"I know. I'm sorry," said Adara. "But if you fight Ondo, we'll have both peoples taking sides, and it could be serious. He'll leave you alone when he sees you won't play. Promise me you won't fight him."

Sulkily, Gair promised. And, having promised, he felt he was forced to keep his promise, much to everyone's disappointment. He ground his teeth and tried not to look at Ondo sitting smugly on his windowsill for the rest of the day. Gest saw Ondo, too. He might disapprove of Gair sitting there, but, like everyone else, he still thought of it as Gair's windowsill.

"What the Ban does Gair mean by letting that little beast sit there?" he demanded of Adara. Adara explained what had happened. "I see," Gest said curtly. He had just come from a long, long argument with Orban over the size of his new house and, though he had managed to keep his temper, he was so annoyed with Orban that he could not help thinking Gair was very poor-spirited not even hitting Ondo once. It did nothing to help any understanding between them.

The next day, Gair got to the windowsill first. It meant leaving his share of the building, but few Garholters blamed him. Gair did not feel at all triumphant. He sat with his knees under his chin, moodily looking out at the flat, deep green of the Moor, nagged at by the unhappy, uneasy feeling he kept having, and fairly sure that Brad and Gest, and probably everyone else, thought he was being a coward over Ondo. He thought he was being a coward himself. But, having made that promise, he did not know what to do. He had almost reached the point where he thought Ondo was right to hate him when he looked round to find Ondo, Scodo and Pad crowded onto the windowsill, too. While Gair was looking out at the Moor, they had quietly climbed up beside him.

Ondo grinned exultantly. Yesterday had convinced him Gair was easily crushed. "Get down," he said. "We want to be here."

Gair pushed on his heels and levered his back up the side of the window until he was standing up. He felt defeated. He knew that if he let Ondo get away with this, he would be giving in. But he had promised Adara not to fight. Dimly, down inside the mound, he could see people stopping whatever they were doing and turning to see what would happen on the windowsill. It looked as if he was going to make this a public humiliation for Garholt. All he could think of to say was, "This is my place—and I didn't ask you up."

"I don't need *your* permission," said Ondo. "Down."

"Gair's scared," said Scodo to Pad.

"Like Gest—he talks big and acts little," said Pad to Scodo.

As before, the suggestion that Gest was a coward was too near Gair's own fears for him to take quietly. "What do you mean by that?" he said.

All three laughed. "Everyone in Otmound knows what a cheat Gest is," said Ondo. "He never did any of those tasks Og set him. He was too scared. So he cheated. Ask your mother, if you like. She told him the answers to all the riddles."

"And of course he was too scared to kill a Dorig," said Scodo. "So he went and swore friendship with one so that he could get its collar. Ask him where his own collar went, if you don't believe us."

"And you know how they say he moved the stone?" asked Pad.

"No. How?" said Gair. Each thing they said made him more blindly angry. He could hardly see them by this time. For he knew they were speaking the truth. It all fitted in. He knew Gest could not answer riddles, and he had always wondered why Gest had come home without his collar. "How did he move the stone?"

Ondo sniggered. "He didn't. He got a Giant to move it for him, of course!"

Gair forgot his promise and went for Ondo. Scodo and Pad stood in his way, but he was so angry he hardly noticed them. His shoulder hit Scodo and his elbow caught Pad, and the two of them vanished. Gair heard both of them yell, below somewhere, and a furious buzzing from the bees, but he was too intent on catching Ondo to bother about them. Ondo, finding nothing between him and the raging Gair, did his best to climb back among the looms before Gair could reach him. Gair got to him when his head was still above the sill and seized hold of his gold collar. "Mother!" shrieked Ondo. There were screams from Kasta, beyond the looms, and screams to Gair, from the looms themselves, to baste Ondo. Gair hardly heard them. With the strength that only blind rage gives, he heaved the large, solid Ondo back onto the sill again, swung him round by his collar and hurled him after Scodo and Pad. "Mother!" roared Ondo.

It was a delicious feeling. For a moment, Gair stood panting, enjoying it. Ondo was rolling and bawling. Scodo and Pad were yelling. The bees were out in a dark cloud as high as the sill itself and as busy as the boys were noisy.

Inside Garholt, Gest pushed his way among the jostling, shouting people. He was very angry, largely because he was going to have to punish Gair for doing something he had been itching to do himself. "*Gair!*" His voice rose above the shouting, and even above Ondo's screams. "*Gair! Come down at once!*"

But, after what Ondo had told him, Gest was the last

person Gair wanted to see. He did not even think what to do. He simply leaped after his three enemies, high and long, so that he missed their rolling, wailing bodies and landed some way down the hillside. A cloud of bees, thoroughly excited and confused, came after him and buzzed round his head. They knew him, and did not sting him. And Gair remembered to do his duty by them. You should always tell bees what happens. "I'm going," he said into the buzzing cloud. "You saw why. I don't know where, but I'm going to find some Dorig."

He set off at a run toward the marshes.

For some time after he had gone, Garholt rang with accusations and insults, outcry and confusion. No one knew why fighting did not break out then and there, as the Otmounders united in blaming Gair, and the Garholters felt they had stood enough from Otmound and said so. But Gest went outside and spoke sharp words to the bees—which sent them back into their hives in some haste—and brought the three swollen, blubbering boys indoors. He did not say much, but the Otmounders recollected that, but for Gest's kindness, they would have nowhere to live, and even Kasta moderated her language. Everyone ran about for remedies for bee stings.

When peace was somewhat restored, Ceri said to Ayna, "What is Gair going to do today?"

"He's going to look for Dorig and find Giants," said

Ayna. The faraway look on her face gave way to excitement. "I say—where *is* Gair, Ceri?"

Ceri was equally excited. "Near a Giants' house. Come on and I'll show you."

Chapter

6

GAIR PLOWED THROUGH SQUASHY MARSH, among hot rustling high grasses. Whenever he came to a peaty pool he said loudly, "Anyone there?" But the only living things he saw were birds flitting among the grasses, which may or may not have been Dorig. At length, he came to one of the straight dikes by which the Giants tried to drain the Moor. It flowed so sluggishly that it almost counted as standing water, and it only had thorn trees planted along its farther bank. Gair loitered along its near side. He was hot and sticky and so miserable that, if a scaly Dorig arm had reached out of the dike to drag him under, he would have been glad to see it.

His broken promise did not trouble him at all. He was glad he had slung Ondo among the bees, and, for all he cared, the Garholters could be fighting the Otmounders till Sundown. What made him miserable was what Ondo had told him about Gest. And it made him even more unhappy that he could not understand why he should be so miserable to find that his father had cheated. It ought to have been comforting, since it meant that his ordinariness was hereditary. But it was not. Gair felt as if the roots of his life had been cut away. Nothing grand or good was left. It would not have surprised him to find that Adara was nothing like as Wise as she was said to be. And he would have given anything to have gone back miraculously to thinking Gest was a hero out of a story — instead of just an ordinary person who had cheated Og.

"No wonder he can't fight Dorig!" Gair said aloud. He felt bitter and contemptuous. Gest had accorded some unknown scaly Dorig the greatest mark of trust and friendship by changing collars with it. The degree of friendship depended on the words Gest had said on his collar, but it must have been strong, or Gest would have risked helping Orban in battle. And he had done it just to cheat Og! This so disgusted Gair that he shouted out as he walked, *"Dorig! Come and get me!"*

No Dorig came. Gair wandered on, miserable, confused and disgusted. The dike petered out and he walked through the moistness of the Moor, not even caring that he had never been so far alone in his life. He supposed that the Dorig's collar must be the splendid one Adara wore. In that case, in spite of what people said, Dorig must be able to work gold — and work it far, far better than any people could. And what of Giants? Gair felt a great surge of misery and resentment. His father had told him never to have anything to do with

Giants. Gest! Gest, who had gone to the Giants and asked them to move a boulder for him!

Gair realized that he had thought of Giants because there must be Giants near. He was in a tufty field. There were trees ahead. Behind them, Gair could just make out the high, square shape of a Giants' house. He stood still. At any other time, he would have dived for the nearest cover and got himself away from that place as fast as he could. Now he said, "Who says you mustn't talk to Giants?" and walked on. If anything, Giants were more likely to kill him than Dorig were.

He reached the trees. He had not quite the courage to shout to the Giants to come and get him, much as he hated himself for it. Indeed, he found himself, purely out of habit, taking a careful look all round, particularly behind. And he was just in time to see Ceri and Ayna drop and freeze behind two tufts of grass.

That did it. Gair's pent-up misery broke in furious anger. He stormed back to the two tufts. They were very small tufts. Even a Giant could have seen Ceri and Ayna lying there. Ceri was quaking. Both he and Ayna knelt up nervously as Gair reached them. It made Gair more miserable and angry than ever to see that even Ayna was scared of him.

"What do you mean by spying on me?" he shouted.

"We weren't," said Ceri. "I asked Ayna what you were going to do."

"And I asked him where you were," said Ayna. "Then we came here."

Gair felt for a moment that the whole world was against him, and Ceri's and Ayna's Gifts in particular. He felt quite helpless against them. "I'm going to that Giants' house," he said. "So now you know."

"All right," said Ayna, and Ceri nodded. Gair saw that they were both prepared for an adventure. He was furious, because it was, after all, *his* adventure. He swung round again and marched toward the trees.

He felt, rather than heard, that Ayna and Ceri were following him. It was extremely annoying, but, all the same, Gair was not as angry as he had expected to be. He was less miserable with Ayna and Ceri there and, to tell the truth, rather relieved, because he could not let Giants kill him with Ayna and Ceri looking on. He stole among the trees much more cautiously than he would have done alone. Ayna and Ceri followed him like two puffs of wind. The trees ended, and they lay in the cover of the last of them, looking at the first Giants' house any of them had seen close to.

Gair's first thought was that it was ugly. It was square and tall and dark, with clusters of tall chimneys. It was built of dark bricks, and the quantities of little panes in its windows were dark too. It looked sealed and sad. Dark bushes had been clipped square above the dark brick wall in front of the house. Dark summer trees stood on either side of it. It seemed to give off darkness into the bright misty sunlight. If you were used to round houses, it was very queer. But Gair saw that it was old and, in its way, graceful. Queerly, it was surrounded with water. There was a dike or moat under the wall with the dark bushes, and this moat had a sort of bridge over it, leading to the front door. A second dike, neither so large nor so full, ran close to the trees where they lay. In between was a stony stretch where an old dog was wandering.

"Standing water," Ayna muttered anxiously. "And no thorn trees."

Gair was laughing at the dog. It was so small. It stood no higher than Gest's favorite hound, and it was so stiff and mild that a puppy of Garholt could have torn it to pieces. He could not see what use the Giants could possibly have for a dog like that. At that moment, it seemed to him that the house was a beautiful, peaceful place.

The dog scented them. It did not bark, but it began to amble stiffly and peaceably toward them. All three, without thinking, said the words to make it ignore them. Looking puzzled, the dog sighed and lay heavily down.

At once, the house seemed uglier than ever to Gair.

Ceri pulled at his elbow. "Those dikes—moats. No thorn trees."

"Who cares?" said Gair. The house was too beautiful and peaceful for the Dorig to trouble them there. It occurred to him to wonder whether Giants and Dorig were friends or enemies. No one had ever told him.

"Where are the Giants?" Ayna whispered.

Then the house seemed ugly again.

After that the house began to pulse, from beautiful to ugly and back again. It went in great, slow, pounding pulsations, and each time it was ugly it was more sinister. A huge sense of foreboding began to grow in Gair. He felt horrified, beyond reason. Pulse, pulse. Ugly, lovely, ugly. Gair's ears rang, and his heart pounded.

"What on earth's the matter, Gair?" said Ayna.

"I don't know. I don't like this house."

"It is a bit square, isn't it?" Ceri agreed, rather amused.

Gair saw he was being stupid. It was silly to be frightened of a house, Giants' though it was, when Ceri and Ayna could look at it so calmly. "Let's explore," he said, and got up. The pulsing stopped.

They drifted silently down the line of trees and came to a small wood just beyond the stony forecourt of the house. It was a lovely fresh place, with a stream winding among the trees. The ground was bare earth, as if it was walked on a great deal, and a number of the trees were thorn trees. They all relaxed and listened to the churring of the stream, the birds and the cool sound of the trees. There was another noise, too. They looked at one another.

"Music?" suggested Ayna.

"Sort of," said Ceri. "Not quite."

They stole forward to investigate. They froze. They inched behind trees and froze again. There was a Giantess. They looked at her and their eyes popped. She was huge. Never had they seen such quantities of pink flesh. She was vast. Her cheeks wobbled when she moved. Her great leg shook a tree just by moving a little on the ground. She was sitting near the stream, her great features drawn into a large-scale map of a moody frown, nodding her head in time to the noise. The noise was coming from a magic box on the ground beside her, and it was clear she took it for music.

All three children stared, fascinated both by the Giantess and her magic box. They wished she would stand up so that they could see how tall she was and, most interesting of all, how she contrived to carry that quantity of pink body even on thick legs like hers. They were so absorbed that they did not notice the ground quake.

"I told you to get out, Fatso!" said a loud voice.

In spite of all their training, all three jumped and turned round. If the Giant on the other side of the stream had not been glaring so angrily at the Giantess, he would certainly have seen them. They edged out of his sight and looked at one another's scared faces, wondering what to do. If the Giantess turned her head, she would see them now. But she was glowering at the Giant.

"That was last Easter," she said. "Snotty!" She did something to her magic box to make it louder.

"You watch it, Brenda. You won't like it if I put you out," rumbled the Giant. "This is our property." He was a dark Giant, tall, thin and gloomy-featured. Beside the Giantess, he was a trifle disappointing. True, he was at least as tall as Gest, but he was not much wider than Gair. His bare arms were not much thicker than Ayna's. He walked menacingly toward the Giantess, and they wondered how he thought he could shift her an inch.

The Giantess did not seem to think he could. She sat where she was. "What are you doing here, anyway?" she said. "Why aren't you away at your school?"

"I had measl—nothing to do with you!" snapped the Giant. "I said out!" About three feet from the Giantess he stopped and breathed windily.

Gair, Ayna and Ceri seized the opportunity to slide round the trees, out of direct view. Ceri, rather half-heartedly, jerked his head back in the direction of Garholt. Both Ayna and Gair fiercely shook theirs. Ceri did not protest. This was enthralling. It was interesting enough to discover that Giants could catch measles, too. But the most astonishing thing was the way they acted as if they were bigger than they were. The tall Giant contrived to make the earth shake even when he was standing still. He breathed like the bellows at the forge. The glare he directed at the Giantess distorted his face in all directions, although his actual features were not very much larger than Gair's. As for the Giantess, her great face was one outsize pink contempt for the Giant. Her bloated hand went out to the magic box and made it louder than ever. Even the combined smithies of Garholt and Otmound did not make such a noise.

"Get out!" yelled the Giant, above the din. "I'm sick of you infesting the place with your music!"

"Get out yourself," said the Giantess, piercingly. "You're not going to order me about, Gerald Masterfield!"

"This is our wood!" bawled the Giant, his pale face reddening. It made him look healthier—more like a person.

The Giantess turned her head and stared indifferently into the wood, beating ground-rippling time to the noise from the box. Ceri dared not move. If the Giantess had been really looking, instead of putting on an exaggerated Giant act, she would have been looking straight at him. "Get lost!" she said to the Giant.

"*I love you love me love!*" sang the magic box, gigantically. It seemed to have mistaken the situation.

There was a sudden flurry of action. The children gasped, both at its speed and its tremendous violence. The Giant pounced forward and tried to seize the shouting box. The Giantess, moving even faster, snatched it into her arms. Her great leg whipped up from the ground, armed with a mighty thick-soled shoe, and caught the Giant a terrific kick on the shin. Gair winced. It must have been like being hit by a sledgehammer. He was surprised the Giant's leg did not snap like a dry stick. But the Giant, being supernaturally strong, merely roared, doubled up and hit out at the Giantess. His hand landed on her face with a huge rubbery smack, and actually bounced off again. Then he hobbled to a safe distance, white and glaring. Gair was not surprised to see very human tears of pain in his eyes.

The Giantess, meanwhile, lumbered to her feet, clutching the magic box to her great stomach. The ground quivered as she did so, like the shifting marsh pools, and such birds as had not already left the wood flew screaming from the treetops. But, vast and heavy though she was, they were astonished to find that, standing up, she was very little taller than Ayna. She was fat— so fat that Ayna could not have put both arms more than halfway round her. She stood monstrously on the bank of the stream, one side of her face bright purple where the Giant had hit it. There were tears in her eyes, too.

"Order me out, won't you!" she said. "There was a girl climbing trees here all yesterday, and you never said a word to her!"

The Giant replied with a bad word. Ayna blushed and Ceri's eyes widened. The box seemed to tumble to the situation at last. *"We have just had news of storms in the South,"* it said. *"The Meteorological O—"*

The Giantess silenced it by briskly snapping a knob. And the Giant dashed forward again, with the same unexpected speed as before. On her feet, the Giantess was not so swift, and she was hampered by the magic box. The Giant caught her, and they wrestled on the edge of the stream with Giant snorts and gasps. The encounter shook the treetops and awed the three onlookers. The Giants swayed, tipped and both landed with one foot in the stream. They were out again the next second, yelling abuse at one another, leaving the stream boiling yellow. The next second, they had wrenched apart, the Giantess holding a handful of the Giant's hair and the Giant with the magic box. The Giant, taller and nimbler, limped quickly away backward, holding the box high over his head and laughing unpleasantly, while the Giantess pursued him, screaming.

"No, Gerald! Gerald, please! Don't you dare!"

The Giant, still laughing, moved the box as if he were going to throw it in the stream.

"Just like Ondo!" Ayna said indignantly. No one could have heard her above the yells of the distressed Giantess. Gair's ears buzzed with the din. He supposed the Giant was behaving like Ondo. In fact, the fascinating thing was the way this was like an enlarged version of the quarrels people had.

The Giantess threshed at the Giant with her feet, but not seriously. She was too much afraid of losing her box.

"Give it me, Gerald! Give it me and I'll go!"

"Promise you'll get out," said the Giant. "If you don't promise, your radio goes in the brook."

"I promise!" she shrieked. "Snotty beast!"

"Fatso!" retorted the Giant. He slung the box at her so hard that she gasped and nearly dropped it. "Now get out!"

Clutching her box, the Giantess made off like an earthquake.

But she was not entirely defeated. Ten feet away, she swung round again. Ceri, who had unwisely started to move, froze. "You may think you own the whole Moor, Gerald Masterfield," she said. "But you don't! *Your* property, *your* wood—you make me sick! You won't sing that tune next year, will you?" The Giant, looking very surly, started to say something, but the Giantess screamed him down until Gair's ears rang. "Behaving like you're the King of Creation, just because your family owns Moor Farm! Well, next year, when they flood the Moor, it'll all be underwater just like the rest! *Then* where will you be? You won't look so grand then, and I shall be glad! *Glad!*"

The Giantess swung round and marched off. The earth boomed under her feet. The sound pulsed through Gair's head. Boom-bad, boom-bad, boom-bad. For a moment it seemed to be the same as the queer pulsing of the Giants' house.

Irritably, the Giant put his hands in his pockets and turned away. Gair was still quivering with the sound of the Giantess's feet. He had no time to move. For perhaps a tenth of a second, the Giant and he stood and stared at one another. It was one of those times which seem to last an hour. What the Giant thought he saw, Gair could not imagine. Gair saw a fierce, moody nature, unhappy deep down, and unhappy, too, on the surface now, because of the Giantess. Then the Giant blinked and started to take his hands out of his pockets. The moment his eyes closed, Gair whisked himself out of sight round the tree and got ready to run. He had a feeling Ayna said something. He waited for the Giant to move. Waited. And waited.

"Funny," said the Giant. He began walking away. Gair could not believe it at first. But, when he dared to look, he saw the Giant's tall narrow back as the Giant limped slowly away toward the pulsing house.

"Whew!" said Ceri. "Narrow escape! I thought he was going to start on Gair."

"He was," said Ayna. "That's why I said the words to stop dogs. Which just goes to prove what beasts Giants are! *Wasn't* he a beast?"

"Foul," Ceri agreed. "Wasn't she *fat?*"

"Sort of tight," Ayna said, chuckling. "As if she'd been blown up!"

"Let's get back," said Gair. He did not like the wood any more. It still seemed to boom with a faint pulsing, though the Giantess must have been a long way off by then. And meeting the Giant face to face had shaken him badly. Gair was not happy until they had crossed the tufty field and reached the marshy meadow beyond. Even then he did not want to talk much. But Ayna and Ceri were thoroughly excited and had plenty to say.

"She wasn't very tall," Ceri said. "Neither of them was. I thought Giants were bigger than that."

"Of course they are," said Ayna. "Full-grown Giants are yards high. Those were only children." Gair knew she was right. If he compared their size with that of the monstrous blurred foot he had seen on his first hunt, he saw they could not have been fully grown. And he realized he had known they were children all along, by their behavior.

But Ceri was dubious. "Then how old were they?"

"Only babies," Ayna said decidedly.

"No they weren't," Ceri said, equally decidedly. "The fat one was older than me, and she was the youngest."

"You're just being silly," Ayna said loftily.

"I'm not. I can tell. So can you, if you think," said Ceri. "Fatso wasn't as old as you. She was more Gair's age. But the Snotty one was older, maybe older than you are, even. Isn't that true, Gair?"

Gair nodded. He had a feeling Ceri had got it right, which was very puzzling.

Ceri turned triumphantly to Ayna. "There! So full-grown Giants *can't* be yards high. You're almost as tall as Mother now."

This seemed to be undeniable. Gair thought again of the foot he had seen. He had been very small at the time, of course, and things seen near to and blurrily always looked larger than they were. Perhaps Giants were not the huge beings he had supposed. Maybe their Giantliness really lay in their violent, larger-than-life behavior.

"Giants," Ayna declared, "grow at a different rate from people." But she did not feel on strong enough ground to continue with that subject. "Wasn't the Snotty one like Ondo! I was quite sorry for Fatso."

"You needn't be," said Ceri, speaking from bitter experience. "You could see she'd done horrible things to him, too. Though at least you don't kick me very often," he added handsomely.

Ayna ignored this. They had come in among the long white grasses, and she pretended to be very busy looking out for standing pools and steering clear of dikes. A thought struck her. "We couldn't get Ondo over there and set Snotty on him somehow, could we? I'd love to see someone make mincemeat of Ondo!"

"Gair did," Ceri reminded her.

Ayna looked at Gair and realized she had been tactless. The gloomy, lonely look she and Ceri knew so well had settled on Gair's face. Gair thought of Ondo rolling among the bees. He rather dreaded what must be in store for him in Garholt. Worse still, he remembered the misery in which he had set out, which the Giants had knocked clean out of his head. It was not so bad now, but he knew he would never see Gest the same way again.

"Do you want us to stay out longer?" Ayna asked, trying to make up for what she had said. Gloomily, Gair shook his head. He felt he might as well get it over.

Ceri looked up into Gair's face in frank fascination. "You know, it's not Ondo Snotty was like! It's you, Gair!" He scuttled sideways as both Gair and Ayna rounded on him. "I didn't mean it!"

"Yes you did," Gair said bitterly. "You mean I'm proud and brutish, don't you?" He feared Ceri was right again. Ceri was far too observant for comfort. And, during that short, endless moment in which he and the Giant had stared at one another, Gair had indeed felt he was looking at someone rather like himself.

Ayna and Ceri did their best to soothe him.

"No, no. I just meant dark and gloomy," Ceri protested.

"You're *not* brutish!" said Ayna. "And a Chief's son has every right to be proud." She saw she was being tactless again. "You're never proud to us." This only seemed to make matters worse. Ayna was wondering what else she dared say, and Gair was thinking that this day seemed to be dedicated to unpleasant discoveries, when the storm the magic box had predicted hit the Moor. The grasses whistled and leaned over. The Sun shot like gold pouring into a mold between racing blue clouds. The stinging rain soaked them in seconds, and hailstones clotted in their hair and their clothes.

They ran for the flimsy shelter of a thornbush and crouched behind it, shivering. "How did that box know?" Ayna wondered.

"Giant's magic," said Ceri, whose teeth were chattering. "I wondered whether to put a Thought on it, to make it shout rude things at Snotty. But I didn't quite dare."

"Good thing," said Ayna. "Knowing you, it would probably have grown legs and run about."

Ceri opened his mouth to explain he could control Thoughts, and decided against it. That was Gair's secret. Gair was dejectedly watching the hailstones hiss through the heaving grass, wondering what made him seem proud. He had nothing to be proud of. In an effort to think of something else, he hit on an uneasiness which had nagged at him for some time now.

"What did she mean, saying the Moor would be flooded next year?"

"I thought she was just yelling nasty things to scare Snotty," Ayna said doubtfully.

"She couldn't have meant it," said Ceri.

But Gair was fairly sure the Giantess *had* meant it.

It had been in her manner, and the Giant had not denied it. And the way her feet had boomed through the wood for some reason made Gair surer still that she had been speaking the truth. He thought about it while the storm raged around and behind them. How could anyone flood such a big place as the Moor? And who would want to? The answer seemed to be the Dorig. They had already begun by flooding Otmound. In that case—Gair had a sudden horrible vision of everyone on the Moor drowning or homeless. Surely not. Surely the luck did not run so much against them as that. He would have to ask Adara. And if this disaster really was coming, the Giants would drown, too. So it looked as if Giants were the enemies of Dorig as much as people.

Ayna was thinking, too, but her thoughts went the other way. "If she did mean it, then that must be the reason the Otmounders are going so far away. You asked me the wrong question, Gair. I knew somebody would! Dorig and Giants are in league against us."

"I don't think they are," Gair said, bowing over as the bush rattled in a stinging gust.

"They are," said Ayna. "That's why the Dorig said they wouldn't attack Garholt. They're leaving us to the Giants. Ask me. Go on."

"Ask you what?" said Gair.

"Stupid!" said Ayna. "Ceri, ask me."

"Will the Giants attack Garholt?" Ceri said, promptly and anxiously.

Ayna gazed out into the swirling grass. "No," she said, with great decision, and laughed, because she was so relieved. "Then we've only the Dorig to worry about. Let's go home. This storm's not going to blow over in a hurry, and we couldn't be wetter if the Dorig had caught us." She stood up, bent over in the wind, with her hair blown sideways. "Come on." Her voice whipped away over the marsh and they could hardly hear it.

Ceri and Gair got up and squelched after her. Gair sighed, because Ceri's question and Ayna's answer did not seem to him to have settled anything. But he had no clear idea what Ayna should have been asked. Nothing was clear. His mind seemed to be a vague cloud of worry, pulsing a little like the Giants' house and the booming of the Giantess's feet. When he looked out across the Moor, it had become hissing gray distance with regular white gusts beating across it. The inside of his head felt the same. He sighed.

He sighed more frequently as they plodded closer to Garholt. Ceri and Ayna took to giving him consoling smiles.

"Don't worry," said Ayna. "It'll all be over by tonight. Father won't stay angry."

Gair was busy with his vague worry and he lost half this in the wind. "What?"

"Father was dying to hit Ondo himself," Ceri called. "She means."

"Saw it in his eye," Ayna shouted.

Gair supposed he must be dreading returning to Garholt. He did not feel as if he was — or not that much. But he could not understand why else he should feel so depressed.

Chapter
7

IT WAS EARLY EVENING WHEN, WINDSWEPT AND drenched, they reached Garholt at last and spoke the words at the hive-gate. It opened on to the warmth and smells of the overcrowded mound, and almost every face inside turned up to look at them. There was a moment of unnatural quiet.

It was like a menace. Gair felt gloom and terror flooding up from inside the mound, swirling and mounting over the tapestries, dimming the faces, dulling the warm smells. It was like the uneasiness he had felt ever since the Otmounders came, but far, far stronger. His mouth went dry with it and his knees weak. Then most people went back to what they were doing. Conversation began, exclamations and laughter, and sour remarks from Otmounders.

Adara came hurrying to the foot of the steps. "Where have you all been?"

Miri pushed past her and panted up the steps. "Caught in that storm! Wet through, the lot of them!"

It was plain she and Adara had been very anxious. But, when she reached them, Gair saw Miri was frightened, too scared to scold properly. "You meddled with nothing outside? No Powers?" she asked breathlessly.

"No. Nothing," they answered, semi-truthfully, wondering what made her ask. Though the feeling of gloom had subsided a little, Gair still felt depressed as he answered—but this could have been because Gest was now standing at the foot of the steps with his arms grimly folded.

"I'll see you, Gair, when you're in dry clothes," Gest said.

All the time Miri was fussing him into dry clothes, Gair tried to feel courageous. It was not easy. Ondo was lying in his bed under a mound of blankets, rolling and moaning, to remind him of his sins. When Miri pushed Gair into the room where Gest was grimly waiting, Gair found he had barely any courage left.

Gest had his belt unbuckled and swinging in his hand. Gair could not take his eyes off it. "What have you got to say for yourself?" said Gest.

Gair thought miserably that Ondo could not have said anything he was less likely to tell Gest. He looked at his father's tall, strong frame and wished he could still think he was a hero. "Nothing," he said. "He got on my windowsill."

"I saw him," said Gest. "You promised not to fight him."

Gair nodded. Just like Gest promised not to fight Dorig, he thought. "I forgot."

"Oh, did you?" said Gest. His mouth parted his golden beard in a laugh. Gair looked at it and shivered. "I'd have done the same myself," said Gest. "But Kasta wants you punished, you know." Miserably, Gair nodded again. "So we'll have to please her," said Gest. "Stand over there."

Gair stood, trying not to quake. Behind him, the belt whistled. He clenched his teeth. There was a heavy thump as the belt hit something—something not Gair. Gair spun round in time to see the belt come down and slash the floor a second time.

"That's for Kasta!" Gest said, between his teeth. "Thinks she can give me orders, does she?" He belabored the floor several more times. Whistle-thump, whistle-thump. Outside, it must have sounded just as if Gest was hitting Gair. Gair could not help smiling—though it was not very happily. Gest was cheating again. Islaw people were as tricksy as Ondo said. Almost—but not quite—Gair would have preferred Gest to hit him.

Gest looked up, hot and irritable from the effort. "What are you looking so glum about?"

"I—" said Gair. "You're cheating."

Gest stared at him. "Do you want me to hit you, then?"

"No!" said Gair. "No—no!"

"And you're going to go and tell Kasta all about it?"

"Of course not!" Gair said indignantly.

"Then you're cheating, too," said Gest. "Aren't you?"

"No," said Gair. "Yes." By now, he was bewildered as well as miserable. The muddles and troubles of the day were suddenly too much for him. He felt his face harden into an angry scowl. The blood rushed up round his eyes and his fists clenched themselves. He wondered where to hit Gest, and how hard. "You made me cheat! You're the cheat, not me!"

Gest's head went slowly up. He became every inch a cold, proud Chief, and, somehow, Gair did not feel able to hit him. "I am, am I?" said Gest. "Then if that's what you think, you can have your punishment. You're forbidden to go on the hunt. You can tell Adara you're staying behind with the babies."

"What hunt? When?" Gair was seized by a sudden unreasonable alarm. It seemed to take him by the throat like a hard hand. "You're not going hunting!"

"We are. Tomorrow. You're not," Gest said, and went to the door. "You and Ondo will be the only boys left behind," he said as he went out. "That'll teach you to speak to me like that."

"Don't go!" Gair said despairingly, though he knew

it was a silly thing to say and he did not know why he said it. But Gest had already stalked out of the house.

At supper, no one talked of much except the hunt. Orban had given in to Gest's argument. Every available man and boy and any girl who had no other job was to go. They had settled to go the following night, so that they could stay out for three days if necessary, until the Moon was nearly full, and bring back as much meat as they could catch, to provision Garholt for the Feast of the Sun at Full Moon, and for as long as possible after that. It was clear Orban hoped, now that he had given in to Gest, that Gest would give in to him and agree to attack the Dorig when they came back.

Little does he know! Gair thought bitterly, sitting silent beside Ceri. Or perhaps Orban did know, but he seemed not to think one need bother to keep faith with Dorig.

No one was surprised Gair was subdued. Miri managed to sneak him several nice tidbits, even though supplies were so low that supper was rather plain. Miri and Fandi were engaged in their usual battle to get their own family the best helpings. It was very wearisome. If Ayna had not told him the Otmounders were going away soon, Gair would have left the eating-square. The inexplicable feeling of alarm grabbed at his throat every time the hunt was mentioned, and he did not want to listen. He wanted to think about Giants and devise some way of asking Adara who might want to flood the Moor without giving away that he had stood face to face with a Giant.

The battle for the best helpings was complicated by Ondo, lying in bed and calling out fretfully from the house. Fandi and Kasta connived together to send Ondo in the best food. Kasta several times took things from Orban when he was not looking.

Orban bore with their fussing until the end of the meal and his fourth mug of beer. Then he said, "You spoil that boy, Kasta. He'd be as well as I am if you let him alone." Kasta at once exclaimed that Ondo was *very* delicate and—with a venomous look at Gair—in *great* pain besides. "Nonsense!" said Orban. "He's as tough as boots. I'm sick of this cosseting. He's going on this hunt, stings or no stings. Make a man of him."

Kasta and Fandi both clamored against him. Kasta clamored Fandi down and went on clamoring alone. She was one of those who could talk and talk and talk. Gair listened to her harsh voice—"Just like a duck," Ayna described it—and hoped she would lose the argument. But Adara once said Kasta had never lost an argument in her life. She just talked everyone insensible. Gair tried to resign himself to being left behind in Garholt with Ondo. But for Ondo, it would not have been too bad. There would be Ayna for company, and he could help with the root-flour, taste preserved fruit, mix honeycakes and shell nuts. It was like being small again, but fun, as it always was, preparing for Feasts—but not with Ondo there, swollen and angry.

Kasta was still quacking away when Banot and the other Chanters gathered between the wells to chant luck for the hunt, and she only fell silent when the chanting began. Gair leaned against the round stone hood of the fourth well to listen, and to wonder, as he often idly did, why Banot's harp had one whitish string that never seemed to break. But the uneasy feeling began to grow out at him from the walls of the mound and snatch at his throat, as soon as the chanting finished and Adara came to tell Gest and Orban how the luck lay. It seemed to lie well. But the feeling pressed and grabbed at Gair, and he felt something was wrong, though he did not know what. When Ayna came to be consulted, he went up onto his windowsill to avoid it.

The windows were now sealed for the night. Gair had no view except the great vault of Garholt itself with its tapestries shimmering shadowily in the light, the ring of old, round houses, the half-built new ones and the inner ring of wells, like little houses themselves. He could see everyone gathered round the space there and Ayna, conspicuous with her fair hair, standing very upright to be consulted. He could faintly hear her answers.

"Deer, in the Northeast . . . yes, beyond the river . . . keep to the hills above Otmound."

Orban looked thoughtful here. He seemed to ask if the Dorig from Otmound were likely to attack the hunt.

"No," said Ayna. Orban did not look altogether pleased. He wanted to abandon hunting for war if he could. The feeling of oppression and gloom grew so strong on Gair that he wanted to shout out to them not to go.

He fell asleep that night to the sound of Kasta quacking at Orban. In the morning, she had stopped. Orban was looking tired and dismal and Kasta smug.

"I think Ondo's staying," Ayna said gloomily. "Lucky Ceri! I wish I could go on the hunt." Ayna, because of the value of her Gift, was not allowed to hunt very often. Ceri wished his Gifts were that valuable. He did not think himself lucky at all. Three hard days in the open appalled him. He would rather have had Ondo.

"I wish you were going, Gair," he said dolefully.

Rather than answer, Gair slid away from the bustle of preparation and climbed onto his windowsill again. Scodo and Pad limped among the looms and called jeeringly up at him. Gair ignored them. He looked out at cloud shadows racing on the flat Moor, over to the hazy hills in the North where the deer might be even now. Below him, Miri's son, Med, who was Beekeeper these days, was kneeling by the hives telling the bees about the hunt and asking them to guard Garholt while it was gone. Behind Gair was bustle, and the clatter of the forges.

There was no reason why he should feel depressed. He had been left behind before. Nevertheless, Gair found he just could not bear to stay in Garholt while everyone prepared to go hunting. A little dazzled from watching Sun and clouds, Gair glanced back into the mound. Scodo and Pad had gone. No one was looking at him. Gair swung himself off the sill in a leap which carried him over Med's head, to land on the hillside just below. There, he waited. You were always polite to bees and their Keeper.

Med looked up and grinned as Gair landed. Med had bees crawling all over him, dark on his arms and legs, gently strolling on his neck and face and whirling round his head. "They were glad to oblige you over Ondo," Med said, "but they lost a lot of workers over it. So don't do it again, will you?"

"No," said Gair. "Tell them I'm sorry." He was sorry. Bees had died to revenge him.

"And they say the strawberries are ripe by the wood," Med added cheerfully. "You'll be first there if you go now."

By this, Gair knew that the bees had freely forgiven him. He thanked them, and Med, and then went off to the strawberries, largely because Med and the bees would expect him to. But he ate only a few. Five minutes later, he was trotting steadily among the marsh grass, in the direction of the Giants' pulsing house.

His depression lifted as he trotted. He began thinking

of the Giants and wondering who could be plotting to flood the Moor. It must be the Dorig. Dorig lived underwater and ate fish. Giants lived by the land more than people and grew things from it to eat, so it followed that they would not want it underwater. Gair, as he trotted, looked round the bare, cloudswept landscape and saw that it would be easy to fill the Moor with water. All the Dorig need do was to complete the ring of hills with a wall or so and dam up the slow, winding rivers. But, surely, if the Giants knew their plans, they were going to stop the Dorig trying? Gair intended to listen to Giants again and find out what they meant to do.

Or he thought he did, until he came upon the Giant Gerald gloomily wandering in the wood beside the pulsing house. After that, he knew why he had really come. He wanted to know if the Giant was like Ondo, or if, as Ceri had said, he was even more like Gair. Or if—which was the most troubling thought—the Giant resembled both because Gair was like Ondo.

He spent the rest of the morning lurking from tree to bush, watching Gerald and trying to decide. It was not truly difficult. Gerald strode about crushing grass and shaking the earth, his dark face set in a lonely, private look which Gair found very familiar. It was not Ondo's look. Gair knew it was his own. The Giant did not look happy. Gair wondered why. He wondered, too, if he looked that unhappy himself.

The difficult thing was that the Giant seemed to sense he was being watched. He kept swinging round irritably, and Gair was several times only just quick enough in sliding out of sight. It happened so often that the feeling affected Gair, too. He turned round quickly a number of times, sure that he would catch somebody sliding out of sight—probably Ayna and Ceri again. But there was never anything but a bird, or a gray squirrel clinging to a tree. It became so tiresome that Gair would have gone away, had he not wanted so badly to know why the Giant behaved like Ondo, too.

When the Sun showed midday, Gerald went back to his pulsing house. As Gair could not follow him there, he was forced to trot back to Garholt without having settled the question. Most of the way, he went very briskly, but, as soon as Garholt was in sight, his trot faltered. He dropped to a walk. Finally he stood still, wondering whether to go on to Islaw to see his aunt rather than face the depression he knew was waiting to clutch him in Garholt. He had not felt it yet, but he knew he would. He decided Islaw was too far, if he was to spend the afternoon watching the Giant again. So he braced himself and went to the hive door.

No sooner was the door open than, sure enough, the feeling was there, climbing up out of the walls of Garholt and clutching at Gair. It was more like a solid thing than a feeling. He had to force himself down the steps against it. And when he was down, there was bustle and bad temper and far too many people. Everyone was irritable. Gest was in a very bad humor and Ceri had fallen foul of him.

Gair could not quite understand what had happened, because the trouble appeared to have something to do with himself. No one quite liked to tell him what Gest had said. But Gest had said it, and Ceri had replied. They had yelled at one another.

"Only fancy!" said Miri. "Ceri threatened to put a Thought on his own father! I don't know what we're coming to, I really don't!"

Gest told Ceri he would risk the Thought and asked him which he preferred: a belting, or not going on the hunt. Ceri promptly opted for staying at home. Gest had replied with some well-chosen words about Ceri's character, and that was that. Ceri was not going hunting either.

When Gair saw Ceri at the eating-square, Ceri looked sulky, but Gair could tell he was thoroughly satisfied. "I don't know what's the matter with Father at the moment," he grumbled, trying to hide a secret smile. "If you say anything, he snaps your head off."

"Gest has a great deal on his mind," Adara explained to Gair when Gair went to find her among the stores, "now that there are twice as many people here. And I don't think Orban is being as helpful as he might.

Don't cross your father."

Gair's one wish was to keep out of Gest's way. There were other things he wanted to say to Adara. "Mother," he said, "what are the lines of luck from now to next year? Are they good or bad?"

Adara screwed her face up thoughtfully. "I hardly know. Nothing's clear at the moment. Why?"

"Is it clear for Dorig, or Giants?" Gair asked.

"Ban's bones!" said Adara. "Let me think. Dorig are clear enough. Their fortunes follow Saturn and the Moon, and both are strong for some time to come. But Giants—Their luck is no clearer than ours. Why?"

Lines of luck were strange and confusing, Gair thought. To look at the Giant Gerald, you would have thought his fortunes followed gloomy Saturn, if ever anyone's did. He suspected his own did, too. But he had other things to ask about. "Mother, could the Moor ever turn into a lake?"

Adara looked at Gair anxiously. One thing she knew all about was the secret unhappiness that made people ask strange questions. But she did not think Gair had any reason to be unhappy. "The Moor was a lake once," she said. "When they were enlarging Beckill, they found skeletons of fish, and shells, embedded in the earth— and even stranger things in Islaw. And sometimes, the way the luck lies, the Moor still behaves like water. The Moon draws it. I think that's why the Dorig live here.

Gair, are you unhappy?"

"Oh no," said Gair. He did not want to talk about his unreasonable depression, and he was afraid of being led to confess to following a Giant about. "There's a certain kind of person," he said hurriedly, "who's private and lonely and—anyway, why do people think those kind of people are proud? Aren't they just ordinary?"

"I wouldn't say they're ordinary," Adara said, hoping this got to the seat of Gair's trouble. "Some people find it more difficult to be easy with other people, and perhaps, if they seem proud, it's the best they can do. Such people usually have a lot going on inside their heads."

"I see." Gair felt his face going red. "Is Ondo that kind of person?"

"Ondo?" Adara said dryly. "I wouldn't say that was one of Ondo's troubles. No. Reserve and conceit are rather different things."

"Thanks," said Gair, and he dashed away, much comforted.

Adara, as soon as she had finished with the stores, went to try and find him. He had worried her. But by that time Gair was halfway to the Giant's house, thinking as he trotted that he was in a fair way to becoming a Giant addict.

The Giant was ranging about in the wood again. And now Gair was comforted by what Adara had said, he almost felt he knew him. If he was in doubt about any feeling which crossed the Giant's gloomy face, he only had to look into his own mind and he knew—or knew more or less. After five minutes of lurking and watching, he discovered that the reason Gerald had been so unpleasant to the Giantess was that Gerald felt the same way about the wood that Gair did about his windowsill. The wood was Gerald's windowsill—his private place—but, being a Giant, Gerald needed a larger place than Gair did. He was jealous of it and, as he had done in the morning, he kept turning round to make sure he was alone.

Gair caught the feeling, just as he had done in the morning. He had a notion that it had something to do with the pulsing house. He could feel it, at the corner of his mind, queerly shifting from ugly to lovely just beyond the wood. It made him uneasy. He kept needing to turn his head.

One time he turned, he found the old mild dog had ambled into the wood out of the Sun. When Gair saw it, it was amiably staring at a gray squirrel, which was clinging halfway up a tree trunk, obviously not at all scared by the dog. Gair softly spoke the words and the dog came amiably to him. He made a fuss of it. It was so old and so good-humored that he wondered again what possible use it could be to the Giants.

The Giant saw the dog and called to it. But the dog was enjoying Gair scratching its chin and did not bother to move.

The next second, the Giant was crashing among the trees toward Gair. "Tober! Tober, come here!"

Gair let go of the dog, slid round a tree and flattened himself against it. He was terrified. All he had been told about the ruthlessness of Giants, all he had discovered about their strength and violence, made his heart bang and his stomach turn. If the Giant found him in his private place—! But he wanted to know Gerald. He yearned to talk to him. He was the only being Gair knew with whom he had anything in common. But he dared not move.

"My father could do it!" Gair told himself angrily. "Why can't I?"

He stayed flattened against the tree while Gerald trampled up and took the dog away.

Later, Gair returned slowly and moodily to Garholt. He was ashamed of his failure. He was also dreading the feeling he knew would meet him as soon as he went inside the mound.

But the feeling took him by surprise by climbing out of Garholt and seizing him by the throat before he had reached the gate. It took Gair and shook him. It was like a great living creature. Gair choked and almost fell over. "What *is* it?" he said. "Stop it, can't you?" It made no difference. The feeling clenched itself on Gair's neck and seemed to wrap itself round his shoulders. But it was all round, too. Gair had to fight his way into the mound against it, and, inside, it was even worse. It made Gair want to shout things, peculiar things. He went down the steps very slowly, biting his teeth together, determined not to open his mouth except to eat. He knew it was going to force him to say something stupid if he gave in to it for a moment.

Garholt was quiet and businesslike by this time. All the preparations for hunting were made. Those who were going were ready to eat supper and be off. The only one bustling was Kasta. Since Ondo was still in bed, wringing the last drop out of his injuries, Kasta was free to fuss noisily round Orban, to remember this, recall that and generally make a stir.

"Must draw attention to herself, that one!" Miri said savagely. Then she looked at Gair's face. "What's the matter? Where have you been?"

"Gair, what is it?" said Adara.

"Nothing," said Gair, and bit his teeth together again. Miri and Adara looked at him so anxiously that Gair wondered what was the matter with his face. But he dared not ask, for fear the feeling made him say something insane. It kept forcing at him and forcing at him, jabbing him with horror, racking him with anxiety, trying to make him shout out nonsense, so that he had to resist it all the time.

Over supper, Gest gave Adara instructions about what to do while the hunt was gone. Everything he said seemed to make Gair's feeling worse. "Don't trouble with the building," he said. "Unless the old men want to do the carpentry. And be careful of strangers—don't let them know we're all away. Will you need to send any parties out of the mound?"

"Yes. The strawberries should be ripe," said Adara. "I was going to send the children, with Gair for a guard."

Gest looked at Gair, who was listening with his head bent and his teeth clenched against the feeling. "Hm," he said. "But do make sure—"

Kasta turned from sending Fandi to Ondo with a plover's egg. "No need to worry, Gest," she said. "I'll be in charge."

Gest looked at her as if he could not believe his ears. "In charge?"

Kasta wriggled and gave a preening sort of smile. "Of course. I am the senior wife, after all."

"*You!*" said Gest.

"Now, Gest," said Orban. "We can settle this reasonably."

"NO WE CANNOT!" said Gest. "I give orders in Garholt. Not you, and certainly not Kasta. Is that clear?"

"Well, I—" said Orban.

"Don't be ridiculous, Gest!" said Kasta. "You can't pass over me for Adara, when my experience—" The quacking noise was in her voice. Everyone sighed.

"Shut *up*!" said Gest. Kasta stopped, with her mouth

open, outraged. "No amount of noise from you," said Gest, "is going to make any difference. Adara is in charge while I'm gone. If you don't like it, you can come on the hunt, too. Now hold your tongue!"

Kasta's face twisted with rage. She opened her mouth again, to point out that she was far too important to go hunting. Gest stared at her, daring her to say another word. And, to everyone's surprise, Kasta slowly shut her mouth again. There was an uneasy, admiring silence, which grew longer and longer, as everyone realized Gest had actually worsted Kasta.

To Gair, it was unbearable. The feeling grabbed him in the silence, and squeezed and squeezed, forced at his throat and squashed words out of him before he could stop it.

"Don't go hunting," he said. "Please. Don't any of you go."

Everyone at the eating-square turned and stared at him. Orban's eyebrows went up; Fandi tittered. Gest looked exasperated.

"Why did you say that, Gair?" Adara asked quickly.

Gair had no idea, except that he had been unable to stop. He felt ashamed and stupid. All he could do was shake his head. He dared not speak.

"Poor little soul!" Kasta said maliciously. "He's over-wrought!"

She could have said nothing better calculated to annoy

Gest. He looked coldly from Gair's shamed face to Ceri's puzzled one. "I seem to have fathered a rare couple of ninnies," he said, and for the rest of supper he pointedly talked only to Ayna and Adara.

The people going on the hunt were mustering by the main gate. Gest got up to join them. The feeling rushed at Gair so fiercely that it was all he could do not to shout out.

Orban said, "Won't be a moment," and hurried into the house.

He was gone some time. The muster by the main gate grew, and was surrounded by ladies tightening buckles and reminding their relatives that they had spare socks in their bag and the *green* blanket was waterproof. Gest became impatient. Kasta ran about wondering what Orban was doing.

Orban came out of the house towing Ondo. Ondo was dressed, and very sulky indeed. There was not a sign of a bee sting on him, except for a small purple blotch on one cheek, but Kasta screamed at the sight of him, and wrung her hands.

Ondo liked hunting even less than Ceri. He took instant advantage of it. "I'm not well enough, Mother! Don't let him make me go hunting!"

"Of course you mustn't, darling! Orban—!" quacked Kasta.

Orban took no notice. He nodded to Adara, and

Adara brought out Ondo's hunting-bag, ready packed, his blanket, his weapons and his belt. Ondo protested that he felt *ghastly*. Kasta, finding Orban and Adara had gone behind her back, shot them venomous looks, and pursued Orban as he dragged the miserable Ondo over to the gate, quacking like a whole flight of ducks. Fandi pursued Kasta, rather put out to find that even the Otmounders were trying not to laugh.

"Serve them both right!" said Miri, and hastened to see that Med was properly equipped.

"Let's go and say good-by," Adara said to Ayna, Ceri and Gair.

Gair would much rather not have gone. He knew it would look stupid and sulky not to say good-by, but the feeling was now so strong that he could only resist it by bracing his legs and clenching his teeth and standing where he was.

They went over to the gate. The feeling tried to push Gair there ahead of the others. He had to lean against it to stay beside them. And once they were among the hunters, it was worse than ever. Through a sort of haze of horror, Gair saw Miri embarrassing Med by repacking his socks; Banot joking with Tille as they did a last-minute repair on Brad's spear-lashing; Dari's little sisters presenting her with a lucky flint; Gest smiling cheerfully at Adara; and Orban firmly buckling equipment onto the sullen Ondo. The feeling beat at Gair and shook him, and he dared not open his mouth.

Gest kissed Ayna and turned to Gair. "I'm relying on you to help your mother," he said. Gair dared not say anything. He dared not even nod, for fear the feeling took control. He could only stare at Gest. "Answer me, can't you!" Gest said irritably.

"Yes, I'll help," Gair said. And, as soon as he opened his mouth, the feeling had him at its mercy. "Don't go," he said. "Please don't go."

Gest was annoyed enough already at the delay Orban had caused. He glared at Gair. Adara, remembering the odd questions Gair had asked her, began to think he was ill. She shook her head warningly at Gest. Gest ground his teeth and said, with terrible patience, "We have to go. We're short of food."

Gair could tell by the patience in his father's voice that Gest had no intention of attending to a word he said. He could not see why Gest *should* attend. But the feeling made him frantic. "Don't go. Something's wrong!"

All the hunters turned and looked at Gair uneasily. Gest was exasperated, for he knew that much more of this would seriously interfere with their luck.

"Poor child!" Kasta said artificially, from the background.

That made Gest really angry. "I'm not going to stand here all night listening to nonsense!" he said. "Open the gate, someone."

Banot said the words. The big opening rumbled and parted, showing blue and white, mist and Moonlight. Orban, calling good-by, pulled Ondo through it, where they at once became vague, bleached figures. The others followed.

The feeling twisted at Gair and jerked him. "Don't go!" he said desperately. And, when Gest simply turned away to the door, Gair was forced to follow him, the feeling scoured through him so. "If you must go," he called out, "you must make sure no living thing comes through here until you come back!" For the life of him, he could not see why he should say that.

"Ban!" Gest said savagely. "Adara, take him away before he spoils the luck completely!"

Adara took hold of Gair's arm, and Gest went out through the gate, calling good-by to Ceri as he went, and bleaching away into the Moonlight like the others. The big opening thumped shut again. Gair stood looking at it. The feeling was dying, now that he had said what it made him say. He was left with the unpleasant knowledge that he had made a fool of himself—as badly as Kasta, he thought miserably.

"Gair," said Adara, "I don't think you're well. You're going to bed, with something to make you sleep. Come along."

"All right," said Gair. He felt very tired. But the feeling had not quite gone. It gave a last twist. "You did hear what I said, didn't you? No living thing," he said anxiously.

"Yes, yes," said Adara. "Come along."

The drink was strong and worked quickly. Gair was asleep when Ayna, driven by her own worries, shook his shoulder fiercely. "Gair! Wake up! They asked me the wrong questions, didn't they? Gair, wake up and tell me what they should have asked!" Gair tried to wake up, but he could not manage it. He mumbled. "Bother you!" Ayna crossly shoved his shoulder and went away.

Chapter
8

WHAT WITH THE DRINK AND HAVING HIS OWN
bed again, Gair slept very well indeed. He woke up feeling calm, rested and happy. It was soon after dawn. He
could tell that, because the windows had been unfastened
and a damp breeze was blowing into the house, smelling
of early morning. He could hear people moving about,
and the double flock of sheep bleating by the gate to be
milked. Then came the slap and hiss of a nutcake going
on the griddle. Miri, at the fire outside, was getting breakfast. Gair lay wondering why he felt so happy—as if he
had thrown off a weight. No Ondo, that must be it.

The smell of hot nutcake swept toward his nose.
Gair found he was ravenous. He sprang up, dressed
and dragged a comb through his hair. When he came
out of the house, Ceri, blinking with sleep, was already
sitting wistfully beside the pile of nutcakes on the
eating-square, waiting for Miri to turn her back. But
Miri, squatting over the cooking-fire, her gold bracelets
flashing as she turned the browned cakes, was wise to

Ceri. She watched him like a hawk.

"Nutcakes!" Gair said ravenously.

Miri laughed. "I see you slept well. All in good time. Nutcakes after the milking."

"Milking?" Gair said. His empty stomach seemed to turn over. "Are they doing it outside?" he said anxiously.

"No," said Miri. "Why should they?"

"*Ban!*" said Gair. "They *mustn't!*" As he said it, he heard the rumble of the main gate opening. He turned to see the big archway filled with wreathing mist, colored orange by the rising Sun, and he knew it was too late. He was too sleepy still to wonder how he knew. His only thought was to stop it. He pelted to where Adara stood by the milking pens, holding a bucket.

"Hallo, Gair. Slept well?" she said.

From outside in the mist came the "Hi, hi, hi!" of Ayna and the other girls, driving the sheep in to be milked.

"I told you not to let in any living thing!" Gair said. "I *told* you! Close the gate."

Adara looked at him anxiously. "Gair! I hoped you'd be better."

"There's nothing *wrong* with me!" said Gair. "Can I close the gate, then?"

"Don't be silly," said Adara. "Not till the milking's done."

As she said it, the first of the ewes came scampering into the mound, bundling and bleating, with their Ondo-like ears cocked and their silly yellow eyes staring. Bleating filled the mist behind them. Out there was a mass of gray backs, sheep ears and yellow eyes, with here and there the curling horns of a ram, or the flitting shape of one of the girls. The cold of the mist struck in with the noise.

"Shut it!" said Gair. "There's still time."

Ayna, as she always did, came through the gate after the first huddle of ewes, and stationed herself to turn them into the pens.

"*Shut the gate!*" Gair screamed at her. But Ayna could not hear him above the frantic bleating of the herd. Sheep poured into Garholt in a solid stream, like a river in flood, more and more and more. Nothing could be heard but their little feet drumming and their loud, ceaseless bleating. Ayna was swept aside. The hurdles of the pens were trampled down. And still the sheep came. Gair could see them, dimly, out in the mist, seemingly going on forever. He felt sick. There were far, far too many.

"Why are there so many?" Adara said, quite bewildered. "Even with two flocks—"

The girls in the gateway screamed. "Dorig! Help!"

The sheep running toward Adara wavered. They became misty blots, which climbed into misty columns. "Gair, I beg your pardon," said Adara. The columns hardened and set into silver-plated tall bodies with pointed heads. They were all long, thin Dorig now, carrying round shields and bent swords. To Gair, the most horrifying thing was that their grim white faces still had yellow sheep's eyes.

Adara threw her pail at the nearest, but it clanged harmlessly on the silver scales. "Gair, get all the children out!" she screamed as the Dorig closed round her.

That was the last Gair saw of her. He turned and ran, his skin up in prickles at the cold of the shape-shifting. There was utter confusion. Gray Dorig flitted everywhere with light, gliding steps. Real sheep with Garholt and Otmound markings blundered about, mad with fear. There were screams, clangs, a queer gluey smell mixed with the smell of burning. A house was on fire. Kasta's voice was quacking, babies were crying. Gair tried to run toward the houses and find some children. If he could find just a few, he might slip out of a side gate and take them after the hunt.

But it was like a nightmare. Gair never could reach the houses. A sheep blundered across his path and melted into a pale Dorig. Gair swerved and raced away. He tried to avoid even real sheep after that. But they were everywhere, and so were Dorig. He found himself running this way, then that. He slipped in something and saw it was blood. While he was down, a Dorig came for him with great strides. Gair scrambled up, slithering, dodging as he slithered, and tried to run for hiding in the half-built houses. As he ran, he saw Fandi lying on the ground and Miri standing astride her, dealing great swipes at Dorig with a broom. There was a hard, hopeless look on Miri's face which Gair well understood. More Dorig came for him as he reached the new buildings and he was forced to swerve away. There were no children anywhere. He seemed entirely alone, running and running.

Then he was in the space by the looms, almost under his window.

"Gair! Help!"

Ceri was pattering frantically up from one side. There were three Dorig on his heels. Gair put Ceri behind him and turned to face the Dorig. He found there was a whole line of tall silvery warriors moving slowly toward them, between himself and the battle among the houses. This end of the mound was comparatively quiet. Gair heard Ayna's feet thudding as she dashed toward them in front of three more Dorig. She was so frightened that her eyes looked mad.

"Gair, I don't want to be killed!"

The Dorig stopped. "That's three with gold collars," one said matter-of-factly. "Haven't they found the fourth yet?"

"I'll go and see," said another. They both had an odd hissing lilt to their voices, but it was easy enough to understand what they said. Gair watched the second

Dorig set off toward the houses with long gliding steps and saw that, confusing though it had seemed, he and Ayna and Ceri had been deliberately herded to this end. He did not care to think why.

"What shall we *do*?" whispered Ayna. "Oh, why didn't they ask me the right *question*?"

"My window," said Gair. "Quick."

They turned and ran among the looms. None of the Dorig moved.

"Come back. You can't get away," one called after them.

"Oh can't we!" said Ayna, boosting Ceri fiercely upward.

Oddly enough, it was not until Ceri slung himself onto the sill and jumped out into the misty daylight, that the Dorig realized they were escaping. They shouted, pointed and flitted hastily after. Gair was still on the ground, waiting for Ayna's feet to climb out of the way.

"Hurry!" he said desperately.

Ayna's feet took wings. Gair grabbed a handhold and climbed as he had never climbed before, with Ayna's heels in his face the whole way. Behind him, the Dorig crashed and clattered among the looms. They seemed to understand looms as little as they understood windows. As he climbed, Gair heard more than one bad word, some strange, but most surprisingly familiar. Ayna reached the sill and jumped away into the low-lying mist.

Gair swung himself up on her heels. The bees were out in some numbers, questioning, worried, feeling disaster but not sure what to do. Gair shouted to them what to do as he jumped. He rolled, staggered up and ran.

He found Ceri and Ayna among the grasses and the mist by the panting and rustling they made. Then he realized they should have scattered, when it was too late. The Dorig were jumping out of the window. They could tell by the storm of buzzing above, and Dorig voices spitting out more bad words. They all three gave unhappy chuckles as they ran. Good old bees!

They ran, trying to put as much distance between themselves and the Dorig as they could before the mist cleared. But they had already run a long way, completely uselessly, inside Garholt. Before they had run half a mile, their chests burned and their legs ached and they were forced to drop to a trot. Almost at the same time, the mist cleared, drifting off in shreds, lying only on pools and dikes, and leaving the Moor in full yellow daylight. They all turned round to see what their situation was.

It was not good. As soon as they saw Garholt, already become one of the line of hills at the Moor's edge, pale green and misty still, they knew they had set off into the marshes at quite the wrong angle to have a hope of catching up with the hunt. And the Dorig were hot on their trail. They could see a cloud of bees above the grass and a glint of silver scales.

"Help!" wailed Ceri.

They forced themselves into a run again, hoping the bees could delay the Dorig until they could hide somewhere. But there was nowhere to hide. They splashed through wet peat, and beat through long grass. A spinney of reedy trees ahead gave them a slight hope, but it proved to be more open than the grass when they reached it. They thrust among the trees, looking wildly over their shoulders and going slower and slower whatever they did. The Dorig were still behind and catching up steadily. The white glint of them was closer every time they looked. There were few bees left now. They had stung and died and defended their owners, and they seemed to have delayed the Dorig not at all.

Beyond the spinney, they burst out into a place where the marsh grass had died and lay blond as hair around a peaty little pool. Ayna stopped, scarlet-faced and croaking for breath.

"I know. One of you get me a thorn tree. Quick!"

The boys were too blown to think. They struggled obediently back to the spinney. Gair seized a little bush, and he and Ceri wagged at it with limp, tired arms until it came free. They could see the Dorig in a shimmering gray group at the other side of the spinney as they took the thorn tree back to Ayna.

"*Endeftala vithy ðan*," Ayna was saying when they reached her. "Thanks. *Endeftala tala ðan*. Get in the pool, both of you." She dipped the branches of the tree in the brown, inch-deep water and shook the drops back in. "*Deftala deftala.*"

"What are you doing?" panted Ceri.

"Making it safe. Get in and don't interrupt," said Ayna. "*Tala tala tala. Dan in endef.* I said get *in*, Gair. *Deftala.*" She jammed the thorn tree in the ground at the edge of the pool, seized her staring, panting brothers each by a shoulder and dragged them, splashing and stumbling, into the center of the water. "Don't be idiots. They can't get us here."

"Oh no," said Ceri. "So they can't. That was clever."

Through the trees of the spinney, the Dorig saw them standing still. Their pointed heads turned to one another, nodding. They shimmered and shrank. Nine black birds flew up from the ground there, flapped over the trees and coasted down beside the pool. A gust of cold air made the children shiver as the birds each piled into a gray pillar and became tall Dorig again.

"They've made the water bad!" one said disgustedly.

"That won't help them much," said the one who seemed the leader. He folded his silver-plated arms and glided as near as he could come to the pool, which was about two yards from the thorn tree. They were fascinated and pleased to see that the left side of his face was swollen and almost as red as their own hot faces. His left eye was a fat yellow slit. "Come on out," he said. "You can't get away, so there's no point staying there."

"And you can't get us," said Ayna. "We're not leaving here until you go away."

The leader shrugged. "As you please. I suppose we'll sit it out then."

They watched helplessly while the Dorig, who were all stung somewhere on their faces and looking rather irritable, spread out in a ring round the pool. Most of them sat down. Two of them slung their shields behind them and lay down, with the shield as a pillow. Three or four pulled at their fingers and presently stripped off gloves made of gray-glinting scales. Their hands underneath were pale flesh-colored. Gair wondered if the rest of the silver scales came off the same way.

"Well?" said the leader. "Coming out?"

"Certainly not," said Ayna.

"Very well," said the leader, and yawned. "I'm going to get some sleep. You—Sathi and Fethil—take first watch." The two Dorig he picked on were the two lying down. They sat up sighing. Evidently he was a tartar. "That's better," said the leader. He lay down in the same way, with his shield as a pillow, and stripped off his gloves. They watched him raise a finger to the Sun before he settled down to sleep.

"I didn't know Dorig did that, too!" Gair said, rather surprised, as the rest of the Dorig not on watch settled down and made the same gesture.

Ayna looked resentfully round the restful ring. "I suppose they've been up all night pretending to be sheep," she said loudly. "Baaa!" The Dorig took no notice. They simply lay, in a ring round the pool, flattened and frog-like, their gray-silver color blending almost uncannily into the bleached-blond grass. "I've not done much good, have I?" Ayna said.

"It was a good idea," said Gair.

"But what shall we *do*?"

"I don't know."

They knelt down in the water. There seemed no point in standing up. The damp crept up their clothes as the Sun rose higher, and they all felt rather too cold. Gnats and midges found them and bit. It was no comfort at all that they also bit the peaceful Dorig. The Moor stretched around, flat, huge and empty. Birds called in the distance. Giant machines droned. Every sound seemed to underline their complete loneliness.

After an hour of kneeling, Ceri took up a scoop of peaty water and gingerly licked it.

"Ceri!" said Ayna.

"I'm thirsty," Ceri said miserably. "And we're going to die anyway, hung up in the Sun for sacrifices."

"Shut *up*!" Ayna and Gair said in unison.

Ceri defiantly swallowed water.

"Ceri," said Ayna, "couldn't you put a Thought on the Dorig? Like you did to Ondo?"

"No," Ceri said flatly. "I can't."

"Won't is more like it! Why not?"

"Mother said I wasn't to." Tears began to pour down Ceri's face. "She said I wasn't to put Thoughts on people. And she's dead and it's sacred."

Gair jabbed Ayna with his elbow, but Ayna was too desperate to care. "Dorig aren't people, silly!" she almost screamed.

"Oh, aren't we?" called one of the Dorig on watch. "Come over here and find out, Lyman."

Ayna stared at him, rather shaken. He was propped on one elbow laughing at them. "Lyman!" she muttered. "What kind of cheek is that?"

"I think that's what they always call us," Gair said.

Ayna could not find words to express what she felt about that. They settled to waiting—none of them knew for what, except that it was better than giving in. The one hope seemed to be that the sentries would fall asleep, too.

Long ages later, when the Sun stood nearly at mid-morning and the damp had crept to their necks, Ayna realized that neither of the sentries had moved for some time. She suddenly felt ridiculous, crouching tensely in a pool of water. The Dorig looked queerly harmless, lying blended with the grass, not moving and almost invisible. Ayna stood up, gently and cautiously. She was about to take a step when she met the yellow eye of one of the sentries. His thin white face was amused. Ayna pretended to be stretching and sat miserably down again.

"That's what they're hoping we'll do," Gair said, sighing.

Soon after mid-morning, the leader woke up and stretched. He glanced casually at the pond and then gave some kind of signal. The other Dorig sat up. They all produced pouches, with food in them. It was yellowish stuff and came away in soft flaky mouthfuls when the Dorig bit it.

"Oh *Ban!*" said Ceri, watching yearningly.

"It's probably very nasty," said Ayna.

The leader turned to them. "Smoked trout," he said. "Want some?"

Their mouths watered. "Yes please," said Ceri.

"Come on out and we'll give you some," he answered.

They realized he was tempting them and shook their heads.

"As you please," said the leader, and bit deeply. "You're being very stupid," he said, with his mouth full, "even for Lymen. You'll have to come out in the end."

"Lymen!" Ayna said disgustedly. Ceri's stomach rumbled.

They were glad when the Dorig finished their trout and put their pouches away. Two more were put on watch. The others lay about lazily, exchanging remarks in low voices, laughing and dozing. They seemed to enjoy basking in the Sun. Gair was rather amazed at their lazy, luxurious air, and the way one laughingly pushed another aside when he got in the way of the Sun. It did not seem right, when the Dorig were the ones who were made to live in water, that Gair should be crouching in a pool, wet to the neck, shivering in the mild breeze that whistled through the reedy trees of the spinney. In fact, everything was wrong. The Sun now stood at its highest, nearly as high as it would ever stand in the whole year, which ought to have meant that Gair's people were in the ascendant. Instead—

Ayna nudged Gair and pointed anxiously at Ceri. Ceri was shuddering. His clothes were dark with water and his face was white and pinched. His collar was turning an ominous green-black in places. No doubt it was shock and misery as much as exposure, but Gair saw that there was a chance Ceri would not live to be sacrificed to the Sun.

"Shall we give in?" Ayna whispered.

Gair shook his head. There must be some way they could escape. The trouble was his brain was dimmed with the boredom and misery of sitting here. He could not think. When he did think, it was useless things. It was no use asking Ceri to put a Thought on the Dorig, or on the hunt. He had promised not to. Lucky Ondo, to have gone on the hunt. Aunt Kasta's voice. The voice from the Giantess's magic box was almost as ugly. It— Wait a moment!

"Ceri," Gair said quietly.

Ceri pushed his chattering teeth together. "Yes?"

"Ceri, can you tell me where that magic box is—the one the Giantess had?" Ayna looked at Gair as if he had suddenly gone mad. "I'm *not* mad," Gair said. "Can you, Ceri?"

Ceri put his face in his hands. "It's a long way, much farther than I usually— There are quite a lot of magic boxes, Gair. I'm not sure which one."

"Then is the Giantess with any of them?"

There was a pause. Ceri bowed over, thinking hard. "Oh yes," he said at last. "I see. She's just come in and picked it up."

Gair looked cautiously round the Dorig. The two on watch were certainly listening, although the rest seemed to be asleep. He could only hope they did not understand about Finding Sight or Thoughts. He beckoned Ceri and Ayna as close to him as they could get and whispered, "Put a Thought on that box to make it tell the Giantess to come and help us."

"I'll try," Ceri whispered. "But is it safe, Gair?"

"Gair!" Ayna whispered. "She's a *Giant*!"

"Anything's safer than sitting here," Gair said. "She may think we're Giants, too. Don't tell her we're not, Ceri." He put his mouth close to Ceri's ear and told him exactly what to make the box say.

Ayna, meanwhile, pulled at his sleeve. "But *can* she help? *Will* she?"

Gair had doubts about that. The Giantess had not inspired him with trust. He would have preferred to ask the Giant Gerald, but he did not have the magic box. But it was all he could think of. He pretended not to hear Ayna. "Got that?" he asked Ceri.

Ceri cleaned his ear out with his finger. "Now that's wet, too. All right. I'll try." He put his hands in the water and knelt on all fours, very quiet and tense. Gair could see from his face that he was finding it difficult. As the minutes trailed on and Ceri did not move, nor did the look of strain on his face alter, Gair saw that he had asked something which was beyond Ceri's power. He saw he would have to persuade Ceri to put a Thought on the Dorig after all, before Ceri's strength gave out completely.

"Well?" Ayna whispered. "Yes or no?"

Ceri relaxed slightly. He seemed puzzled. "Yes—I think."

"Don't if it's too difficult," Gair whispered.

Ceri shook his head and sat damply back on his haunches. "I think I did it. It's working by itself now. But the music and things still keep trying to interrupt."

"So we wait?" Ayna whispered, trying not to sound too eager. Ceri nodded.

They waited. Half an hour passed, as slowly as a fortnight. The Sun stood at its height, then began to move down. The water in the pool was almost warm, but they all shivered even so. Seven of the Dorig slept. The two sentries lay lounging, only shifting from time to time, looking marvelously comfortable.

"How I hate this pool!" Ayna said.

The Sun marched down the sky, another half hour. Gair's hopes went down with it. Nothing was going to happen. He had been a fool to think it would. He let the Sun march for another half hour, the longest of all. Then he gave up and turned to Ceri. Ceri's collar was now more than half black. He was shivering in spasms, with a minute between each spasm. His teeth rattled like the trees in the spinney. Gair hardly had the heart to bother him again.

"Ceri—"

Ceri's head came up. To Gair's surprise, he was excited. He put his finger across his mouth and shook his head. Ayna craned round to see, and her face went bright with hope.

"What?" Gair said soundlessly.

Ceri frowned. "Someone," they understood his mouth to say.

A few seconds later, the wind brought a faint sound. All of them looked at the Dorig to see if they had heard it, too. Not one moved. Each one lay silvery and near invisible, stretched among the white grass. If they heard the sound, they must have thought it unimportant.

A few seconds later, the sound was louder. Gair, with his eyes watering, thought he caught a movement against the Sun, somewhere south of the spinney. It could have been someone dark and large. He lost it in the Sun and the grass. When he caught it again, he was sure it was a Giant, but it did not seem wide enough for the Giantess. He lost it completely after that glimpse and squatted in the pool, puzzled and worried, not knowing whether to hope that the Giant came their way or not.

The thread of sound persisted. It was very small and coming closer. But there was no quivering in the ground and no swishing of grass. The distant Giant, if it was a Giant, was walking with most un-Giant-like caution. Yet he or she seemed to be talking to itself all the time. The Dorig did not seem worried by it. They basked and slept as before.

The Giant suddenly emerged from the grass to one side of the spinney, much closer than Gair had calculated. I don't believe it! Gair thought. It was Gerald. The Giant had a businesslike, almost angry, look. One arm was crooked to carry a long iron object with a wooden handle, clearly a Giant weapon. In his other hand, Gerald was carefully carrying a magic box. It looked quite different from the Giantess's box, but Gair could tell it was one because the thread of voice was coming from it. Gerald was turning the box slightly, using it to guide him in some way, and he was walking most unusually cat-footed, as if he had grasped that the situation was serious.

Ceri and Ayna looked at him in utter dismay. Ceri took painful hold of Gair's ear and whispered, "What shall we do? I got the wrong box!"

Gair did not say anything, because he was not at all sure that one Giant boy with one Giant weapon could possibly be a match for nine full-grown Dorig warriors.

Chapter
9

THE GIANT CAME ON QUICKLY, SURE OF HIS direction now. Though he kept looking keenly their way, he did not as yet seem to have seen Ayna, Gair and Ceri crouching in the pool. Probably, in his unobservant Giant way, he took them for a clump of reeds. Ayna and Ceri were so frightened of him that they hoped he never would see them. Gair longed to wave or shout, but he knew that would alert the Dorig, and it seemed to him that Gerald's best hope was to take them by surprise.

When Gerald was five yards away, they could hear the box quite clearly. The voice seemed to be Ceri's, talking and talking, with faint gusts of music behind it.

The Giant saw them. He stopped, looking uncertain and rather accusing. The box fell silent, with a sharp click. Ayna and Ceri shrank. If it had been possible, they would have got right under the water. Before Gair could say anything, the Giant was coming toward them again, this time with his usual heavy stride, calling out in his normal haughty-sounding voice. He had not noticed the Dorig at all.

"I say, are you the people who—"

Then he trod on a Dorig.

The Dorig sprang up with a howl of horror. The next second, a huge green and gray pike was twisting and snapping under Gerald's great foot. The Giant jumped clear hastily, yelling louder than the Dorig. The noise woke the others. All round the pool they sprang up, flopped down again as fish, rose into pillars of fog and hardened into Dorig again, while the Giant backed this way and that toward the pool, looking as if he might be sick. Then the leader came to his senses and shouted, "*Birds!*" All nine Dorig dwindled and blackened and became nine large crows, hopping together into an agitated group. The Giant stared at them, breathing heavily and shivering in the cold they made. Ayna could have wept. If every Dorig had been sound asleep, they might have escaped without calling the Giant at all.

Gerald recovered a little. He turned to Gair. "I see your problem," he said. "What do you want me to do?"

Gair stood up, feeling awed by the largeness and strength of the Giant, and tried to smile. "Can you help us get away?"

"Well, I've got a gun—" Gerald began dubiously. There was a shrill shout from the spinney. He looked up and looked disgusted. "Oh no!"

The Giantess was forcing her way among the trees. The magic box dangled from one fist and, in the other, she was holding a mighty iron poker. The trees bent and clashed under her fierce progress. Ripples spread in the pond. And, when the Giantess stumped out into the grass, her feet left deep holes filled with water. It was plain she was very angry. "If this is your idea of a joke—!" she said ferociously.

"Ceri," said Ayna, "how many boxes did you put a Thought on?"

"Ban knows!" Ceri said hopelessly. "Just the one in the wood, I thought."

Gerald moved to one side so that the Giantess could see the pool, and bowed ironically. "Your mistake, Brenda."

Brenda's mouth fell open. She approached with great squelching strides. From the box in her hand, Ceri's voice said, "—in a pond beyond the spinney. We are surrounded by Dorig and in great—" Absentmindedly, the Giantess clicked it off. Her attention was wonderingly on Ayna, Gair and Ceri. Ayna and Ceri thought it polite to stand up beside Gair while the Giantess stared. "Whatever *are* you?" she cried out. "Are you fairies?"

Gerald's face went deep red and he made a disgusted noise.

"Of course we're not!" Ayna said. "Fairies are little silly things with butterfly wings. And they're not true."

"Then what are you?" said the Giantess suspiciously. "And where are these Dories of yours? I don't see any."

She was so large and purple and awesome that Ayna dared not answer. But Gerald took the Giantess by her poker-wielding arm and turned her toward the crows. They were hopping and clustering and cawing together anxiously, as if they did not know quite what to do about the Giants. Gerald pointed. "Those are the Dorig."

"What? Those birds? No one's afraid of birds!" said Brenda.

"They're not birds," Gair and Gerald said together. That made them look at one another and smile. After that, there was no doubt that they were friends. Gerald said, "I saw you twice—in the wood."

"Twice?" said Gair.

"These kids are soaked," said Brenda. "Let's take them to my house and get them dry. Are you hungry?"

"Horribly," said Ceri.

The Dorig came to a decision. As the Giantess said cheerfully, "Come along then," and turned to leave, the crows lengthened into nine gray pillars. The pillars tremblingly grew arms and legs and hardened into silver-gray scales. Cold air swept across the grass. Nine yellow-eyed Dorig warriors drew their curved swords and glided toward the pond in a half-circle.

"Ooh-er!" said the Giantess. It was the most expressive noise they had ever heard. Her big face lost its pink completely. She raised her poker uncertainly. Gerald, quite as pale, jerkily did something to his gun and held it ready.

The Dorig halted. "You Giants," called the leader. "Those Lymen are our prisoners."

The pink flooded back into Brenda's face. "*Giants!*" she said. "What blinking cheek!"

"*Lymen!*" said Ayna, quite as crossly.

Gerald swallowed. "They're not your prisoners any longer. Keep off!"

"I warn you," said the Dorig leader. "There are nine of us. Hand the Lymen over and we'll leave you alone."

Gerald swallowed again. Gair could see his gun quivering. "And I warn you," he said. "I can kill you all before you can get near us. Keep off, or I'll start firing."

"Start what?" said the Dorig contemptuously. He jerked his head and the nine warriors began to advance.

Gerald's face went whiter still. "Stupid idiots!" he said. He pointed the gun low and fired at the Dorig's feet.

The sudden *crack* sent Ayna to her knees in the water again. Peat, water and clods of grass sprayed over the Dorig. They scattered hastily and, while long echoes of the shot rolled back from the distance, they regrouped near the spinney.

"See?" called Gerald.

It was clear the leader was angry. "Don't think you

can scare us with noises!" he called back. To their dismay, the Dorig began to advance again.

"You'll have to hit one," said Brenda. "That'll teach them."

"I know," said Gerald, jerkily putting something into the gun. "But it's not like *rabbits*, damn it!" He raised the gun very carefully toward the gliding Dorig and fired. Crack-*thump*. The leader cried out and dropped down, holding his leg. There was bright blood on the silver-gray. The other Dorig either threw themselves aside or went down on their knees beside the wounded leader. "Come on," said Gerald, looking sick. "My house is nearest." He seized Ceri by the arm and set off with long strides through the grass. Gair and Ayna followed as fast as their stiff legs and numb feet would let them. The Giantess lingered to wave her poker menacingly before she came puffing and pounding after.

Gerald's dark house was not much more than a mile away. They went straight to it, crashing through nettles, wading dikes, bursting through a hedge and scampering across squashy fields. Ceri began to flag badly, and so did the Giantess. Gair turned, waiting for her to lumber up, and saw a line of crows flapping across the field behind them.

"That's them!"

Gerald looked up. "Yes," he said. "I can see his leg trailing." He raised the gun and moved it menacingly along the line of birds. They at once scattered to left and right and seemed to land. "Scared them," said Gerald. He thrust the gun at Gair. "You take it and keep doing that at them." Then he swooped on Ceri and bundled him into his arms. Ceri yelped with surprise and gave Gair a shamed look over the Giant's shoulder.

"Thanks," said Ayna. "He's worn out."

Gerald took Ceri away with vast strides, almost faster than Gair could run. Gair followed with the strange weapon. It felt awkward, cold and heavy, and he would have been very much afraid of it had not Gerald assured him breathlessly that it was harmless—not loaded. Several times more, Gair had to turn and menace the pursuing Dorig, before they crashed between the trees in front of the pulsing house. Gair did not want to go near it, but it was preferable to being caught by Dorig. As they crossed the bridge to the front door, the nine crows swooped over the trees and flew straight for them. Gerald slung Ceri down and snatched the gun from Gair. Brenda rattled frantically at the front door and could not get it open.

But the crows ignored them. They folded their wings and dived straight into the moat in front of the house, entering the water in a black mass, without a splash and almost without a ripple.

"They can go in there," Ayna said shakenly. "There are no thorn trees."

"They live in water," Ceri explained to the Giants.

"Oh I see," said Gerald. "Then I suppose they're all right. It's locked," he said to Brenda, who was still trying to open the front door. "They're both out. Go round the back."

Brenda turned and heavily led the way through an archway in a wall and then down the side of the house. The house was much bigger than it looked in front. It stretched back to a low, sloping part, where Brenda opened a door and led them in among strange smells and unfamiliar shapes, which she called a kitchen. There she collapsed in a chair with her feet out in front of her, puffing alarmingly.

Gair did not like it in the house. A faintly pulsing feeling of depression took hold of him there, rather like the feeling he had had in Garholt, only not so strong, and colder somehow. He would have been very troubled by it but for the interesting strangeness of the house. It smelled of water, and mustily of old, old building, with newer, cleaner smells on top. Everything possible was square. Giants seemed to want things square as naturally as people wanted them rounded. Gerald led them to a square, hard-white room, full of silver things, where they took off their sopping clothes and dried themselves with vast towels. Brenda had recovered. They could hear her shouting to be told where the bacon lived, whatever that meant. Gair and Ayna were alarmed by the strange silver fitments. But Ceri, who was recovering rapidly now that they were safe, looked thoughtfully at one and made it send out a stream of hot water. It was he who discovered the use of the thing Gerald called the loo, for which they were all grateful and which amused them considerably.

Then Gerald came back with an armload of old clothes and took theirs away to dry, looking at the garments with interest as he gathered them up. They found Giant clothes quite as queer. The most fascinating things were the magic fastenings called zippers. Once again, it was Ceri who discovered how they worked.

"We might almost be Giants!" Ayna said, when they were zipped into the clothes which fitted best. "We must thank them. I'd no idea Giants were so kind."

In the kitchen, Brenda was making achingly appetizing smells at a box where there seemed to be no fire. Nevertheless, when she turned the food onto plates, it was perfectly well-cooked. They were a little embarrassed at having to sit at a table to eat, instead of round an eating-square, but, as Ayna said, it was not so different except that your feet dangled. Brenda, as might have been expected from the size of her, put out a stacked plateful for herself, too. And Gerald, when he smelled the food, said he thought he could manage a second lunch. Shortly, they were all tackling strips of fried salt meat, huge eggs and quantities of wheat-bread and butter. Brenda made a hot drink called tea, but they found they preferred the mild-tasting cow's milk.

"Ayna, Gair and Ceri," said Brenda. "Have I got that right? Funny names! Where do you live and all? What happened?"

Before they could be sidetracked by the explanations Brenda clearly wanted, Ayna and Gair tried to thank the two Giants for their help. "I mean," Gair said shyly, "it was the way you came and said 'What do you want me to do?' which was so good."

"Not asking questions, just helping," Ayna agreed.

Gerald seemed embarrassed and said it was nothing. But Brenda said, "Don't be silly. You needed helping, so we helped. That's what you're supposed to do, isn't it, Gerald?"

"Yes. It was like a call for help at sea, when all the ships in the area go," Gerald said. "Even if it turns out to be a practical joke. I thought yours was, actually. I thought it was Brenda, or the yobboes up in the village."

"So did I," said Brenda. "Or Gerald."

This explanation cast a new light on Giants. Gair thought about it while Ayna told how they came to be marooned in the pool. And here he found another peculiarity of Giants. Though they were both sympathetic about the disaster in Garholt, Gerald awkwardly, Brenda heartily, it was the unimportant details that really interested them.

Brenda said, several times, "Fancy the Moor being full of—er—you all, and those Dories, and us never knowing!"

"Well, the Moor is supposed to be haunted," Gerald said, equally interested in this fact. "Now we know why."

It was the same when Ayna said she had made the pool safe from the Dorig. The Giants' chief interest was in how she had done it.

"I said the words and planted a thorn tree, of course," Ayna explained. "Then they couldn't touch the water."

"Magic, you mean?" Brenda asked, sharply and eagerly.

"No," said Ceri. "Words."

"That's what she meant," said Gerald. "A magic spell."

"No it wasn't," Ceri insisted. "It was words, and words are quite ordinary. Magic is things like your talking boxes and the box that cooks without fire."

"Those aren't magic. They're science," said Brenda.

"And electricity," added Gerald.

There was silence, as each side discovered it did not understand the other. Gair found Ayna and Ceri looking at him, trusting him to be wise enough to explain. Though he did not feel very wise, he did his best.

"There's nothing magic about words," he said. "They just do things if you say them right. Look, if I say, 'Pass the bread, please'—no thanks, I didn't mean it really— you give it to me." This practical demonstration made

160

both Giants laugh until the table shook. "But," said Gair, "if I just said nonsense, like — er — gobbledygook or something, then you wouldn't give me the bread. And it's the same with everything else. You just have to say the right words."

"Well," said Gerald, "I'd still call that magic. But about electricity —"

"See here," Brenda interrupted. "Those Dories. They fair give me the creeps — sort of fishy and snaky, with those starey yellow eyes. Can they turn themselves into anything they want?"

"Yes, I think so," said Gair.

"Then what's to stop them turning themselves into fleas and hopping in here under the door?" Brenda said, lowering her voice and glancing uneasily over at the back door.

Ceri and Ayna looked, too, much alarmed. "Do you think it would seal like our doors?" Ceri asked.

Gair was sure all doors did. He was about to say the words, when it occurred to him to give the Giants another practical demonstration. He turned to Gerald and told him the words. "Stand in front of it and say them," he said. "Then see if it opens."

Gerald did so, in the most awkward and unconvinced way. Then he put out a large hand, lifted the latch and tugged. The door would not open. "Blimey!" he said. "It works!"

"How creepy!" said Brenda, shaking the table with a happy shudder. "Did you use words to broadcast on our radios?"

"No, that was a Thought," said Ceri. "And I didn't get it right, either."

This caused another wave of interest from the Giants. They were not satisfied until Ceri had explained both his Gifts to them, found a penknife Gerald had lost a week before—it was behind the cooking-box—and broken and joined the butter dish.

"That's better than Uri Geller!" said Brenda. "You could make your fortune!"

Ceri felt suddenly shy, which was a most unusual feeling for him. He tried to divert Brenda's quite overwhelming interest by explaining Ayna's Gift.

"Ooh!" said Brenda. "You tell fortunes! Tell mine!"

Ayna put her head up. "Sorry," she said. Her voice shook. "I—I'm not going to use my Gift again. Not—not until I'm sure someone asks me the right questions. None of this would have happened if—" She had to stop there.

There was a difficult moment. Brenda did her best to smooth it over by asking Gair, "And have you got a Gift, too?"

Gair had been afraid one of them would ask him that. Glumly, he shook his head. Brenda yelped as he did so. He rather thought Gerald had kicked her under the table.

"Oh yes you have, Gair," Ayna said. "If they'd listened to you, they'd have asked me the right—" She had to stop again.

"What do you mean?" said Gair.

"You warned them," said Ceri. "You said not to let any living creatures in—and the Dorig came in as sheep."

"But—but that was just—" Gair wanted to explain that it was simply a feeling he had had. Then it occurred to him that he had no idea what a Gift should feel like. For all he knew, Ayna and Ceri were right. And if they were, then it meant Gair had the rarest Gift of all. Only five people since King Ban the Good had had Sight Unasked. That took some getting used to. So, too, did the discovery that, whatever he was, no one could call him ordinary now—now when the Dorig had conquered Garholt and it was too late to make any difference. Depression pressed in on Gair. It took him a second or so to see that it was caused not only by this discovery, but by the pulsing of the house he was in. Rather uncertainly, since the whole thing was so new to him, he said, "I think there's something wrong about this house. It feels—oh, threatened."

Brenda gasped. Gerald looked gloomy. "It's more than threatened," he said. "This time next year it's going to be under water."

"Our house, too," Brenda said mournfully.

"Now do you believe me, Gair?" Ayna asked, wiping her eyes on her hand.

"But why is it going to be under water? How?" said Gair. "Is it the Dorig?"

"No. People in London!" Gerald's gloom and bitterness were large even for a Giant. "They want to make the whole Moor into a beastly reservoir and then drink it."

"Has your dad had any luck?" Brenda asked anxiously.

"I don't know. I hope so," said Gerald. "He's got some high-up from the Ministry that he used to be friends with coming here tonight. But Aunt Mary says they hate one another's guts now, so the high-up will probably flood the Moor just to spite him. Aunt Mary's gone to that meeting about it. I wish I could do something!"

"Me, too," said Brenda. Sighing gustily, she lumbered to her feet and began, very noisily, to clear away the plates.

The others sat quietly, overcome by the disasters dogging the Moor. First the Dorig—now this. None of them could quite understand why the Giants should be so thirsty that they needed to fill the Moor with water, but none of them quite liked to ask. Gerald and Brenda were miserable enough about it. They wondered what they should do when the Moor was a lake, only fit for Dorig.

Gair felt a sad sense of triumph, because he had connected the pulsing of the house with Brenda's talk of flooding from the first. The pulsing depression weighed on him harder as soon as he thought of it, and, as he had in Garholt, he found himself bracing himself to resist it. And the more he resisted, the harder the feeling pressed. After a second or so of fierce, private battle, Gair realized it was trying to tell him something else. He was scared. But he was also ashamed of himself. He had forced Ceri to come to terms with his Thoughts, and yet he was too frightened himself to do anything but try to ignore his own Gift. The trouble with Sight Unasked was that it was a Gift so rare that there was nobody alive who knew enough about it to help Gair come to terms with it. He knew he would have to do it on his own. It was a very lonely feeling.

So, hesitantly and timidly, dreading what might happen, Gair tried to give in to the feeling. It was unpleasant, but not as bad as he feared. Once he was not trying to resist it, the Gift did not batter and press at him. It simply showed him something evil. It was very evil. It was cold, venomous and insatiable. It lay pulsing somewhere in this very house and, what was more, pulsing and chill at the heart of all the troubles on the Moor. It poisoned Giants and, through them, people. Gair, shuddering, realized he would have to find whatever it was and try to destroy it.

Meanwhile, Ayna pulled herself together and told Ceri

to clean his collar. "It's a disgrace, all black like that."

"Yours aren't much better," Ceri said sulkily. He took his collar off and rubbed it with a Giant checked table napkin. Ayna and Gair took theirs off, too, and found they were black all round the inside. They took up napkins and rubbed away as well.

Brenda was exceedingly interested. "They're ever so pretty!" she said. "Do you wear them always? Aren't they heavy at all?"

"No. They're quite light," said Gair. And, glad to be distracted from the cold evil he had felt, he explained, as he rubbed, how you had to wear gold or keep it warm, or it would turn back to black ore again. A thought struck him. "Dorig must be warm-blooded," he said. "Or they couldn't have collars."

"Do they?" said Ayna. "Oh yes. Father got one."

Gerald and Brenda were looking oddly at one another. "Green gold," said Gerald. "I wonder."

"That turns to dead leaves in the drawer overnight!" said Brenda. "Oh, that settles it. You *are* fairies!" She drew a deep wistful sigh. "Do you grant wishes at all?" At this, Gerald scowled and turned away.

"No," Gair said patiently. "We don't grant wishes. How can we? We're not fairies. We told you. We're people."

"Oh no, you can't be!" Brenda exclaimed. "You're so little and sort of delicate, and so pretty!" Gair felt his face going as red as Gerald's at this, although, when he looked at Ceri and Ayna, he knew what Brenda meant. Though neither of them was much smaller than the Giants, they looked little and fragile beside Gerald's large features and thicker frame. And both of them were much prettier than Brenda. "And you live forever, don't you?" Brenda added, rather accusingly.

"No, we don't!" Gair said, truly astonished.

"Shut up, Brenda!" growled the heartily embarrassed Gerald. "They're *not* fairies. They've told you."

"They must be," Brenda insisted. "They can't be people, because *we* are."

"No. You aren't people," Ceri explained. "You're Giants."

"Well!" said Brenda, very pink. "Big I may be, but Giant I am *not*! Giants are huge, big as houses. And they're not true. Anyway, I thought you were called Lymen."

"That's what the Dorig say. We say people," Ayna said. "We haven't any other name but people."

"Well, neither have we!" said Brenda. "Giants indeed!"

"Why worry?" said Gerald. "Anyway, they're nothing like as different from us as those Dorig. Why can't they be People and we be Humans?"

"Gerald, you ought to be a politician!" said Brenda.

Gerald's face bunched up. "Is that meant to be funny?"

Brenda and he suddenly remembered they were enemies. They stared at one another with such ferocity that

Gair feared they were going to come to blows. He was not sure he could stand it in the confined space of the kitchen.

Ceri put a stop to it by bursting into tears. "Oh don't do any hitting!" he wailed. "Everyone was hitting everyone in Garholt this morning. Don't! Ayna, please can't I ask you what's going on there?"

"No," said Ayna.

"Gair," said Ceri, "don't you know? Make her tell me!"

Gair shook his head, feeling tearful himself.

"But you must want to know!" Ceri wailed.

"Of course I do. Be quiet. We'll have to go and see."

By this time, the Giants had forgotten their quarrel. "You can't go and see," said Brenda. "Those Dories will snap you up the moment you set foot outside the door." She looked worried. "Gerald, what *are* they going to do?"

Gerald looked equally worried. "It looks," he said slowly, "as if we ought to know what happened at Garholt before we can decide anything. Suppose I take the gun and go and see? Dorig seem to have a healthy respect for us Giants."

"And I'll come with you," Brenda offered. "Put them in your room and let them put a hex on the door so that no one can find them there."

Ayna and Gair consulted together anxiously about this plan. Neither of them dared think what Gest would say to it. But, since Ayna utterly refused to use her Gift, they could think of no other way of finding out what had happened in Garholt. They agreed to let the Giants go. Gerald showed them where his room was and Gair, wondering what his father would think if he knew what he was doing, gave the Giants exact instructions how to find Garholt and open the main gate.

"I say," said Gerald, "if there's any of your people . . . there, how are they going to know you sent us, and we're not just marauding Giants?"

"Don't keep calling us Giants!" said Brenda.

"Marauding humans then," said Gerald.

This was not difficult. Gair took his collar off. "They'll know this is mine, if you show them." He was about to hand the collar to Gerald, when it came to him how grateful he was to Gerald and how glad he was to have met him properly. He took the collar back and spoke words over it.

"Gair!" said Ayna.

"Why not?" said Gair. "I think Father did it." He passed the collar to Gerald. "There. You can keep it now—keep it warm."

Gerald turned Gair's collar this way and that, almost said something, changed his mind and said something else. "I ought to give you something in exchange. Here." He took his watch off and handed it to Gair. "That's gold, too." The collar was uncomfortably tight for him. He had to keep it in an inner pocket. Then he picked up his gun and Brenda her poker and they tried to open the back door. Of course they could not.

"Say the opening words we told you, silly!" said Ayna.

Gerald said them, this time with great conviction, as if he had been using words of power all his life, and Brenda mouthed them with him. The door opened and the two Giants clattered out.

"They're almost like people," Ceri said. "I'd rather have them than Ondo and Aunt Kasta any day."

Chapter
10

MOST OF THE WAY TO GARHOLT, THE TWO GIANTS, in their different ways, were wondering what to do about Ayna, Gair and Ceri.

"Poor little souls!" Brenda said, in the sentimental way which never failed to set Gerald's teeth on edge. "I feel so responsible! Can we hide them? Or should you tell your dad?"

"No," said Gerald.

"We ought to tell someone," said Brenda. "What'll any of them do when the Moor's flooded? Tell that man your dad's having tonight. Tell him the Moor's crowded with—Lymen and he mustn't make it into a reservoir."

"You don't understand!" said Gerald, fingering Gair's warm collar. He had never been more surprised and honored by any gift in his life, and he felt he owed it to Gair to stop Brenda doing anything so stupid. "Those people have a whole way of life. If we go and show them to a stupid Government official, that'll be the end of it. He'll probably make the Moor a reservation and trippers will drive over on Sundays to goop at them. Ceri would probably end up in a circus—and Ayna—and the rest would all be selling carvings and gold collars. Like the Red Indians."

"They'd make a lot of money," Brenda observed.

Gerald made a rude noise.

"Well, it's better than being drowned," said Brenda. "And you're still the rudest boy I know."

"Good," said Gerald.

Luckily for the peace of their mission, Brenda saw a bird just then. She shied like a carthorse. "A Dory! Look!"

"It isn't," said Gerald. "And what would you expect me to do about it if it was?"

"Shoot it," Brenda said simply.

"Only if it goes for us," Gerald said irritably. He sighed, and a gloomy, sick feeling, which he was rather used to, came over him. One way or another, he had shot quite a quantity of birds in his life. He had shot rabbits and hares, and a number of things moving in the long grass which he had never found. Any of them could have been Dorig. Some of the vanished ones could have been Gair's people. He found himself remembering, with unpleasant clarity, the red blood on the silver leg of the Dorig leader. He wished he had not had to shoot him.

Brenda distracted him by insisting they had missed

Garholt. "He said beyond the wood. That's two woods we've passed."

"When he said wood, he meant wood, not three bushes," Gerald said grumpily, and kept on.

They passed the steep banks which concealed the village. Soon after, they passed the wood. It was unmistakable.

"There's nothing," said Brenda.

Gerald was dismayed, too. He had thought there would be some sign to show Garholt was there. But all there was was a rounded stretch of green hillside. He plodded crosswise up it. Brenda lumbered and gasped behind him.

"Ow!" she shrieked. "There's bees in holes!"

Gerald slithered back to see. Where Brenda stood sucking her finger, a few bees were buzzing around what seemed to be rabbit holes. A few more came out to investigate Gerald. Gerald retreated hastily downhill, hoping they would realize he meant no harm. But the bees remained out, menacingly, and followed Brenda as she galloped heavily downhill after him. "We're here," Gerald called up to her.

"Are you sure?" Brenda puffed, landing squashily in the marshy ground at the foot of the hill. "It's just part of the hill—not a mound at all, really."

Gerald was sure. He could see a number of paths, which looked like rabbit paths, converging on this place from above and below. He walked slowly along the soft ground, looking for the door. Gair had said, "You'll see a stream coming out. Then it's ten paces to the right." There was the stream—an oozing trickle, soaking out of the sheer face. Gerald carefully took ten short paces, remembering how much shorter Gair's legs were than his. Then he and Brenda, rather uncertainly, faced the smooth green hillside. They saw clover, rabbit droppings, trefoil—but no sign of a door.

"You say it," Brenda said.

Gerald said the words he had used on his own back door.

There was a faint rumbling sound. Quite suddenly, neither of them saw how, there was an arched opening in the side of the hill. It was as tall as Gerald and wide enough to take two Brendas. There was light somewhere inside.

"I told you," Brenda whispered. "They *do* do magic."

They bent forward to look in. They did not see much, except that Garholt was big, much bigger than they had expected. But the main thing they saw was a silvery crowd of Dorig running toward the open entrance. They jumped back, and Gerald faltered out the words of closing as fast as he could remember them. The doorway rumbled again and vanished. The only sign it had been there was a sparse but angry cloud of bees buzzing over the spot.

They looked at one another, shaken and rather glum. There seemed nothing to do but go back and give Ayna, Gair and Ceri the worst possible news.

"Let's go," said Brenda. "Ooh-er!"

The doorway was there again. In it was packed a group of silvery, froglike Dorig, whose drawn swords were wickedly sharp close to, and who were blinking unfriendly yellow eyes at them.

"What do you Giants want?" one snapped.

By this time, both Brenda and Gerald were poised to run away. They might have fled in earnest had not the bees homed in then. They fell on the Dorig with angry buzzing and the Dorig, to a creature, were forced to cover their faces with one hand and beat at the bees with their swords. Brenda and Gerald took courage at this.

"We've come to find out how many of the Lymen you killed," Brenda said. "We've got friends here."

Amid zooming bees diving to the attack, the Dorig managed to exchange significant looks. "Yes, we've had word they've made friends with the Giants," one said. Then, as a bee settled on his right eyebrow, he added angrily, "Don't you clumsy great fools know better than to trust Lymen?"

"I'd rather trust them than you lot!" Brenda said. "Sneaking in disguised as sheep, and killing them all before breakfast!"

The bees retreated a little and hung, a much sparser

cloud now, buzzing between the Dorig and the two Giants. Most of the Dorig were left with a pale pink swelling somewhere on their pale faces. Most kept a wary eye on the bees as they drew themselves up angrily to face Brenda.

"Watch it, Brenda!" said Gerald. There were at least twenty Dorig, and they were all taller than he was.

"We only killed a few," a Dorig said contemptuously. "You can talk to one if you like. Which one do you want?"

This offer puzzled Gerald considerably. Dubiously, he said the only name they knew. "Adara?"

"Oh, her," said one of the Dorig. "If you want. But don't believe a word she says."

"Why not?" demanded Brenda.

"She's a slippery Lyman," said another of the Dorig. "They all know how to twist you with words until they've taken your mind away. They pretend to be friendly, but all they want to do is kill you or use you. You Giants shouldn't let yourselves be used."

Brenda and Gerald looked at one another uneasily. They saw that, in a way, Ayna, Gair and Ceri had used them. And there was no question that they could use words in a dozen different ways to bend things to their will. So why not to bend humans?

"Aren't Lymen like—like people at all?" Brenda asked miserably.

The silvery group in the doorway shouted with laughter. Each froglike warrior had something to say about that, and they all said it, speaking at once, until, what with the scornful hiss of their voices and the whining buzz of the bees, Brenda and Gerald felt quite bewildered. "Lymen aren't people!" they heard. "They only care about themselves— Can't shift shape to save their lives— They're mean and sly— You can't trust them an inch— They eat caterpillars— They hate water— They're killers— Speak fair and act nasty." And when the clamor had died down somewhat, the first Dorig asked, "Do you still want to speak to Adara?"

Brenda thought she did not. Gerald hardly knew. It was not pleasant to think one had been used by three aliens for their own ends. On the other hand, Dorig were not human either. "Look here," Gerald said, "what do you think of Giants?"

There was the kind of pause that happens when people do not like to say what they really think. "You're very strong," one Dorig said politely. "And," added another "they say you work wonders with the fruits of the earth."

Gerald felt like laughing. He wondered what the Dorig really thought of Giants. At any rate, he was sure it was not unlike the things they said about Lymen. He took hold of Gair's collar for encouragement, and he knew it had been given to him in real friendship, as a real honor. "Could we speak to Adara, please?" he said.

The Dorig shrugged, as if they gave him up. Some of them went away inside the mound, while the others stayed. One or two of them looked marvelingly at Brenda's pink bulk and whispered in a way which made Brenda self-conscious and peevish. Then the other Dorig came back with not one, but two ladies. One was behaving with dignity. The other was rushing along behind.

"Let me through! I insist on talking to them! You've no right to stop me!"

"What an awful voice!" said Brenda.

"Just like a duck," agreed Gerald.

The Dorig in the doorway sighed and seemed to brace themselves. There was a muddle in the entry, and a great deal of quacking. A Dorig said angrily, "What did you bring that duck for?"

"Couldn't stop her."

The quacking lady was somehow bounced away farther inside, where she continued to rush about quacking. The other lady was allowed through between two Dorig. They knew she was Adara. She had the same dark hair and big gray eyes as Gair. Her skin was very white, so that the thick, ornate collar on her neck showed up dazzlingly. Though she was not quite as tall as Brenda, she had such dignity that both of them were impressed. She had not the face of someone who would twist you with words. They thought she looked kind.

Brenda drew a deep, wavering breath. "Oh," she said. "You are beautiful!"

Adara smiled at her. "I was told you wanted to speak to me."

"Yes," said Gerald. A little embarrassed because the Dorig were all round watching, with the bees whining overhead, he took Gair's collar out of his pocket and held it out to Adara. "Do you recognize this?"

Adara's pale face became much paler, and her eyes widened. "It's Gair's. What—?"

"It's all right, your ladyship," said Brenda, seeing what she was thinking. "They're all safe, and they sent us to find out about you. Gair gave us that so that you'd know we weren't—you know—marauding or something."

"Oh, I see." Adara was evidently very relieved. She smiled, but, at the same time, they found her looking at them both in a kind, careful, penetrating way which suggested that she might be at least as clever as the Dorig thought. "Tell Gair," she said, "that not many of us were killed. But they're keeping us prisoner. They want us to take the words off the wells here, and of course I've told them that no one but Gest can do that. It would help if Gair could go to Gest and tell him. Ceri can find Gest. Can you tell them that?"

They said they would.

Adara said, "I'm very grateful to you. Can you tell me another thing—who is turning the Moor into a lake?"

She turned to the listening Dorig. "You did say it wasn't you, didn't you?" They nodded and shook their heads and shrugged.

"It's us," Gerald said glumly. "I mean, the other Giants in London."

"I understand," said Adara. "Not very convenient for you, or for us. Thank you. May I have Gair's collar, or did he give it you to keep?"

"Er—to keep, I think," Gerald said. "But you can have it if you like."

"Did he say words on it?" Adara asked. Gerald nodded. "Then I wouldn't dream of taking it," said Adara. She seemed about to say something else, but, at that moment, the quacking lady made a determined effort to break out and the Dorig heaved back against her. The bees, seeing them busy, once more zoomed in.

"You'll have to finish now," one of the Dorig shouted over his shoulder, sounding very irritated.

Adara was borne away backward. The next second, the hillside rumbled and became smooth turf again, with bees angrily buzzing against it. They were the only sign that Adara or the Dorig had ever been there.

"Like a dream!" sighed Brenda. "Wasn't she lovely?"

As soon as the two Giants were on their way, Gair knew he would have to find the chilly pulsing evil in the house. Though he did not want to in the least, he said,

"Let's seal all the doors and windows and explore."

Ayna and Ceri were surprised at his sudden enthusiasm, but they agreed willingly enough. For the next hour or so, they enjoyed themselves more than they had thought possible, rambling through the vast square spaces of the Giant house. The amount of room Giants seemed to need astonished them. "I suppose it's because they're so clumsy," Ayna suggested. But none of them could explain why the Giants needed to possess so many things. Each room was crowded with clocks, candlesticks, boots, guns, jugs and many other things. One room downstairs was full of stiff chairs and dozens of little statues made of varnished and painted clay. They wondered if this meant it was a holy place, and shut the door reverently. Then Ayna opened another door down a short passage.

As soon as she did so, Gair knew they were near the evil thing. The whole square space reeked of it. He was amazed that Ayna and Ceri did not feel it. They were delighted with this room. It was a dark paneled room whose diamond windows looked out on a garden. It had easy old chairs, a shabby desk, big bookshelves and things stacked carelessly in corners. Ayna and Ceri inspected a stuffed pike, which Ceri thought might be a Dorig, and a long wooden thing with a blue blade, which Ayna thought might be a special kind of spade. They opened some of the books. But the writing was quite strange and the only thing they understood was the pictures. Ayna gave the books up and went through the drawers of the desk. She found sets of false teeth in the first and burst out laughing. Then she opened the second.

A wave of cold pulsing horror hit Gair. It was so searingly strong that he had to push his way across the room toward it.

"Oh!" said Ayna. "Look, Ceri. This is almost like Mother's." She put her hand out to pick up the thing in the drawer.

"Don't touch it!" shouted Gair.

Ayna snatched her hand back and stared at him. "Why not?"

"It's got a curse on it." Gair brought himself up to the drawer and made himself look in. A beautiful gold collar lay there, rich and lustrous, in spite of a film of dust. It was almost the twin of Adara's, except that where the knobs at each end of hers were in the shape of hawks' heads, this one had two staring owls. The cold blast of evil beat off the green gold into Gair's face. Every twist in the pattern was loaded with horror. It was so strongly bad that Gair felt weak and ill. No wonder the house had pulsed, with a thing like this in it!

"How do you know it's got a curse on it?" said Ceri. "You're just guessing."

"Use your sense," said Gair, gasping from the deadly cold of the thing. "No one's wearing it, and you can see by the dust it's been in that drawer for years. It ought to have gone back to ore ages ago. Only a curse can keep gold like that."

"Quite right," said Ayna. "Only you shouted at me before you looked at it." She began shivering. "I'd rather have your Gift than mine, Gair."

"Would you?" said Gair. "It makes me feel dreadful." He stood, turned sideways to look at the collar because the emanation from it seemed easier to bear like that, feeling sick and helpless. He could not touch the thing. He had no idea how to raise a curse, and yet he knew he should try. He owed it to Gerald, for his help, and he was fairly sure this collar was poisoning not only Gerald's life, but all the lives on the Moor.

"You do look sick," Ceri said wonderingly.

They all looked sick the next second. There was a violent clattering. A shrill Giant voice shouted, "Gerald, *Gerald*! What have you done to this door? Let me in at *once*!"

"Oh dear!" said Ayna, and guiltily slid the drawer shut.

"*Gerald!*" shrieked the voice. *Clatter, clatter.*

"We can't keep someone out of their own house," said Ceri.

Bunching together for safety, they hurried toward the clattering front door. It was bouncing in its frame.

Tremulously, Ayna spoke the words, and they all prepared to run.

The door flew open and a tall Giant lady in an ugly hat darted in before they could move. "Gerald— Oh!" She stared at the three strange little children, wondering why two of them were wearing necklaces. "Who on earth are *you*?"

Ceri looked at his speechless sister and brother and saw that it was up to him. And it was going to be difficult. This Giantess was tired and cross already, and he could tell she did not care for strangers or like children. He went forward, shamelessly using his most charming smile, and held out his hand politely.

"The Sun bless you. We were waiting for Gerald."

The Giantess looked puzzled. Her hand came jerkily forward, and stopped before it reached Ceri's.

Ceri allowed his smile to fade and his big blue eyes to stare sadly. "I'm glad you've come. We were lonely."

The Giantess's hand reached out to Ceri's. An uncertain smile flickered at her mouth and pulled it wider. "Are you all alone in the house? That's too bad of Gerald! How do you do? I'm Gerald's Aunt Mary."

Gair and Ayna did not dare look at one another, but they relaxed and sighed.

The two Giants stopped short, seeing the square brown car beside the moat.

"My aunt's back," said Gerald.

"I'd better go home," Brenda said uneasily.

"No, don't. We may have to rescue them," said Gerald.

He left Brenda loitering heavily in the hall and tiptoed to the kitchen, not knowing what to expect. He could hear clattering. The first thing he saw was Ayna and Ceri slowly and seriously buttering scones. Next, he heard Aunt Mary's voice, more cheerful than he had ever heard it before, calling out to Gair as he pattered about with crockery. And they said they didn't do magic! Gerald thought.

Aunt Mary saw Gerald. Her face took on its more usual sharp shape. She pulled him out into the passage and began to talk in a flustered whisper. "Really, Gerald, you might tell me when you invite your friends here! It was fearfully awkward. And there's this Mr. Claybury coming here this evening, too, and you *know* how important that is!"

"I'm sorry," said Gerald. He wondered whether they could get Ayna, Gair and Ceri to Brenda's house without going past the moat where the Dorig lurked. "I'll take them away, shall I?"

"Don't be so thoughtless!" hissed his aunt. "Of course they must stay. But Mr. Claybury's got to have the good spare room, so will the boys mind doubling in with you? Ayna can have the small room next to yours."

"That—that's perfect," said Gerald, trying not to

show his amazement. He knew how Aunt Mary hated strangers and loathed having visitors. Wondering whether he was trying her unusual hospitality too far, he added, "Brenda's here, actually. She could help with beds and so on."

Aunt Mary disliked Brenda and Brenda's parents, too. But she said, "That would be a help. I suppose I'd better give the child tea in return." Then, just as Gerald was breathing deeply and thinking that the crisis was miraculously over, Aunt Mary bobbed her head down and whispered, "Those extraordinary names! And they are so small for their ages, Gerald. But I think I see. Tea's ready."

Wondering wildly just what Aunt Mary thought she saw, Gerald went to fetch Brenda. Over scones round the kitchen table, it emerged that Aunt Mary thought Ayna, Gair and Ceri came from Malaysia. Brenda looked at their faces and breathed in half a scone.

While Gerald was pounding Brenda on the back, Ceri leaned back from the vibrating table and looked Aunt Mary limpidly in the eye. "I'm afraid we don't remember Masaylia at all."

"Malaysia!" hissed Ayna.

"Or that either," said Ceri.

Gair looked at Gerald over Brenda's coughing back, and they both prayed.

"Of course not, dear," said Aunt Mary. "More tea?"

After that, Gerald took them all away upstairs to make beds as soon as he could.

"I'm sorry," said Ayna. "Ceri never knows when to stop. I wish our aunt was as nice as yours. Did you— Garholt—?"

For a while, Gerald feared there would be a crisis of a different kind. When they heard Brenda and Gerald had actually talked with Adara, Ayna and Gair turned chalk white. Ceri sat bolt upright on Gerald's bed with big tears rolling down his cheeks. Brenda, at the sight of him, forgot all the suspicions the Dorig had raised in her and threw both large arms round Ceri. Ceri gasped rather, but it seemed to comfort him.

"This is silly," Ayna said shakily.

"We should be laughing," Gair agreed. "Aunt Kasta, too!"

"The duck one?" said Gerald. Ayna nodded.

"But I don't understand," said Ceri. "Why can't Mother take the words off the wells? Anyone can. I could!"

"Don't be silly!" said Ayna. "It was pretty clever. She told the Dorig that so they wouldn't kill them until Father comes. And she wants us to warn Father."

"How can we, with the Dorig in the moat?" Ceri objected.

"We'll think of something, first thing tomorrow," Gerald promised. "What I don't understand is why the

Dorig want your wells."

"That must be for when the Moor's flooded," Gair said. "Ours are the only safe wells, and I suppose the water would run out into the rest and make it all bad for the Dorig. Look—this important Giant who's coming here. If we explain to him about the mounds, do you think he'd agree not to flood the Moor? If the Moor wasn't filled with water, the Dorig wouldn't want Garholt."

"They didn't attack Garholt because of the wells. They did it because they hate your guts," Gerald said gruffly. "You should have heard the things they said." He was shocked that Gair should think of telling someone like Mr. Claybury about his people, and he could see Ayna and Ceri were equally shocked. He was wondering how to explain to Gair about Civil Servants and Red Indians, when Brenda said:

"You don't really eat caterpillars, do you?"

Ceri nodded. He was about to tell Brenda which were the good kind and where to find them, when, luckily, he saw Ayna glaring at him. He looked up into Brenda's face and found it puckered with pink, Giant disgust. "Of course we don't," he said.

Gair was still thinking of Mr. Claybury. "I suppose if I did tell him," he said, "all the Giants would want to come and look at us, wouldn't they? I know I'd hate that, but we can't all be drowned or sacrificed, can we? And we've made a start by asking you for help."

"We're different," Gerald said crossly. He was annoyed with Gair for seeing so clearly and rendering his explanation useless.

A Giant machine crunched on the gravel below. Everyone surged to the window to watch Mr. Claybury and Gerald's father arriving. Gair caught no more than a glimpse of Giant faces inside the square, sturdy machine, but that glimpse was enough to make him doubt whether he had the courage to explain about his people. Ayna and Ceri felt equally dismayed. Those faces looked more distant from them and their troubles than the Moon. The door banged. Soon they heard Aunt Mary hurrying up and down in a flurry of nervous hospitality. Brenda left the rest of them struggling with Giant sheets and blankets and dashed thunderously out. Presently, she rolled in again, beaming.

"Hey, I told your aunt my mum'll lend me to her for a waitress this evening! I'm going to give that Mr. Claybury something to think about. You'll see."

"That's right. Pour soup down his neck," Gerald said.

Then he was called away downstairs. He came back with a dour, gloomy look Gair felt he recognized.

"My old man's in an awful mood," he said. "I'll have to find you some decent clothes for supper."

Giant cupboards with high shelves were searched. Brenda and Ayna sat on beds and altered things with big hasty stitches. This did not add to the comfort of the clothes when Gair and Ceri put them on. Ceri was particularly miserable, since he finished with a tie, over a shirt, over his double collar. It did not soothe him when Brenda pointed out that the shirt would not have fitted him otherwise. He was disgruntled and morbid and said he wished he were back in Garholt. When Ayna told him sharply that he would be a Dorig sacrifice if he were, Ceri burst into tears.

Here Gerald went away and, to Ayna's surprise, came back with a girl's dress. "My sister was about your size when she died," he said gloomily. "Try it on."

The dress was a pretty soft green. It went beautifully with Ayna's collar and Ayna was delighted with it. While she and Brenda were admiring it and Ceri sulking, Gair seized the chance to talk to Gerald alone. "Have there been many deaths in your family?"

Gerald looked somber even for him. "My sister. And my mother died when she was born. All right," he said angrily, before Gair could ask any more. "You've got some kind of feeling. Well, you're right. Nothing ever goes right with us. We're always miserable as sin and my father keeps losing money and Aunt Mary's always ill. And now we're going to be turned out to make room for drinking water. Is that what you wanted to know?"

"Yes," said Gair. "It's that gold collar in the desk with the false teeth."

"Oh that!" said Gerald. Though he sounded contemptuous, Gair knew he was not. Gerald must have had traces of a feeling about the collar, too.

"You haven't touched it, have you?" he asked anxiously.

"I—Only once," Gerald admitted. "It felt cold as the grave. What about it?"

"It's got a curse on it," said Gair. "I think a very strong one. And it's like—"

"Like your mother's," said Gerald. "Do you know where it comes from then?"

"No," said Gair. "I don't know much about either of them, but I *think* they may both be Dorig collars. I was hoping you'd know."

Gerald's large face moodily scowled. "I don't. I could try asking my old man, I suppose, but I wouldn't get very far—well, you'll see soon enough."

Chapter
11

IT WAS PROBABLE THAT NOBODY ENJOYED THE
Giant supper-party that evening. Gair and Ceri certainly
did not. They crowded silently behind Gerald into a tall,
square room at the front of the house, with a tall, square
table in the middle and a number of transparent cupboards round the walls filled with remarkably ugly
painted plates. Gerald's father, whom they had learned
they were to call Mr. Masterfield, was standing in front of
the unused hearth. Giants had a habit, which struck them
as most uncomfortable, of going without fire in the summer months. Mr. Masterfield looked as tall and cold and
dark as the empty chimney. They had to tip their heads to
see his face. It was as dark, private and proud as Gerald's,
and they could tell from the way Mr. Masterfield looked
at them that they were not welcome and that Gerald had
been in trouble for inviting them. That accounted for
Gerald being so dour and gloomy.

"This is Mr. Claybury," said Mr. Masterfield.

They were troubled to find Mr. Claybury a most disappointing Giant. Though he had the Giant thickness and heaviness, he was no taller than Gest. The top of his head was bald, with a tufty rim of dark hair below, and he wore two round pieces of glass, one to each eye, which enlarged and rounded the mild brown eyes underneath, until Gair was uncomfortably reminded of the staring owls of that evil collar, which he could feel all the time pulsing out its curse into the air of the house. Mr. Claybury looked trim and fussy and pleased with himself. It seemed all wrong that he should be the Giant with the power, and not the tall, cold Mr. Masterfield. He smiled at them all and said, "Hallo, nippers."

Wondering if Giants called them Nippers the way Dorig called them Lymen, Ayna politely went to shake hands. Mr. Claybury gave her hand a firm, fussy squeeze and said, "Live near here, do you?"

"Yes," said Gair.

"No," said Ceri, who was beginning to think it safest to lie to Giants when he could.

Gerald's face went red. "They're visiting me," he said hurriedly, and rather too loudly. Mr. Masterfield glowered at him. Gerald looked back at him defiantly. Gair saw that they did not get on with one another at all. He sighed, because it was just like himself and Gest, except that the puzzling thing was that Gerald and Mr. Masterfield were really remarkably alike. Perhaps they were too much alike for comfort.

In an awkward silence, they all sat round the tall, square table, which Ceri was appalled to find covered with strange implements and little silver containers. Aunt Mary bustled brightly in, followed by Brenda carefully carrying a tureen of soup. Aunt Mary was nervous. She chattered in a loud, high voice and forgot to finish sentences.

"This soup is very," she said. "But I forgot to put in the. At least, up to the last minute, so I hope you'll forgive the."

There was a long, puzzled pause, while Brenda carried round the soup. Brenda was nervous, too. She panted loudly and wheezily, as if she had been running. Gerald and Mr. Masterfield gave her irritated looks, and Mr. Claybury craned round to see her and seemed to be wondering if she was ill. *Wheeze, wheeze, wheeze,* went Brenda, while Ayna, Gair and Ceri sat wondering helplessly if they were supposed to lift the steaming bowls and drink, or use one of the rows of eating-things. Gerald caught Ayna's eye and held up a heavy, round spoon. Very relieved, they all picked up spoons and dipped them in the soup, only to find Aunt Mary frowning at them. They let the spoons go again and waited. *Wheeze, wheeze, wheeze,* went Brenda, endlessly. Then at last Aunt Mary and Mr. Claybury picked up spoons. Thereafter, they were careful not to do anything until Mr. Claybury had done it first.

But this awkwardness was nothing beside the awkwardness between Mr. Masterfield and Mr. Claybury. It was clear from the first that they were not getting on. But they were pretending to be friends. Mr. Masterfield turned to Mr. Claybury with a broad, comradely smile, which sat on his gloomy features as heavily as the great stone on top of Otmound, and asked him if he fished much these days.

Mr. Claybury, beaming with false friendship, shook his head. "I don't get much time these days, Jerry old man. Too much to do with water to think of the fish in it. How about you?"

"I thought you'd remember, George," smiled Mr. Masterfield savagely. "I never could understand your passion for fishing."

"I've put those days behind me," beamed Mr. Claybury. "A man in my position is too much in demand at the office to think of old times."

Everything Mr. Claybury said seemed designed to point out what an important Giant he was. Every time Mr. Masterfield spoke, his smile was more of a savage grin. Gair could not help being reminded of his father and Uncle Orban, on larger, Giantly scale. The odd thing was that Mr. Claybury seemed to be the one who really had a cheerful, open nature, like Gest's. Yet he was behaving like Uncle Orban, because Mr. Masterfield made him feel small. And Mr. Masterfield was being forced to be jolly against his nature, because he needed badly to please Mr. Claybury. But he was not pleasing Mr. Claybury. It was obvious to Gair, and Ayna, too, that Mr. Masterfield had made a mistake in asking Mr. Claybury to stay with him.

Nobody else in the dining room seemed likely to please Mr. Claybury. Aunt Mary puzzled him and Brenda's wheezing alarmed him. Gair and Gerald were somber and subdued. Ayna looked at Ceri, hoping he could use his charm on Mr. Claybury. But Ceri felt tired to death, lost and homesick. He had burned his tongue on the soup. His collar was uncomfortable and it was as much as he could do to follow Giant table manners. So, when Mr. Claybury happened to glance her way, Ayna tried to please him herself with a rather desperate smile.

Mr. Claybury's slow, Giant features looked first surprised, then pleased. Ayna could almost see him thinking what a relief it was to find somebody friendly at that awkward table. Then he smiled back—a natural, jolly smile. In spite of his glasses and his bald head, the smile was exactly like Gest's. Ayna went pink with hope. Perhaps the Moor need not be flooded after all. For, if there was one thing Ayna knew how to do, it was how to get round someone like Gest.

After that, in a way, Ayna became as shameless as Ceri. She leaned forward, smiling, and asked Mr. Claybury about his work. And when Mr. Claybury protested that it was too dull to interest little girls, Ayna told him she knew it was very interesting indeed. But that was the most shameless thing she said. Mr. Claybury suddenly opened out. He smiled, he chuckled, he told a silly story about a man in his office, and, though Ayna did not understand the story very well, she found herself liking Mr. Claybury very much. She could see Gair watching her hopefully, Ceri critically and Gerald with slightly scornful admiration. Aunt Mary looked relieved, and Mr. Masterfield, after seeming at first as if he wanted to shut Ayna up, sat back and looked a little cynical. Ayna was annoyed with them all. Mr. Claybury was a kindly Giant, who liked to be friendly, and she was becoming truly fond of him. And, thanks to her understanding, by the time Brenda had finished two pints of leftover soup in the kitchen and wheezed in again with a joint of meat, she found the dining room almost gay.

Mr. Masterfield almost smiled as he fetched a bottle of wine. "Ladies first," he said to Ayna. "Wine?"

"Yes please," said Ayna, feeling rather flustered. She could see Mr. Masterfield was trying to show he was grateful to her, but he frightened her rather.

"Oh no, Jerry," Aunt Mary said anxiously. "Ayna, surely your mother doesn't allow you to drink wine?"

"Yes she does," Ceri said, afraid of missing his share. "We all do."

Aunt Mary looked worried. "You shouldn't. You're

all far too small for your ages."

Brenda let out a large, nervous wheeze. Ceri protested, "I grow all the time."

"How old are you?" Mr. Claybury said teasingly to Ayna.

Ayna blushed. She suspected Mr. Claybury was thinking of her as a little girl, rather younger than Ceri, and she was afraid he was going to be disillusioned. "Nearly fourteen," she admitted.

"That settles it," said Mr. Masterfield, and he poured Ayna some wine in spite of Aunt Mary's frown.

Mr. Claybury, to Ayna's relief, threw back his bald head and laughed. "Would you believe it!" he said. "You're the same age as my little niece!" It was plain he thought his niece was wonderful, so that, Ayna thought thankfully, was all right. "And here was I thinking you were a bit young to be trusted with that great gold necklace of yours!" Mr. Claybury said, pointing to Ayna's collar. His face became thoughtful. Slow, Giant memories came into it. "I know what it's been reminding me of." He looked at Mr. Masterfield. "Jerry old man, do you still have that gold collar that funny little fellow gave us for shifting that stone?"

Gair's heart bumped. He avoided looking at Ayna's and Ceri's startled, troubled faces, and looked at Mr. Masterfield instead. His face was blank, bitter and crafty. "What on earth are you talking about, George?" he said.

Gair felt the pulsing of the collar strongly as he said it. It was working to make Mr. Masterfield cheat and lie, perhaps even kill, to keep the thing which could only do him harm.

Mr. Claybury's face became less pleasant, too. "Maybe you don't remember," he said. "You were very drunk. But I'd like to know what became of that collar. It was half mine, after all."

"I've no idea," Mr. Masterfield said flatly, and went round the table with the wine. Mr. Claybury's mouth pursed up and he looked almost murderously at Mr. Masterfield's back. It was only too clear to Gair that the collar had destroyed any friendship there had been between them.

Gerald took a deep breath. "I think I know the collar you mean, Mr. Claybury. It's in the study." Mr. Masterfield whirled round and glared at him, and Gair was not the only one who held his breath.

"There *is* a gold torque in the study," Aunt Mary said nervously. "Torque is the word, Gerald. A very fine one."

Mr. Claybury laughed and drank some wine. "I think I'll tell you a story," he said suddenly.

"How kind," Aunt Mary said uncertainly.

"The nippers'll like it anyway," said Mr. Claybury. "It starts on a fine moonlit night, years ago. There were two young men called—well, let's call them Jerry and

George, shall we? They had just come down from Oxford and Jerry was to be married the next day. George was going to be best man. And, the night before the wedding, the night I'm talking about, these two proceeded to get unbelievably, monstrously, extravagantly drunk—so drunk that they were never quite sure afterward what really happened. However, they did distinctly remember going to a farm called Marsh End—"

Brenda gasped from beside the sideboard. "My Auntie Marianne lives there!"

"Does she?" said Mr. Claybury. "She was a very comely young lady." After that, he turned his chair to include Brenda as he told his story, and much of his good humor seemed to return. Gair kept an eye on Mr. Masterfield and thought he had seldom seen anyone, Giant or person, look more dangerous. He hoped Mr. Claybury knew what he was doing. "These young men," Mr. Claybury said, "rollicked all over the Moor, and several times returned to sing songs under your auntie's window. And then, somehow, they ended up at a place where three roads met, on one of those little triangles of grass. There was a signpost there, and without that signpost they would have fallen down. They were as drunk as that. Shall I go on?"

"Ooh, yes!" said Brenda.

But the question was aimed at Mr. Masterfield and, to Gair's astonishment, Mr. Masterfield laughed, and laughed quite naturally. "Why not?" he said. This had nothing to do with the collar. Gair could feel it pulsing as coldly and strongly as ever. Either Giants had some source of strength Gair did not know about, or Mr. Claybury had worked powerful magic.

"Very well," Mr. Claybury said happily. And this was the story he told—and he told it very well, too, Gair thought, as well as Banot might.

George and Jerry were hanging onto that signpost and howling out a song about someone called Nelly Dean as hard as they could howl, when a strange little man suddenly hopped out of the ditch and came toward them.

"I wonder if you two could do me a favor," he said.

They stopped their song and did their best to look at him. They found him rather hard to see in their state. His clothes kept melting into the moonlight, but they could discern that he was fair, with a fair beard, and that he was laughing at their condition. Jerry was somewhat incensed at this, and drew himself up with dignity. Unfortunately, he forgot to let go of the signpost. The post came out of the ground and George slid in a heap to the grass. But Jerry was never one to let details bother him. He simply cradled the signpost in his arms and demanded, "Who the devil are you, you funny little man?"

George thought the little man was rather annoyed at

Jerry's tone, and also much impressed by his strength. But he was tired of being on the ground, so he said, "Put the signpost back, Jerry. I need it."

Jerry seemed rather surprised to find he was carrying a signpost. "How did I get this, George?" he said. "It seems to be a signpost. Shall we take it home as a souvenir?"

"No," said George. "I need it. Put it back."

Jerry did his honest best to put the signpost back, and George did his best to help him, but they got into great difficulties, because George could not find the hole to put it in and Jerry found several, all over the place. Every time the signpost fell over it seemed funnier. The little man seemed to find it quite as funny. They were all helpless with laughter by the time the little man planted it himself in the right place. And the darned thing started to fall over again. But the little man was not having that. He said one or two strange words, rather severely, to the signpost, and it promptly stood as firm as a rock.

"I think it's the wrong way round," George said, peering at the names on its arms, but, as nobody felt this mattered, he sat down to have a rest.

Jerry, meanwhile, had decided that the little man was one of his best friends. "Good old Titch!" he said, and made the little fellow utter a sort of croak by flinging an arm round him. "Didn't you want us to do you a favor?"

"That's right," said the little man, sounding rather

surprised that he should remember. And he pointed to something in the field beyond the hedge. "Would you mind very much moving that stone for me?"

Jerry hurt George's head by laughing. "Hey, George! Titch wants us to move the Gallows Stone!"

"Shan't," said George. He was getting sleepy. "Don't hold with capital punishment."

"Don't be a fool. It's not been used that way for centuries. Take a look."

Titch kindly helped George flounder up beside Jerry, and he seemed to find it quite a strain when George leaned on him. This was quite odd, because, in actual fact, George and he were much the same size. It was just that Titch *seemed* smaller, if you see what I mean. Anyway, George was finally able to stare across at a mound, near the edge of the Moor, which had a huge boulder balanced on top of it. On a rough estimate, by moonlight, it was about half the size of a haystack. "We can't move that!" George protested.

"Not if we both heaved?" said Jerry, who was much taken with the idea.

George remembered that he had certain responsibilities toward Jerry. "Got to get you to church in one piece," he said.

"True," said Jerry. "Sorry, Titch. Home, George. I need a drink." There was nothing he needed less just then.

Titch, at this, became curiously desperate. "Would you try to move it if I offered you a reward?" he said.

"George," said Jerry, "Titch is now offering us a reward if we move the Gallows Stone."

George woke up, feeling unmistakable interest. "How much?"

"This collar," said Titch, and he put his hands to his neck. As far as they could see, he was not wearing any kind of collar. Titch seemed to realize he was not, too, and took his hands away again, looking rather at a loss. "I'll give you a solid gold collar," he said. He seemed to mean it.

"I had a gold collar-stud once," George said wistfully. "Mind you, I prefer my collars made of cloth, come to think of it. *Gold*, did you say?"

"Yes, a gold collar," said Titch.

"It's no good, George," said Jerry, who had been considering the matter. "It's too big. We couldn't move it for a whole gold suit. It would take a bulldozer."

Here, both Jerry and George were struck with the same splendid idea. They turned to one another, swaying in the moonlight.

"Do you think we could?" said George. "I can't drive."

"I can try," said Jerry. "It would be a lark, and we haven't done anything yet tonight, have we?"

"The night is young!" shouted George. "Come on."

Jerry shouted to Titch to come on, and they all three

ran like madmen, down the branch of the road which the signpost now wrongly asserted led to Oxford. In fact, it led to Marsh End Farm. Now, it is one of the more remarkable things about being drunk that, even when you can hardly stand, you can run like the wind and even find breath to talk.

"We have to do something," George explained to Titch as he sprinted. "We've just finished Finals, and Jerry's getting married tomorrow. Silly fool, isn't he?"

"You don't think I'm a silly fool, do you, Titch?" Jerry said plaintively.

Titch, who did not seem in the least out of breath, although his legs were fairly twinkling along, said that he did not think Jerry was a fool at all. "If you can move that stone," he said, "I shall be married tomorrow, too."

"Hear that, George?" Jerry panted. "Titch is getting married tomorrow, too!"

It occurred to George that Titch's family must have some very odd marriage customs, if they required bridegrooms to heave stones about, but before he could say so, they arrived in the dark and odorous farmyard of Marsh End Farm. They had, as I said, been there several times that night, and, as happened each time, a confounded dog stood up on the end of its chain and tried to eat them, making the air hideous with its barking. But Titch said something to it quietly, and it stopped, just like that, and lay down again. Which left Jerry and

George free to hurl handfuls of farmyard at the upstairs window and yodel for Marianne.

After a while, the light went on, and this young lady's auntie stuck her tousled head out of the window. By this time, she was understandably irritated. "If it isn't you two again!" she said. "Go away. I've had about enough of your drunken yelling."

They sang to soothe her. "Please, Marianne," sang George. And Jerry caroled, "We want to borrow a tractor."

"The idea!" said this young lady's auntie. "I'll have our dad come after you with his shotgun if I hear any more tonight!"

"A tractor!" they sang.

"Go away," said Marianne, and she shut the window and turned out her light.

"How about that?" said George. He did not like shotguns.

"The old man's down at the pub still," said Jerry. "We did ask, and she didn't say no." And he boldly led the way to the shed where the old man kept a tractor. Titch, when he saw it, pulled his little fair beard and looked dubious, but he did not say anything. George said they would need some rope, too. "Chains," said Jerry. "They're much stronger." He found a whole lot in a corner of the shed and told Titch to put them in the back of the tractor. Titch carried them easily enough, but he seemed more doubtful than ever. They asked him why.

"You people put so much faith in iron," he said. "I don't altogether trust it myself."

"Carry them over and don't argue," said Jerry.

Titch did so, but as soon as he reached the tractor he looked sick and asked why it smelled so horrible. Jerry told him it was only diesel oil. But, since Titch seemed on the way to getting really ill, and the sight affected George profoundly, too, Jerry told them to wait outside while he tried to start the tractor. Much relieved, they went and leaned on the gate, where the dog watched them placidly, and George became confiding.

"I'm going to be a great man, Titch," he said. "I want you to believe that. One of these days, everyone's going to be talking about George Claybury, self-made man." And he said many other absurd things as well, being young and foolish and, as I think I have remarked, very drunk besides. Titch, to do him credit, listened very patiently and did not try to interrupt with advice. And, fortunately, just as George had got onto his unhappy childhood and started to cry, he was interrupted by a vast, vibrant chugging. Jerry and the tractor came backward out of the farmyard at an unexpectedly high speed. It was halfway to the crossroads before either of them came to their senses.

"After him!" howled George.

As they pelted up the road, the lights came on in the farmhouse and Marianne leaned out of it, screaming abuse. The dog, released from whatever hold Titch had had on it, joined in the clamor. But neither George nor Titch could spare any attention for the farm. Jerry, having knocked the signpost crooked again, went through the hedge on the other side of the road and across the field beyond in a series of sumptuous loops. His companions scrambled after him, wondering if he could stop before he came to Edinburgh or not at all. Luckily, the tractor stalled on its way up the mound which held the Gallows Stone.

"I got here!" Jerry bawled proudly. "Backward."

"Splendid fellow!" gasped George. "Eyes in the back of your head!"

The next step was to harness the tractor to the Gallows Stone. George and Jerry thought they did it rather well. They scrambled over and around that huge boulder, looping their chains, until it was in a sort of chain cage. Then they took the last length of chain to hook to the back of the tractor. But it became more and more evident that Titch did not trust those chains at all. He seemed to find it necessary to go round touching every place where the chains crossed or joined, muttering more of his weird words to them.

While he was doing it, Jerry and George suddenly found they were cold sober.

Now it may have been the drink wearing off with the hard work in the fresh air, but I think it was more likely the queer way Titch was muttering, combined with the fact that they could see the farmhouse from the mound, angrily lit at every window. At any rate, they both found themselves thinking of shotguns and Magistrates and suchlike unpleasant things.

"Look here, you!" Jerry called to Titch.

"If you've quite finished that muttering," added George. "Who are you and why do you want this stone moved anyway?"

They did not mean to be unfriendly, you understand, just firm. But when Titch came from behind the stone, he was so downright dismayed to see them sober that they became thoroughly suspicious. It seemed to them that, if Titch was not wrong in the head, he was trying to get them into trouble.

"You've got us into a fine fix, haven't you?" said George.

"We'll have to pacify the farmer," Jerry explained. "And my old man, too, I'm much afraid. Not to speak of all my relatives who are down for the wedding."

"Not to mince matters, there'll be a Stink," said George. "If you really want this stone moved, you prove your good faith and show us that gold you promised us."

"Yes. Produce it. Prove yourself," said Jerry. "We don't shift this ruddy rock an inch otherwise."

Titch looked both dismayed and exasperated. But he seemed faintly amused, too, as if Jerry and George were behaving according to some absurd pattern. "All right," he said. "But I shall have to fetch the gold. Will you wait here five minutes?"

"Uh-uh!" said George. "We know that one, little man."

"I'm not trying to run away," Titch said. Then he unbuckled the sword he had at his side and laid it in Jerry's hands. "You can keep that till I come back."

They looked at it. It struck them as something you might find in a museum, and they thought it might fetch a fair price in an antique shop. George nodded. "O.K. Fair enough," said Jerry.

Titch set off at a run across the field. It was hard to see far in the moonlight, but they both thought they saw him reach another, slightly lower mound there. Then he vanished. They were fairly sure they had seen the last of him, and they began to calculate whether the sword was likely to fetch enough to make up for the Stink. They were tinkering with the tractor, trying to start it again, when Titch suddenly reappeared beside them. He seemed breathless and rather triumphant.

"Got the gold?" George asked, not really thinking he had.

"Here," said Titch. He held up into the moonlight a fabulous fiery green torque. It was not only solid gold.

It glittered and twisted with the most intricate and delicate patterns. It was probably the most valuable thing either George or Jerry had seen in their lives. They both reached out to take the golden horseshoe. Titch, naturally enough, held it out of reach. "When the stone's moved," he said.

"If you like," said Jerry. "This is a bit of all right, eh, George?"

"I'll say!" said George. "Get her started, Jerry. Where to, Titch?"

"To that mound over there," Titch said, and pointed to the mound across the field where he had seemed to disappear.

This did not seem a very tall order, for a thing like that collar. Jerry got the tractor started in seconds. It began to roar and vibrate. The chains scrawked and tightened. The stone jerked, then shifted. Titch stood there, and so did George, to tell the truth, marveling at the strength of that machine. It growled. It juddered. Once or twice it stood still with its great back wheels whirling, but the stone, securely netted in the chains Titch had muttered to, went on moving. It bumped down the mound it sat on, and Titch was not the only one who encouraged it with strange noises. George shouted things, too. And it began to crawl like a huge snail ponderously onto the level.

Then—this was the queerest thing of all—as soon as that boulder had reached level ground, George felt a gush of cold air and a whirring behind him. He and Titch both spun round to see what it was. There was nothing, nothing at all to see. But the whirring went on upward into the dark blue sky and, with it, faint sounds of laughter and music. Jerry heard it, too. He turned round and shouted from his shaking perch on the tractor, "What was that? Something went up out of the mound, I swear!"

George shivered and shouted to him to keep going and not to stall. "What was it?" he asked Titch.

"I don't know." It was clear Titch had no more idea than George. "Something glad to be free, by the sound of it," he said.

After that, the stone crawled and bumped over the field and then up the other mound almost without interruption. There was a bad moment when it was halfway up this mound, and the tractor was halfway down the other side, and the two forces seemed exactly equal. But George and Titch set their backs to the stone and heaved, and it went on again. A minute later, it was perched on top of this second mound much as it had been perched on the other. Titch walked proudly up to it and spoke a few more of his well-chosen words, whereupon the chains literally fell off it into George's arms and the stone looked as if it had been in that place for centuries. While George was staggering about with the chains, Jerry must have given Titch back his sword and Titch passed him the gold collar, but George never knew for sure. He became very vague about everything around then. In fact, neither he nor Jerry quite knew how they got home or what they did with the tractor. When the inevitable Stink started, they were both hard put to it to explain. George would have thought he dreamed the whole thing, but for the fact that, while he was looking for the tractor after Jerry had left on his honeymoon, he found the marks the stone had made being dragged across that field, and the stone at the end of them, perched on the lower mound.

"Well?" said Mr. Claybury. "What do you think of that?"

"Lovely!" said Brenda, clearing away the last of the plates. Ayna looked at Gair's grave face and was not so sure. It had become ever more clear, as the story went on, that Mr. Claybury's little man had indeed been Gest. She did not like to think of her father blithely passing two drunken Giants a collar with a curse on it. She could only hope Gest had not known it was cursed. So did Gair, but he was not at all sure. Gest had already parted with his own collar to the Dorig, and it had plainly been urgent to find another. He had an idea that the story, as told in Garholt, suggested that Aunt Kasta came into it somehow—but, as Gest had cheated Og by asking the Giants to move the stone, why should he not have cheated the Giants, too? Gair did not like it at all.

Mr. Masterfield, who had been laughing more heartily than anyone, and was still smiling, turned jokingly to Ayna. "The collar in question," he said. "Whose is it going to be?"

Because he put it like this, Ayna's Gift took over. She might have vowed not to use it, but she could not help answering when people asked her things like this. "It's not going to be anyone's," she said. "It's going back where it came from to have the curse raised from it."

There was an uncomfortable little silence, except for Brenda's awed wheezing. "Coffee—?" suggested Aunt Mary.

Mr. Claybury stood up, looking at Ayna in a puzzled way. "You meant that, didn't you?" he said. For a moment, Ayna could have sworn he was connecting her with the little man in his story. But he said nothing else, and followed Aunt Mary to the room with the varnished statues.

They were perplexed to find that this was not holy after all—unless coffee was a special drink, like the Sun-wine you had at Feasts. If it was, Ceri did not care for it at all. The taste made him shudder. He felt more tired than ever and longed for this Giant gathering to be over, so that he could go to bed. But he was fairly sure no one would stop until they had asked Mr. Claybury not to make the Moor into a lake. And no one had so much as mentioned it yet.

Ceri thought this was ridiculous. Mr. Claybury must know why he had been invited. And, in his experience, you got a thing quicker if you asked for it straight out. "Mr. Claybury," he piped up, "we don't want you to flood the Moor. You can't. You really mustn't."

Ceri could tell from the reactions of the Giants and Ayna that they had wanted to lead up to this gradually. Mr. Masterfield hastily said something about "our young guest's unilateral enthusiasm," which Ceri saw meant Mr. Claybury should take no notice of him. But a slow, Giant shrewdness, mixed with amusement, was spreading on Mr. Claybury's face.

"I'm glad the nipper spoke up, Jerry," he said. "I'm not sorry for a chance to make myself clear. My position's going to be exactly the same, whether we talk all night first or not. May I explain?"

"Go ahead," Mr. Masterfield said grudgingly. Behind him, Brenda gently put down the coffeepot and sat down to listen.

"Now," said Mr. Claybury, "what you're all wanting to say to me in various ways is: Don't make this Moor into a reservoir because people live here. Right?"

"But people do!" Ceri said urgently. "Lots more than you think."

"Ah yes," said Mr. Claybury, but he was not really attending, because he was now making a speech, which was as much of a set-piece to him as his story had been.

"But pause for a moment to consider the number of people who *don't* live here. There are over fifty million of them." Ceri and Gair exchanged shaken looks. Never had they imagined there could be so many Giants. More than the stars in the sky! "And this number increases every year," Mr. Claybury continued, "until it has got to the point when the ordinary rivers and lakes simply do not contain enough water for them all. If you reckon that the smallest amount each person uses every day for drinking, washing, cooking and so on, is ten gallons—and the actual figure is a good deal higher than that—you will see that it is an awful lot of water. And it has to come from somewhere. So my office had to start looking for somewhere, not too far from London, where we could store some millions of gallons of water. We needed somewhere that could easily be made into a lake—and the Moor can be, because of the ring of hills round it—and where fewer people live than average. We went over Southern England with a fine-toothed comb, and the Moor was the *only* place that will do."

Gair spoke up despairingly. He knew this should be his opportunity to explain about his people, and about Dorig. Mr. Claybury had met Gest. He would have believed Gair. But Gair knew this would mean explaining also that his father had, perhaps knowingly, given an extremely evil thing to two harmless Giants. In the face of all those other Giants and their huge thirst, he just could not bring himself to do it. "But why should a few people suffer a lot," he said, "so that a lot of people shouldn't suffer at all?"

"Couldn't they all use less water?" Ayna suggested.

Mr. Claybury smiled and shook his head. "Only as a last resort. This is a very old argument. The greatest happiness of the greatest number. If you think about it, you'll find it always works out that a few suffer for the good of the rest."

"In stories," Gair agreed hopelessly, "brave men die defending the rest. But this isn't like that!"

"Call it the modern version," Mr. Claybury suggested kindly.

"I can't!" Mr. Masterfield said, so loudly that Gair's ears buzzed. "It isn't like that. The boy's right."

Mr. Claybury turned to him. "I know. I do understand. Believe me, I'm not being vindictive, or anything ridiculous like that. I like this Moor. I've had some good times here. That's one of the reasons I was glad to come here today, to see it before it's gone for good. But I do not know any other possible source of water in the quantities we need. So what am I to do, Jerry?"

The two Giants looked at one another. Gair wondered if he would ever understand Giants. He was sure it was the curse on the collar that had caused one friend to flood the other's land. They ought by rights to hate one another. Perhaps they had, earlier in the evening, but, by telling that story, Mr. Claybury had somehow blocked that cold, pulsing curse. He still liked Mr. Masterfield. Probably he had come to visit him hoping their old friendship might revive. And the signs were that it was reviving, against all odds.

Mr. Masterfield said, "You really can't get water any other way?"

"If I could," said Mr. Claybury, "I'd be using it now. If someone came to me—now—tomorrow—next week— and told me I could get it some other way, I'd cancel all plans for the Moor—like that! That's a promise, Jerry. But no one will. There *is* nowhere else. I know. You'd have to be some kind of amphibian to know more about water than I do."

Gerald's head came up, as if he had been struck by an idea. "Mr. Claybury, is that a real promise? If I told you how to get water another way, would you cancel the plans?"

"I really would," said Mr. Claybury. "Provided you were right."

"Go to bed, Gerald," Mr. Masterfield said irritably. "Take your friends with you."

Gerald stood up, looming among the little statues, wished everyone goodnight, and took Ceri, Ayna, Gair, Brenda and the coffee cups out to the kitchen. An extremely noisy magic box was washing the crockery there, using precious water, as Brenda bitterly pointed out. Gerald seemed to want to have some kind of conference, but the others were too tired. Ceri tried to go to sleep under the table. Gair sat miserably on a stool, suddenly longing for his lost windowsill. And Ayna, who felt as if her best efforts had gone for nothing, said tearfully that they had to find Gest first thing tomorrow.

"I'll get my old man to drive you anywhere Ceri says," Gerald promised. "But you'll have to promise to help me, too, with a sort of idea I've got. After all, you owe us for our help." They could not but agree they did. "Come back first thing tomorrow," Gerald called to Brenda, as she took her poker from a corner and gloomily opened the back door.

"O.K.," said Brenda. "Look at that, now! It's raining. You'd think it rained enough in this blessed country to turn us all into Dories. Where does it all go?"

Chapter

12

THEY SLEPT LATE IN THE SOFT GIANT BEDS.
They awoke in the bright rain-specked mid-morning to
find that their own clothes had dried overnight, somewhat shrunk and wrinkled, particularly their boots.
Nevertheless, they put them on with relief and went
downstairs feeling much more like themselves. Ayna
thought Mr. Claybury looked rather sharply at them,
but he and Mr. Masterfield were busy bustling off for
a tour of the Moor in Mr. Masterfield's car. They
seemed the best of friends, and there was a strong suggestion that they were going to pay a visit to Brenda's
Auntie Marianne. Ayna could not imagine that she
would be pleased to see them. Aunt Mary was also
driving off, to a place called Church, so, when Brenda
crashed into the kitchen brushing toast-crumbs off her
generous front, Gerald and his three visitors were
alone there having breakfast. Brenda promptly had
more breakfast with them.

Gair had waked with his head full of disturbing

thoughts. He felt weak and inadequate, and blamed himself for not explaining to Mr. Claybury. And he did not want to see Gest yet. He was glad both cars had gone, and ashamed of being glad. For some reason, it did not occur to him to connect these feelings with the fact that he had spent the night close to a powerful source of evil. The nearest he came to it was to think constantly of the way Mr. Claybury had counteracted the curse. It seemed to him that the Giants had behaved better than people would, and he longed to know why.

"What do you Giants do," he asked, "to stop being enemies?"

They did not quite understand him. "We talk," Gerald said gloomily. "Peace conferences, summit conferences, conferences. Talks about talks, preconference talks, treaty-talks, talks."

Brenda said, "I think we use talk the way you lot use words."

"Does it work?" Ceri asked, in surprise.

The two Giants looked at one another. "I think it stops the big wars," Gerald said, after a moment.

"Talking to old Claybury hasn't stopped the Moor being flooded," Brenda said dismally.

"That's more or less my idea," Gerald said. "Talk. We didn't do any good with Claybury, so what if we talked to the other lot who want the Moor flooded?"

"The Dories?" said Brenda. "What good would that do?"

Gerald looked at Gair. "Didn't you tell me the Dorig managed to flood whatsit—Otmound? Doesn't that sound as if they might have control of a water supply somewhere?" Gair nodded, beginning to feel much more cheerful. "So if we talk," Gerald said, "we might just settle the flooding and your war as well, if we played it right. We know there are nine Dorig in the moat at the moment. Can you think of any way we can get them out and talk to them?"

"I think you've got some hopes!" Brenda said frankly. "The Dorig are these lot's deadly enemies. They want them flooded out. And don't forget you shot one. He won't love you for that."

As Gerald began to look gloomy and obstinate, a perfect idea came to Gair. It was so good that he chuckled. "I can catch a Dorig," he said. "All I've got to do is sit on that bridge as bait and wait for them to grab me. You can all hide behind the hedge and grab him as he grabs me."

"And then talk to him!" said Gerald. "Or use him as a hostage to make the others talk. Bravo, Gair!"

Though the others exclaimed at the risk, the idea took their fancy thoroughly. They had all been longing to turn the tables on the Dorig, and the fact that the idea was peaceful seemed to justify it. The real trouble was

222

that the Dorig would certainly shift shape when he found himself grabbed. Some time was devoted to persuading Ceri to shift it back with a Thought. Ceri refused obstinately, until Ayna took a hand.

"Mother isn't dead, so it's not a sacred promise, stupid!" she said. "You know that as well as I do. You're just scared."

"Yes, I am," said Ceri shamelessly.

"Well, it's Sun day. You shouldn't be," said Ayna.

"What's Sunday got to do with it?" said Gerald.

"It's our day," said Ceri sulkily. "The Sun's on our side. All right. I'll do it. But I'm still scared."

Gair was scared, too, when he went out onto the bridge, in spite of it being Sun day and in spite of Aunt Mary's clothesline tied round his waist, with the other end in Gerald's hand behind the hedge. Out of the corner of his eye he saw Gerald's large hands tying the rope to the gatepost. He did not really think that would do much good. Once he was in the water, he was as good as drowned. He had not the first notion how to swim. None of his people had. He sat cautiously down on the bridge, with his shrunk and battered boots hanging just above the blue sparkles and peat-brown shadows of the moat, to give the Dorig a good chance. They were certain to recognize him. Apart from his missing collar and Gerald's watch softly and rapidly ticking on his wrist, Gair was the same small figure in Moor-colored clothes whom they had chased and surrounded yesterday.

He was fairly sure the Dorig were in the moat. He looked casually round, as if he was admiring a fine fresh day, and he could see nothing that looked like a Dorig. White mist rose distantly, from the marshes beyond the trees. A few birds twittered. The mild dog lay on the gravel and slept as if there was no enemy for miles.

"They're not here!" Brenda hissed in a huge whisper.

"Shut up!" Gerald hissed back.

Gair waited, pretending to be deep in thought. Behind the hedge, the rest waited, too. Nothing happened. After a while, Gair dared to look down into the water of the moat, where the soles of his battered boots were reflected, and his white face in the distance between them. But the water inside the reflections was deep, dark and impenetrable. Like the Dorig themselves, it was fearsome and it gave nothing away. Gair thought that one reason he was sitting here, scared and tense, was that he wanted to know more about the Dorig. They were so mysterious.

It did not occur to him that the main reason he was sitting there might be that collar, though he looked up at the dark bricks of the house and thought about the thing itself. He could feel it lying inside, like a cold pocket of poison under a tooth. He knew he owed it to Gerald to do something about it if he could, but for that moment he thought of it only as the thing which had first made him aware that he had a Gift. And it seemed to him he was really sitting there because the Gift had made no difference at all. He had had it all along without knowing it, and now he knew of it, he was still ordinary.

Something jumped in the water.

Gair's head jerked round in time to catch ripples spreading away from something about five feet from the bridge, something which was already sinking out of sight. He waited, tense as a cat. Behind the hedge, they had seen it, too. Gair heard Brenda breathing as noisily as a Giant tractor. He looked across the placid moat and tried to hum a tune.

The fish jumped again—if it was a fish. And it was nearer.

The ripples faded. There was nothing. For a long time there was nothing at all. Gair tried to look at the water while seeming to look at the sky, until his eyes ached. He was forced to rub them. And while he did, there was movement in the reflection of his feet. Gair stared, with his hands at his eyes. The water there swirled and piled into a hummock. There was a grayness. A long thin hand reached up out of it and seized Gair round the ankle.

Tense as Gair was, it happened so quickly that the Dorig all but got him. The thin gray hand had dragged his leg underwater before he could move. But the cold water filling his boot brought Gair to his senses. He shouted. He felt the clothesline jerk as somebody hauled on it. Then he rolled sideways on the bridge and grabbed down into the water beside his leg. His fingers met something slippery and firm. He seized it and pulled with all his might. The water boiled and seethed. Gair was soaked in seconds, but he had hold of what seemed to be an arm and he did not let go. He felt the bridge tremble as Brenda and Ayna dashed from behind the hedge and hung over the edge of the bridge to pull, too.

Gair was astonished how light and weak Dorig were. By the time Brenda seized it, he had the gray Dorig body half out of the water single-handed. One heave from Brenda, and it was on the bridge. The next second, it was not a Dorig any longer, but a yard-long green pike, flailing and snapping and almost back in the water again. Brenda fell on it. The whole bridge juddered.

"Ceri!" Gair shouted.

Ceri appeared in the gateway, white with concentration.

The pike let out a piercing yell and became a Dorig again at once, without the usual dissolving. A wave of cold air rolled between it and Ceri, and the Dorig yelled again. Gair had an idea that it hurt it to change so abruptly. But no one had much time to think. The Dorig, though it was not much taller than Ayna and probably lighter than Ceri, fought Ayna and Brenda like a tiger and screamed piercingly for help. The mild dog woke up and hovered anxiously around, getting in Gair's way, and the bridge became dangerously slippery with the water splashed in the first struggle. Gerald stormed out from behind the hedge, bellowing at the dog and bawling to Gair to untie the rope before it swept everyone off the bridge.

"Hafny, *help*!" screamed the Dorig. "They've stopped me shifting shape!" Gerald pounced on it and held its beating arms to its sides.

"Get it into the house before any more come," Gair said, scrambling out of the rope.

But it was too late. The water was surging again some yards away beside the bank. Glistening gray hands seized the stones there, and another thin, silvery Dorig body slid upward onto the gravel. This one seemed smaller than the first, though it was hard to see for sure, for it remained crouched where it was, with water rilling off it, staring at the crowded bridge. The mild dog, to Gair's disgust, ambled up to it wagging its elderly tail. That dog did not seem to know an enemy when it saw one. It actually let the crouching Dorig pat it.

"Don't just sit there!" screamed the captured Dorig, twisting in Gerald's hands. "Do something!"

"What do you want me to do?" the smaller Dorig asked, rather unhelpfully.

The captured Dorig wailed with annoyance. "Stupid! Go and tell someone. Quick! Before they stop you shifting shape, too."

"Ceri," said Ayna.

"I already have," said Ceri.

"I can't tell anyone," said the smaller Dorig. "You know we—"

"Oh be quiet and do as I tell you!" howled the larger one, and tried to bite Gerald.

"But I'll get into trouble if I do," said the smaller Dorig, crouching where it was with singular calm. "You know we aren't allowed in this moat. We'll have to make them let you go some other way."

"Give us a few suggestions," Gerald called to it, and made a face at Brenda.

Brenda nodded and lumbered slowly sideways off the bridge toward the smaller Dorig. It rose to its feet and slithered cautiously backward away from her, along the edge of the moat. It did not seem nearly as frightened as it should have been with a Giantess the size and shape of Brenda after it. They thought it must be assuming it could easily escape by turning into something else. But the other Dorig did not seem so confident. "Shift shape, you idiot!" it screamed.

"I can't," said the smaller one. "They've stopped me, too."

"Then jump into the moat!" commanded the other.

"Not yet," said the smaller Dorig. "That wouldn't do any good."

Its air of assurance was beginning to irritate them all

as much as it annoyed its fellow. "Then I can't think what you're aiming to do," Ayna said. "You might as well surrender."

"And I can swim, too," Gerald added.

"I know—like a fish out of water. I've seen you," the Dorig retorted, keeping a wary eye on Brenda. Brenda, knowing she did not maneuver well, was shuffling forward until she had a chance to pounce. The smaller Dorig held itself ready to dodge, its deep yellow eyes flickering between her and the crowded bridge. "What are you trying to do?" it said. "It won't help you to kill us. Our people will only kill you."

"We're not trying to kill you," Gair said.

"We wouldn't know how," said Gerald. The Dorig he was holding relaxed considerably at that. "We want to talk to you."

"Why?" said the smaller Dorig, still backing.

"About the Moor being flooded," said Gair.

"That's nothing to do with us. Or you either," said the Dorig Gerald was holding. "You—"

"Shut up, Halla," said the smaller Dorig. He stopped backing, although he was near enough to the moat to jump in if he wanted. "Suppose I agreed to talk. What then?"

Brenda looked doubtfully over her shoulder to see what the others thought. "It's probably a trick," said Ceri.

They all thought Ceri was right. But the only way to get anywhere seemed to be to treat it as real and to hope to turn it to some advantage. Gerald said, "Then we'd ask you to come into the house of your own free will and discuss things."

The two Dorig exchanged looks. "In there!" the larger one said dubiously.

"If we did," said the smaller one, "would you agree to take the Thought off us, so that we could shift shape again?"

"No," they said, all five, in chorus. Gair added, "But we'd promise to take it off you after we've talked."

"By the Three Powers?" said the larger Dorig quickly. "And the Sun and the Moon, and the strange gods of the Giants?"

"Yes," they said, and Gerald asked, "Well?"

"But if we agree," persisted the smaller Dorig, "that means we're in your power without any defense. Would you agree not to use your magic?"

"We haven't got any magic," said Gair, to which Gerald added, "And *we* certainly haven't."

"I wish we had," said Brenda, sighing.

"Yes you have," said the smaller Dorig. "Lymen have words and thoughts, and Giants have unnatural strength and things that work by themselves. If you use any of those, it's not fair."

Gair and Gerald looked at one another. Gerald

shrugged. "Well, I wouldn't call most of that magic, but we won't use them if you want. Now will you come indoors?"

Considerably to their surprise, the smaller Dorig said, "Yes. All right."

"I hope you know what you're doing, Hafny," said the larger one. "All right. I agree, too. Now let me go."

Before he let go, Gerald cautiously asked Gair, "Have they got any other powers you know of?"

"They can use words a bit," Gair said. "But you'll have to risk that."

So Gerald let the larger Dorig go and they all trooped across the bridge and through the door of the house. It seemed safest to Gerald to keep the two Dorig as far apart as possible. He went in front with the larger one. Brenda and Hafny brought up the rear, as queer a pair as you could hope to meet. Gerald led the way into the dining room. "Around the table conference, Giant-fashion," he said.

The size of the room made the two Dorig seem smaller, and more slender, than before. They stood side by side and gazed round wonderingly, particularly at the ugly plates in the cupboards. Gair was interested to see that the gray-silver of their bodies did not seem at all wet now. Indeed, it was sagging and wrinkling from their joints in a way that you would expect from clothes rather than skin.

"You know," said Brenda, "those clothes aren't like the armor the lot in Garholt were wearing. They're more like the suits people wear for skin-diving."

"I've got one," said Gerald. "Only mine's rubber."

It seemed there were things Giants and Dorig understood better than people. Both Dorig looked interested. "Rubber's that black stuff that stretches, isn't it?" Halla said to Hafny.

"It's no good. It doesn't go with you when you shift," Hafny said.

"Giants can't shift shape, stupid!" said Halla, and Hafny was embarrassed. A pale pink flush flooded the white of his face. To cover it up, he stripped off his gloves, revealing long thin hands whiter even than Adara's.

"Do we give names?" Ayna said, rather formally.

"You have ours," Halla said, quite as stiffly.

Hafny looked up. "And I have the Giants'," he said. "They're Brenda and Gerald. And"—he pointed at Gair—"yours, too."

Now it seemed there were things Dorig and people understood better than Giants. Brenda and Gerald looked quite bewildered when Ayna stepped defensively in front of Gair and demanded, "How did you come by his name? If you've dared misuse it—!"

"I've known it for two weeks," said Hafny. "And I've kept it in my head. Have you heard me speak it yet?"

Ayna glared at him, quite unconvinced. Gair was aching to ask how Hafny came to know his name, but he never got a chance. The two Giants were loudly expressing their bewilderment. "What's in a name? What's the fuss about? He knows ours and we know yours. What does it matter?"

"Giants don't know words," Ayna said scornfully. "And it makes you quite stupid, the way you throw your names about."

"You don't let enemies get hold of your name," Ceri explained, so that the Giants' feelings might not be hurt. "Suppose the enemy put words on it. Even Dorig can do that."

"Even *Dorig*!" said Halla. "Don't call us that! We're people!"

"No you're not. *We're* people," said Ceri.

"You!" said Halla. "You're just a miserable little Lyman."

"*Lyman!*" said Ayna. "Listen—"

Gerald made both Dorig jump by uttering a great bark of laughter. "Haven't I heard this conversation before somewhere?"

"Yes," said Brenda. "And I'll have you Dories know that *we're* the only people around here. The rest of you are all fairi—something else!"

The outraged expressions on the narrow white Dorig faces made Gair want to laugh as well as Gerald. "But you're a Giant!" said Hafny. Brenda went purple and began to breathe heavily.

Gair gave up trying to ask how Hafny knew his name. It was clear there was more fertile ground for disagreement here than he had ever known, and if he did not do something about it, none of the things they wanted to talk about would get so much as mentioned. "This won't do," he said. "We came here to talk."

"You called for talk, not us," Halla said coldly.

"But we agreed," Hafny said. "And I needn't have done."

"What, when I was a prisoner!" exclaimed Halla.

"Well, that was your own silly fault for trying to drown a Lyman on Sun day," Hafny retorted. "I warned you. And I told you that one"—he pointed at Gair again—"was probably very clever. He got away yesterday, and he tricked you properly today. So you see I was right." Hafny was looking at Gair as he spoke, and Gair was surprised to see interest and a great deal of curiosity in his strange face. It had not occurred to him before that a Dorig might be as interested in him as he had been in Gerald, but it might well be so. And Hafny was making such a point of not using Gair's name that it seemed as if his interest might outweigh the fact that his people and Gair's were at war.

Gair made a peaceful gesture in his turn. "My name

is Gair," he said, formally. "And I was sitting on the bridge as bait."

At this, Halla looked extremely mortified, but Hafny laughed, the thin, sibilant Dorig laugh. "I told you so, Halla!" He looked from Halla's cross face to the dining table. "Is that an eating-square? Do you want us to sit round that and talk?"

"That was the idea," Gerald said, glad to see things moving the right way at last.

Hafny, rather uncertainly, went toward a chair. But, before he sat in it, he put his hands to his neck, undid a catch and peeled the silver-gray covering off his head. It was just like a hood when it was off. He laid it carefully on the table, in a way Gair felt sure was significant, if he only understood. Underneath, Hafny had hair—dark-honey-colored hair—as curly as Ceri's, and ears only a little more pointed than Gair's. Quite suddenly, in spite of his queer golden eyes, he seemed much less strange. Fascinated, they watched him next rip apart the top part of his silver-gray garments—which opened much in the manner of the Giants' zippers Gair and Ayna had struggled with, to become a jacket over a leathery-looking shirt. It showed them that Hafny wore round his neck a bright green-glinting collar of such magnificent work that Ceri could hardly take his eyes off it.

Halla, a little grudgingly, did the same. Ayna gasped and Brenda sighed wistfully, as a cascade of hair fell

235

from the gray hood—hair so silver-fair that Ayna's almost looked brown. Halla was revealed as an extremely pretty girl, in a collar as rich as Hafny's above a gold-embroidered shirt. Gair felt a little foolish. All his life he had heard Dorig talked of as "he"—or, most frequently, "it"—and it had never occurred to him until this moment that there must be Dorig girls. That there might be Dorig children was something he was more prepared for. He had suspected for some minutes that neither Hafny nor Halla was very old. And now that they looked more like the kind of people he was used to, he could see that Hafny was much his own age and Halla no older than Ayna—though their long, thin Dorig bodies made them more like the Giants in height. Gair was puzzled. He could not think how they came to be in the moat instead of the nine full-grown Dorig of yesterday.

Gerald was frankly disgusted. He leaned over and growled in Gair's ear, "They're only a couple of kids!"

"They must have important parents," Gair whispered back. "Look at those collars."

"I'll take your word for it," Gerald said dubiously, and sat at the table.

Everyone sat down, and Ayna and Ceri reluctantly gave their names. For a short while, it did almost look as if this Giant way of talking round a table was a magic to produce good will. Brenda brought the little barrel of biscuits with her from the sideboard when she sat down. In her greedy Giant way, she took one herself and munched it while she offered the barrel to the Dorig. Hafny refused. But Halla, seeing Ceri's hand reaching out and Brenda munching herself, doubtfully took a biscuit and put it cautiously to her mouth.

"Hafny!" she said. "It's *sweet!*"

Hafny's face lit up and he stretched out a hand as greedily as Ceri. "May I?"

"Go ahead." Brenda pushed the barrel his way. "Don't they allow you sweet things then?"

"Only at Feasts," Hafny said, crunching busily.

"Nothing sweet grows underwater," Halla explained.

Brenda and Ceri were so horrified at this state of deprivation that they got in one another's way to tip a heap of biscuits in front of the Dorig. But when Gerald, hoping to take advantage of these kindly feelings, tried to get down to business, disagreements began almost at once.

"See here," Gerald said. "All of us want to stop the Moor being flooded. Your lot want it flooded. Can you think of any way we can come to an agreement?"

Hafny shrugged. "No," he said frankly, with his mouth full.

"It's you Giants who are doing the flooding," Halla said. "I told you it had nothing to do with us."

"*Some* of us Giants," said Gerald.

"These Giants live on the Moor," Gair explained.

"They don't want their houses and land underwater any more than we want our mounds flooded."

Halla shrugged. "Then ask the other Giants."

"We did," said Ayna. "And there are so many of them that they need the water to drink. The chief Giant has told us that there's nowhere but the Moor where they can get it. But he said that if there *was* water anywhere else, he'd use it."

"I'm glad there isn't," said Halla. "We need the Moor flooded for living-space."

"Couldn't you live somewhere else?" asked Gair.

"Couldn't *you*?" retorted Halla.

"Not very easily," said Gair, struggling not to get angry.

"Neither can we," said Halla.

"And neither can we," said Gerald. "Why do you need all that room?"

"Why do you?" Halla countered.

Gerald sighed angrily. Ayna said disgustedly, "This is getting nowhere!" Gair tried to swallow his mounting annoyance. Halla was no doubt angry still at the way they had captured her, but all the same, Gair was beginning to see why his people and the Dorig had always been enemies. He looked irritably at Hafny, who seemed quite content to sit gobbling biscuits and letting Halla talk, while he stared speculatively from face to face. Hafny was looking at Gerald as if Gerald's size and restrained strength both awed him and made him feel rather scornful, when he felt Gair's eyes on him. He looked at Gair and shrugged.

"Our people are very short of space," he said quietly. "They've been hopelessly overcrowded all my life."

"And of course the smaller kings keep pestering us for action," Halla said. "Luckily, the Giants are acting for us. As soon as the observers reported that, we took steps to move the Lymen. The bad wells at Garholt are a real problem, but we're dealing with that now, quite kindly."

"Kindly!" said Ayna.

Gerald looked at Halla with deep contempt. Gair could see Gerald had formed a very low opinion of her mental powers. He thought Gerald was right. Judging by the unreflecting way she spoke, he suspected she was simply repeating what other, older Dorig said. "You know what you sound like?" Gerald said to her. "You sound just like newspaper propaganda. Next thing, you'll be saying you invaded Otmound and Garholt for defense, or peace, or something."

It was hardly to be expected that Halla would understand this. Nor did she. "Well, it would be more peaceful if there weren't any Lymen," she said. "And flooding Otmound was defense, in a way. The Otmounders attacked the refugees from the Halls of the Kings, fifteen years ago, when all they were doing was peacefully crossing the Moor, and they killed a whole lot of them."

"But what about Garholt?" said Ayna. "We hadn't attacked you."

"If you wanted the words off their wells, why couldn't you have asked?" demanded Brenda. Halla looked at her as if she had formed much the same opinion of Brenda as Gerald had of her.

"How did you flood Otmound?" Gair asked, remembering Gerald particularly wanted to know this.

"With pumps," Halla said carelessly, in the way people do when they have not much idea. "They'd been planning it for years."

"Where did the water come from?" Gerald asked eagerly, forgetting his irritation.

Halla looked blank. Hafny, grinning a little at her ignorance, came to her rescue. "It was the water from the marsh that always has to be pumped out of our halls anyway. They piped it to the Otmound wells and pumped it out of them into the mound."

Everyone digested this. Dorig were plainly ingenious.

"Pumped out of your halls?" Gerald said slowly, disappointed and puzzled, too.

"Hey!" said Brenda. "I thought you lot lived in water!"

"Not *in* water. *Under* water," Hafny said. He looked round at their puzzled faces and seemed almost as puzzled himself. "We breathe air," he said. This was plainly true. Now they came to look, everyone could see him breathing, and Halla, too. They had noses. Their chests went up and down. There was no indication that they had gills or anything fishlike about them. "And we have to pump water out of our halls and let in air to breathe," Hafny said. "Don't you understand?"

Gair thought he understood. He had a sudden perception of the Dorig living in something very like their mounds, only under the bottom of the marsh or river. He turned to Hafny to ask if this was indeed the case, and he had a feeling Hafny was quite ready to tell him anything he wanted to know, but, at that moment, disagreement flared up worse than before. Gerald, who must have understood somewhat as Gair had done, said, "Then you don't have to live underwater at all. You could leave the Moor and live anywhere you wanted."

"No we can't!" snapped Halla. Gerald's lordly tone irritated her, and she was annoyed that he had made her look foolish over the pumps. "My people will never take orders from a Giant. You Giants are nothing but great crude robbers. You descend from bears!"

"Nonsense!" Gerald said angrily.

"Like you descend from frogs," said Brenda.

That made Halla angrier than ever. Her face went pale pink and her yellow eyes snapped. "You dare! You say that, when you stole the land from us! Then you pour filth into lakes and rivers until they're not fit to swim in, and then you expect us to leave the Moor to please you! I tell you, we have a right to live here! We were the very first people here."

"No you weren't," said Ceri. "We were."

Ceri, perhaps, had simply been putting Halla right. But when Ayna joined in, Gair could see it was because she disliked Halla. "And the Giants took the land from *us*!" Ayna said heatedly. "But that hasn't stopped us trying to be friends with them." And she looked at Brenda. From the way Brenda looked back, it was evident the two of them were closing ranks against Halla.

Halla saw it and nearly spat. "Yes, licking the foot that kicked you! Everyone was saying yesterday that that was just like Lymen. Listen, *we* were here before either of you. You came and drove us into the water. And when the Giants came and drove you into the ground, we were glad!"

"We did not drive you into the water!" Ceri said. "You were always there."

"No we weren't," Hafny said, seriously and quietly. "Once we lived on the land like the Giants do."

He was clearly trying to smooth things over. But his reasonable tone irritated Gerald, as it had done all along. "Well, what do you want me to do about it— apologize?" Gerald demanded, so thunderously that Hafny flinched. "That all must have been thousands of years ago. We're all here now. And we've all got a right to live on the Moor if we want!"

At that, Brenda's resentment of Gerald flared up. "Who says?" she said in her piercing Giant voice. "*Your* people came with the Normans and pinched the Moor off us! My folks were here from the year dot — or before that. If anyone's got as much right here as the Lymen and the Dories, it's me, and not you, Gerald Masterfield!"

"No you haven't," said Halla.

"If nine hundred years isn't long enough, what *is*!" roared Gerald.

Gair, with his ears quivering, looked round their angry faces and felt really frightened. It was not merely that the talk had not got anywhere. It was rapidly getting out of hand. He had counted on Gerald to behave in the reasonable Giant manner, but Gerald was fast getting violent. And Hafny, who was behaving reasonably, was irritating everyone with his dry assurance. Gair saw that it was stupid to expect anything else, when they were all gathered in a house shot through with the dark influence of that collar. Their age-old differences were being aggravated into personal dislike. Gair was about to suggest that they go outside to talk, when a sudden perception came to him. Ayna, Brenda and Halla were glaring, Brenda at Gerald, Ayna and Halla at one another. Each had her head tilted in identical angry haughtiness. And it did not matter that Brenda's face was wider and pinker than Ayna's, or that Halla's eyes were yellow where Ayna's were blue. They were all faces. And the hair that grew from the heads of each, though it varied from silvery to dark straw, was the same kind of hair.

"Have you noticed," Gair said loudly, "that we're all people really?" All the faces turned to him, surprised and wondering, Gerald's, Ceri's and Hafny's as well as the girls'. "I mean," Gair explained, "that we're all far more like one another than—well, dogs or spiders."

"I should hope so!" said Halla. But they all turned and looked at one another thoughtfully.

"I see what you mean," said Gerald.

"Five fingers," said Ceri. "Giants' are thicker and Dorigs' longer, but we all have five. You mean we're all the same underneath?"

"Are you people warm-blooded?" Gerald asked Hafny.

"Of course," said Hafny.

"But what about the way they can change shape?" Brenda asked. She sighed. "I can't."

"I've been wondering about that," said Gair. "Do you," he asked the two Dorig, "do it by thinking? Or how?"

Halla and Hafny looked uncertainly at one another. "I—I *think* so," Hafny said. "It's—well, it's a bit like moving your leg or your arm, really."

"Only much harder," said Halla. "You have to concentrate. And you feel tired if you keep it up for long."

"Particularly if you shift to something bigger than you are," said Hafny. "Yes, I suppose you *think* in a certain way, and it happens."

"Like my Thoughts," Ceri said.

"That's what I meant," said Gair. "Ceri, I bet you could shift shape if you turned your Thoughts on yourself."

Ceri's mouth fell open. "I'd never dare."

"You're not even to *try*," said Ayna. "Suppose you stuck! Gair, really!"

"People don't usually stick," Hafny said encouragingly.

"He's not the *same* as you!" Ayna said crossly.

"But he is—in a way," said Gerald. "That's what Gair's getting at. There are stories about people—er, Giants—doing it, too. Werewolves and suchlike. It's not very common among us, but there is that chap who breaks forks, and they say some—er—Giants can see into the future a bit. Is that the sort of thing you're talking about, Gair?"

"Yes," Gair said thoughtfully. "I *think* we must all descend from the same stock."

"You mean you—some of us—are mutants," Brenda said wisely.

"Only, which of us is normal?" said Gerald. "Suppose we're the mutants, Brenda?"

Before the two Giants could indulge in more theories, Hafny firmly interrupted. "I'm sorry," he said, "but it's the differences between us that are important. You'd better get that clear." Somehow, they gathered from his manner that the talk was likely to get somewhere at last. Hafny did not seem unfriendly, but he was very much in earnest as he said, "Giants and Lymen and us are all different. We all want different things. We usually leave you Giants alone to quarrel among yourselves, and occasionally some good for us comes out of it. And it has now, because the Moor is going to be flooded, just when we need more room most. You see, it isn't simply that there are more of our people every year. About fifteen years ago, the places in the West called the Halls of the Kings filled up with water. Water came in where the air should have come in, and no one could pump it out. So everyone had to leave and come to the halls here. There were thousands of them —"

"Just a moment," Gerald interrupted. "How big are these Halls of the Kings?"

"I've never been there," Hafny said cautiously. "But I believe they were enormous."

"And where are they?" Gerald asked eagerly.

"Under some chalk hills," said Hafny. "That's what caused the water, they say — a fault in the chalk. I've heard that the Giants call that part the Downs."

"Which Downs? Berkshire or Sussex?" Gerald demanded, thoroughly excited. "And would you say there was a lot of water?"

"A great deal of water," Hafny said wryly. "People drowned. But those names mean nothing to me, I'm afraid." Gerald, red in the face with excitement, made an annoyed noise. Hafny looked at him in a way that was both shrewd and satisfied. Gair could have sworn he had told Gerald this deliberately, hoping to arouse just the interest he had aroused. Hafny was plainly a deep one. Gair was wondering just what Hafny was playing at, when Hafny looked at him. "Now we come to the Lymen," he said.

"We hadn't anything to do with the Otmounders attacking the fugitives," Ayna said.

"I wasn't meaning that," said Hafny.

"In that case," Halla said warningly, "you'd better not say any more, Hafny."

"Yes I shall," said Hafny, losing his dryness and becoming simply a younger brother arguing with his elder sister. Gair was fairly sure by now that Halla was Hafny's elder sister. "I'm going to tell them because I owe it them. Try and stop me." He turned to Ayna, Gair and Ceri. "The fact is, the bad wells in Garholt are just an excuse, I think. My father has sworn not to leave a Lyman alive on the Moor. If you want to live, you'll have to leave the Moor. If you stay, you'll be killed before you're drowned. Find your father and tell him that."

Gair could see Hafny meant this. A gust of dismay

swept over him, as he thought of the prisoners in Garholt.

"Gair," said Ayna, "we must go and find Father straightaway."

"You can't," said Gerald. "Unless—Are they still chasing them—the ones who were after them yesterday?" he asked Hafny.

Hafny shrugged. Shrugging, Gair was beginning to think, was very characteristic of Dorig. "No. My father called that off," he said, to their great relief. "I told you, we leave Giants alone. My father thought the Giants would kill you anyway."

"Who *is* your father?" said Brenda. "Chief Dory or something?"

Halla's chin lifted proudly. "He's the King."

"Well, fancy!" said Brenda.

"Halla," said Hafny, "you shouldn't have told them that."

"Why not?" said Halla. "We've unhooded to them."

"But none of them have hoods." Hafny shrugged again as he looked round the table. "I expect you're all thinking what good hostages we'll make."

"It never crossed my mind," Gerald said, rather angrily. "We promised to let you go."

Gair was glad Gerald had chosen to behave with Giant honorableness. For a moment, he had been very tempted. Yesterday the Dorig had been rounding up children with gold collars, no doubt to use as hostages. It would turn the tables splendidly if today those same children took the King's son prisoner and sent the King's daughter with the news. It would be that way round, Gair knew. Nobody cared for Halla, but Hafny was interesting. Gair would have liked to have known him better. But it was not to be. Gair looked regretfully at the two Dorig. That they were King's children explained a lot. It explained Halla's haughtiness and Hafny's queer self-confidence, and the way both seemed to speak for the entire Dorig race. It explained their splendid collars. But one thing it did not explain was why Hafny felt he owed them his warning.

"Before you go," Gair said, and he put it that way so as to place temptation firmly behind him. "Before you go, why did you say you owed us that warning?"

He was surprised to find Hafny blushing the pale pink Dorig blush—though less surprised when he also shrugged. "Well, it's your father I owe really," Hafny said uncomfortably. "I think he was your father, from the collar and the likeness. That's how I came to have your name. Ceri kept saying it—but perhaps you don't remember. It was the day we flooded Otmound. You were out hunting and I was—well, I'd got into trouble and run away."

"He keeps doing that," Halla said, in a weary, elder-sisterly way.

"So what? I did it last year. Sometimes you get mad," Gerald said.

"I did it, too," said Gair. "Go on."

"I walked most of the night," said Hafny, "and about dawn your hunt came by, and I had to hide in a pool. I stayed under until I'd no air left. I couldn't feel any more footsteps, so I came up and hoped. And the first thing I saw was you dragging Ceri along and both of you armed to the teeth."

Ceri's face was brilliant red, and Gair knew his own was the same. "You mean that was *you*?" Ceri said. "We were scared stiff!"

Hafny laughed. "I *know*," he said. Gair, looking at Hafny laughing, wondered if he would ever understand the Wisdom. The Wisdom said Dorig were ruled by Saturn, as Gerald seemed to be, but Gair knew that if he had ever seen anyone ruled by Mercury, it was Hafny. "I was quite as scared," Hafny said. "I didn't think, I was so frightened. I just shifted straight to a deer. And of course you both did your best to kill me. I was still so frightened that all I could think of doing at first was to get bigger. And I got to the point where I was so thin on the ground I couldn't move, and you still didn't run away. So I thought of shifting to a warrior. That meant I was still pretty thin on the ground and I couldn't speak—it's hard to talk if you're spread out—so I just walked at you and prayed to the Powers you'd run away now. And you wouldn't. I'd never met anyone so maddeningly brave. And before I could think what to do, your whole hunt was all round me. I thought my last hour had come, because they always tell you Lymen kill you at once if they find you on your own, and I couldn't speak, and I was spread so thin it hurt — I've never felt so horrible in my life. Then your father told me I could go. I've never been so grateful to anyone. I was back in that pool before I knew I'd moved, and I lay there and swore I'd do something in return if I could."

It was queer to have the story from the other point of view. Ceri and Gair were exchanging uncomfortable looks, when Halla made Gair even more uncomfortable by saying:

"And I suppose you've been following Gair around ever since?"

"Not all the time," Hafny protested, looking as uncomfortable as Gair felt. "Mostly here, when you were watching the Giants. We watch you quite a bit," he said to Brenda and Gerald.

Gair felt foolish. He remembered that squirrel when he had been in the wood, and he prayed to the Sun that Hafny had not chanced to be near the time he had walked along the dike shouting to the Dorig to come and get him.

"Flipping follow-my-leader," Gerald said. "Why on earth couldn't somebody have talked to somebody before now?"

"Do you think it's done any good?" Hafny asked him, as if he was hoping for something.

There was a gloomy pause. "No one's talked about that collar yet," Ayna remarked. As soon as she said it, Gair felt the collar break into pulsing life—as if it had been dormant and Ayna's words had wakened it again.

Chapter

13

"WHAT COLLAR?" SAID HALLA.

"It's a Dorig collar," Ceri said. "You can see it is. The work's the same, and both theirs have birds' heads in front, too." And he explained that it had a curse on it and that Gest seemed to have given it to Gerald's father years ago.

The Dorig were interested but puzzled. "I never heard of a curse," said Halla.

"Where is this collar?" Hafny asked.

Brenda's face glowed. She wrung the maximum drama out of the answer. "In this very house!"

She annoyed Gerald heartily. He said, far more casually than he felt, "I'll show you if you like."

"All right," said Hafny.

So Gerald led them all to the study, where Halla and Hafny stared round as curiously as Ayna and Ceri had done the day before. The cold blast of power from the collar made Gair feel ill. When Gerald opened the drawer, he had to hold onto the back of a chair and clench his teeth.

"Oh!" Brenda cried out, enchanted by the richness of the thing, its greenness and its beauty. She put out a large mauve hand to pick it up.

"Don't touch it!" shouted everyone else in the room.

Brenda snatched her hand back, looking puzzled and hurt. "Why ever not?"

"The curse will come off on you," said Halla. She and Hafny were almost as badly affected as Gair. They both stood sideways to the drawer, as if they could not bear to look at the collar straight on, and both had gone pale. When Dorig went pale, they went ashy.

"Yes, it's cursed all right," Hafny said. "As strong as could be."

He and Halla snatched sidelong looks at the collar. "Hafny," Halla said. "Owls belong to our family. Whose could it have been?"

"I don't know," said Hafny, looking like death. "The work doesn't look all that old. Halla, do you realize? This room must be right above our halls."

Halla's hands went to her thin white cheeks. "Powers! Then it must be causing our troubles, too! Where did it come from?"

"Otmound," said Ayna. "We think."

"Father hates Otmound," said Halla.

"Do you know how we can get the curse off it?" asked Gerald. "You're not the only ones it's making trouble for."

To Gair's disappointment, both Dorig shook their heads. "I know you can't destroy a thing that's cursed," said Halla. "You have to lift the curse first. How to lift a curse is one of our Songmen's secrets. We could take it to them—"

"No!" said Hafny. "Put it away. Shut it up. Let's go."

Gerald, rather pale himself, slammed the drawer shut. Immediately, Gair felt better and the two Dorig recovered their color. But none of them felt particularly happy as they trooped away into the hall, except Brenda. Brenda was brimming over with excitement.

"Oh," she said. "It was lovely. *Evil* beauty!"

"Shut up!" growled Gerald. "I suppose you two want to go now?"

"Yes please," said Halla. "If you could take the Thought away."

Ceri concentrated briefly, and Halla and Hafny both disappeared in a wave of cold air. The rest looked round the hall in bewilderment. Then Brenda nearly stepped on a mouse. She recoiled with a squawk, and all but tramped on another.

"You'll get squashed, you stupid fools!" said Ayna.

The next moment, the mice were piling into gray pillars in that way that Gair thought he would never get used to, not if he lived among Dorig for the rest of his life. Hafny and Halla hardened out of them, laughing.

"Funny how Giants are always scared of mice!" Hafny said.

"You wouldn't think it so funny if I'd stepped on you," Brenda told him angrily.

Gair found he had come to a decision. How he had reached it, he was not sure. He did not think that the collar in the drawer was at the moment pulsing with evil, and that, of all the people there, he was the most responsive to it. He simply knew he had decided. "Hafny," he said, "could I talk to your father? Would you take me to him?"

There was a shocked silence in the hall. Then everyone began telling Gair at once he was insane. Halla went off into hissing laughter. But Gair ignored them and watched the expressions on Hafny's narrow face. Hafny looked surprised, alarmed and rather scared, but he did not seem, like Halla, to find the idea ridiculous. Gair might have thought, but he did not, that Hafny was almost as sensitive to the collar as he was himself. What he thought instead was that, in his queer way, Hafny was honorable; that Dorig, now he knew a little more about them, were not as alarming as he thought; and that the Giant way of talking was worth trying on the King.

"You'd be taking a risk," Hafny said at length. "I think you'd be better off going to find your father. What would you want to say?"

"Hafny, you're not going to *agree*!" Halla exclaimed.

"Gair, you are *not* to go," said Ayna. "We should have gone to find Father hours ago."

"You must do that," Gair said. "Go as soon as I've gone, and I'll come to Garholt when I've seen the King. I'd like," he said to Hafny, "to ask your father to make peace. I'll be a hostage if necessary."

"No. Be a messenger," said Hafny. "No one hurts messengers."

"All right," said Gair. "Would you mind if I took the collar with me and asked your Songmen how to raise the curse?"

Hafny shivered a little before he shrugged. "If you wrap it up thoroughly."

Gair looked at Gerald. "I could ask about those Halls of the Kings, too."

But Gerald's large Giant features showed that he had also come to a decision. "I'm coming, too. I'll ask. You'll be safer with me, if they don't touch Giants, and I've got to find out which Downs he means. I can't ask old Claybury to dig up all Sussex and Berkshire on spec, can I?"

Then Gair did think of the collar. He remembered that Gerald was an only child, and that he had lived beside the collar all his life and admitted to touching it. "You mustn't. You won't be safe."

Gerald looked mulish. Hafny said dryly, "He's likely to be safer than you are."

"Stop it, Hafny!" said Halla. "I refuse to take them. It must be a thousand years since Lymen or Giants came down to our kingdom. Everyone will be furious. I won't help you."

"Good for you!" said Ayna.

Hafny turned to Halla. "Halla, listen. If this went right, you wouldn't need to be afraid every second you were up on land. You could come up whenever you wanted. Walk in fresh air. Climb trees. You'd like that."

To Ayna's misery, a thoughtful, dreamy look came over Halla's face. "I do love climbing trees," she said. "All right."

"Good," said Hafny. "Then the only trouble is how good you are at holding your breath. It's a fair way down."

Gerald said he was all right. Gair, like everyone, had often tried to see how long he could go without breathing. He could do a slow count of a hundred. He had no idea if that was long enough, but he said he was all right, too. At this, Ceri saw that Gair really meant to go. He summoned up all his courage and said he would go, too.

"Oh, no, you won't!" said Ayna.

"You're the only person who can find father," Gair reminded him. He was glad when Ceri's face broke into a broad, relieved smile and he confessed sunnily that he had forgotten. That meant Gair would not need to point out that it was the duty of one of them to stay alive to be Chief after Gest—always supposing there were still people in need of a Chief by then. He knew Gest would prefer Ceri to Ondo any day. By this, Gair knew he did not expect to come back himself. He was annoyed with himself for thinking that way, but he found he could not help it. He watched with a sense of shadows closing round him while Brenda—who had become unusually subdued—went to the kitchen and came back with several paper bags and a bag of thin, strong stuff you could see through.

This bag much intrigued Halla. She stroked it and stretched it and looked at her fingers through it. "We've nothing as fine as this," she said.

"It's only plastic," said Gerald. He fetched a long pair of tongs and with them he picked the evil collar out of the drawer and put it in the plastic bag. Then he put that in the paper bags and the whole package into a piece of sacking. "There. Shall I carry it, Gair, or you?"

Gair did not like to touch even the package. But he felt it was his responsibility. After all, it was Gest who had given it to Gerald's father. "I'll take it," he said. As he buttoned it into the front of his jacket, he had a dreary suspicion that he had received his own doom.

Gerald left a hasty note to Aunt Mary, in which, as Ceri asked him, he promised that the three visitors would come and see her later. Hafny and Halla put on their hoods and gloves, fastened their jackets and became again the silver-headed Dorig most people knew. They all went out on the bridge. The Dorig at once slid down into the moat. They had such an air of it being their natural element that all the others envied them. Halla swirled round and held up her hand to Gerald, and Hafny held up his to Gair.

"Rather you than me!" Brenda said, with a shudder that shook the bridge.

Ayna had tears in her eyes. "Good-by, Gair," she said. "I shall pray to the Sun."

Gair was embarrassed. He turned away and attended to the instructions Halla was giving Gerald.

"Sit down and slide in," Halla said. "When I say *Now* take the deepest breath you can and then go limp."

Gerald and Gair obediently sat on the edge of the bridge. Gair felt Hafny's thin, strong hand jerk at his. He had a moment of horrible mistrust. Then he was gasping and splashing in the incredible cold of the water.

"*Now!*" said Halla.

Gair took the biggest breath his gasping lungs would let him. Next second, Hafny had pulled him underwater. The shock was so enormous that Gair let out a huge gollop of air. He saw it go up past his eyes in a big golden bubble. I'm going to need that, he thought, watching the green-gray water against his eyes, and the silver swirl of Hafny beyond, pulling him downward. Gerald was a dark bulk below, almost out of sight.

Down they went, and down. It was suddenly green-dark, as if they were under the house as well as under the water. Gair's ears poppled. Quite suddenly, his lungs told him they had come to the end of their air. He told himself it was nonsense: you could go on for a long time after you first wanted to breathe. All the same, it was as much as he could do not to fight loose from Hafny's tight grip on his wrist and thresh about screaming. He told himself it was Sun day. Hafny was *not* trying to drown him. Hafny dreamed of walking freely in the open air. It must be terrible being a Dorig, Gair thought frantically, to take his mind off air. The whole earth was dangerous to them.

But whatever he thought, Gair's chest ached and his whole body roared at him to breathe—to take a breath even if it was water. Imaginary lights flickered in the roof of his head. *Sun!* Gair thought. He thought words to the Sun and to the Moon, words to the water not to harm him, words, words, words. He could feel Hafny working harder. The grip on his wrist hurt. Everywhere was dark, as if they were deep under somewhere. And Gair's chest screamed it must breathe or die.

Hafny swirled to a stop, and swirled again. Utter darkness fell. Gair knew they were shut in a small space deep down underwater and he was going to die. Hafny did not understand. Dorig were different. Frantically, Gair grabbed for Hafny, but, before his fingers closed on Hafny's slippery suit, light came and, with it, a rushing and surging of the water. It swept Gair away backward and he felt Hafny seize him. But the rushing was air—surely it was air! Gair took a deep breath, and it was water.

A short time later, he came to himself coughing and choking, in a clear light, on a slippery stone floor. Beyond him, Gerald was coughing and gasping, too. Above him, Halla said, "Oh do be quiet, Hafny! They'll both be all right. They ran out of breath, like babies do the first time."

Gair did not feel particularly all right, so he lay where he was. He heard Gerald climbing to his feet. "I say," said Gerald's voice, booming round a narrow space. "Isn't this some kind of air lock?"

"We just call them locks," said Halla. "I didn't know Giants had them."

"Yes, on submarines and spaceships," Gerald boomed. "How does it work?"

"That's one of our secrets," Halla said, with dignity. Gair could tell from her voice that she had no idea, any more than he knew himself why the doors of Garholt opened with the right words.

"And where does the light come from?" Gerald asked.

"The walls," said Halla.

Gair had already seen it was the same light that they used in Garholt. He rolled into sitting position and said, "We make ours with words. Do you?"

"Yes. Are you all right?" Hafny said, looking very relieved.

Gair looked up into anxious yellow eyes and realized, with a jump of surprise, that Hafny liked him. Hafny had been scared stiff that he had drowned him. Beyond Halla, Gerald, who seemed much smaller with his hair and clothes soaking, was looking anxiously at Gair, too. And Gair thought that it was just his luck that the only two people who had ever, as far as he knew, spontaneously liked him, should be a Giant and a Dorig.

Halla, whom Gair did not like so much, said, "You look like two drowned rats. Shall I open the door?" And Gair suddenly wished, ignobly and strongly, that Ayna had been there, too.

"Go ahead," said Hafny.

Halla reached up and pulled a big lever. The end of the room at once swung inward, like a big thick door. They went out into a well-lit passage with a warm draft in it. Gair looked back before the door shut again, and saw that the far end of the room was another thick door, with dark trickles of water coming in round the edges.

The passage outside was dry enough. It was so warm that neither Gair nor Gerald felt cold, wet as they were. The air came through it in hot gusts, bringing gluey, fishy smells. It led them into a much broader, higher passage, with arched openings on either side. Halla told them that the openings led to living-quarters. Some seemed to be working-places, too. Clouds of gluey-smelling steam came out of one. Through another, Gair glimpsed hundred upon hundred of fish skins hung or stretched on racks. In a third, there was a smithy, where Gerald wanted to linger and watch.

There were crowds of people. Halla and Hafny had once more taken off their gloves and hoods and opened their jackets. But it took Gair only a short time to see that theirs were outdoor clothes. The Dorig men, women and children who flitted so busily in and out of the openings all wore garments longer and looser than any Gair had seen before. The main color favored seemed to be a pinkish purple, but there were bright yellows, blues and greens among them, too. Gair began to understand that the peculiar gliding walk of the Dorig was due to the robes they mostly wore. The most outlandish thing about the robes was that they were not woven, but made of cured skin. It was no wonder that the Dorig had not understood the looms in Garholt — nor the windows either — since their life must be passed almost entirely underground.

Most of the people stared. Many looked outraged.

"They're messengers," Hafny said authoritatively. "For my father."

Some people fell back at this, watching and whispering. Others followed, whispering, too. Gair could feel the whisper hissing behind them, and spreading away in front.

"Take no notice," Halla said. "Everyone here's from the West. They're terrible busybodies."

She and Hafny took them by what were evidently side-passages as far as possible. But the whisper was always with them. So was the warm wetness of the air. Gair and Gerald sweated badly, but it did no good at all. Gair became almost grateful for the deadly chill of the collar against his chest. He became really oppressed and longed to get away. The most oppressive parts were when they had to cross a number of large halls which were being used as living-quarters. They edged among the temporary beds and families gathered round eating-squares. People were packed in, making the air hotter than ever. Children teemed in the spaces, adding to the whispers that followed them. Old, old Dorig with wrinkled faces sat on stools and made strange curselike gestures at them.

"You see," said Hafny. "We *are* crowded."

"I should just say you are!" Gerald agreed.

Gair said nothing. He thought of the discomfort when the Otmounders came to Garholt. This was ten times worse. The number of people camping in the last hall they crossed was, alone, more than twice that of

Otmound and Garholt together. Gair was sorry about it. He was also scared. He saw that his people had been frightened of the Dorig for the wrong reasons entirely. He had just found out that there were Giants by millions. Now he saw the numbers of the Dorig were second only to Giants. His own race was tiny. Unless something was done, it would vanish altogether, squashed out of existence by the needs of Giants and Dorig. Gair saw, in quite a new way, that his people were going unthinkingly about their lives, just as they always had done, too set in their customs to know how they were threatened. And he knew that what he was trying to do was even more urgent than he had supposed.

The last part of their way lay entirely through halls, halls narrower and taller, perhaps older, than the earlier ones, though no less crowded. Many of the people in them wore gold collars and seemed important. They pretended not to see the two strangers, whether out of politeness or contempt, neither of them knew. It was here that a gold-eyed woman in a blue robe pushed her way up to Halla.

"Halla! At last! Your mother's turning the halls inside out for you. Come along."

Halla looked beseechingly at Hafny. "You go," Hafny said. "I can manage."

So Halla was snatched away and they continued with Hafny.

"Won't your mother want you, too?" Gerald asked.

"I shouldn't think so," said Hafny. "Mine doesn't fuss like Halla's." Seeing Gair staring at him, and Gerald looking confused, he said, "Why? Do you and Ceri and Ayna all have the same mother?"

"Of course," said Gair. "Adara."

"I've heard of her," Hafny said. "She's famous for wisdom and healing. How many husbands has she?"

"Only my father," Gair said, rather indignantly.

"Don't be offended," said Hafny. "I was only trying to think of customs as different from ours as I could. What do Giants do?"

"Giants," Gerald said, a little stiffly, "only have one wife at a time. Like Gair's people."

"That must be a bit boring," said Hafny. "Even the poorest man among us has at least two wives. And, being the King, my father has five. And I'm still the only boy. I've got seven sisters. I know you don't think much of Halla, but you should see the other six, then you'd—"

A tall Dorig, whose face was a thin white wedge of self-importance, interrupted by taking hold of his arm. "See here, boy, I have to see your father this morning."

Gair was impressed by the polite way Hafny got rid of him. "I'll do my best for you," he said. "But something urgent has come up and I must take these messengers to him first."

The tall Dorig looked from Gerald to Gair with

unutterable contempt. He turned away and said to someone else behind his hand, "That child's consorting with Giants and Lymen now. Someone should tell his poor father."

Hafny's face went stiff. "Powers!" he said. "I hate that man! I'd do anything not to have him living here!" Gair found he understood. In his way, the tall Dorig was not unlike Aunt Kasta.

At the end of this hall they came to an open archway. In front of it stood a line of Dorig in full silver armor — the first they had seen down here. And Gair saw it was true what Brenda had pointed out. Armor was different from the suit Hafny was wearing. It looked thicker and tougher, and it was made deliberately in large fishlike scales. To judge by their shiny faces, the men wearing it were as hot as Gair was.

"Will you let me in to my father?" Hafny asked them. "It's important."

"You're to go in," one of the warriors replied. "He's already heard."

They separated enough to let Hafny, followed by Gair and Gerald, slip through into the room beyond. "Don't Dorig ever use doors?" Gerald wondered in a rumbling whisper. He stopped suddenly, as he realized he was standing before the King already.

There were six robed and collared men in the room. Two were white-haired and stately. The rest seemed young. Dorig had a way of looking either quite young or very old, with no stages in between. Three of the young-looking ones were probably Songmen, to judge from their collars and the way they had their heads together over a harp. The harp had curious white strings, just like the one string that never broke on Banot's harp. The fourth young-looking man was sitting in a low chair with one leg bandaged and propped on a stool. He was dressed in wide blue robes, with a cloud of dark-honey hair loose on his shoulders, and they might not have recognized him but for his bandaged leg and a slight pink swelling round his left eye. He recognized them. His brown-gold eyes widened and his face became as blank as a carving. Gerald went red, and redder, and redder still, and finally as purple as Brenda, as he took in the fact that he had, yesterday afternoon, shot a hole in the leg of the King of the Dorig himself.

"I'd like an explanation of this, Hafny," the King said. His soft Dorig voice sounded quiet and reasonable, but they all knew he was ferociously angry. And as soon as he spoke, Gair knew they had been mad to come. Perhaps it was his Gift again, but it hardly needed a Gift to tell him that the King would never forgive Gerald, nor Gair for calling Gerald to the pool. Gerald had made him look ridiculous. He had trodden on the King, and the King had lost his head and turned into a fish three times in quick succession, and Gerald knew he had.

Gair needed no Gift to tell him that this was the cause of the King's fury. If there was one thing Gest could not forgive either, it was being made to look ridiculous.

Hafny saw, quite as clearly, that he had been mad to bring Gair and Gerald. His assurance went, like water from a pricked blister, though he tried hard to pretend it was still there. "These two are messengers," he said. "I brought them here because they have something to say."

"And how did you meet them?" the King asked.

"Up on land," Hafny said, with false airiness.

"Unfortunately for you, I know exactly where," said the King. "You've been in that moat again, haven't you?" Hafny could not deny that, and he did not attempt to. "Consorting with creatures like Giants and Lymen," said the King. "And you have the face to bring them here. What have you to say?"

Hafny had nothing to say. He looked wretched. Gerald hung his head in embarrassment. Gair looked at the other men in the room, hoping they might defend Hafny, but their faces were serious and shocked, as if they thought Hafny had been very wrong indeed. Gair risked making things worse for Hafny by saying, "We asked Hafny to bring us because we wanted to talk to you."

It did make things worse. Gair saw from the expression on the King's face that he should have pretended not to know Hafny's name. "Did you?" said the King.

"And he doesn't know a spy when he sees one?"

"We're not!" Gerald and Gair said together.

"Be quiet," said the King. "Hafny, did you promise them anything?"

Hafny was alarmed. "I promised to bring them here."

"Nothing more?"

The pale flush filled Hafny's face. "Listen," he said. "I unhooded to them."

"As I see," the King said coldly, raising his eyes to Hafny's curly head. "I can't think what you thought you were doing." Suddenly he seemed sick of Hafny. He turned his face away. "Go away," he said. "Get out."

Hafny shrank into himself and almost slunk to the doorway. He did not look at Gair and Gerald, and neither of them liked to look at him. They heard him say, behind them, "You mustn't hurt them. They came in good faith."

"*Get out!*" said the King. His voice put Gair in mind of Gest's belt whistling through the air. From the way Gerald's face twisted, it had the same kind of associations for him. They heard Hafny's soft footsteps leaving. Then the King looked at them and Gair again wondered how they had been mad enough to come here. The answer was not far off. It lay, sickeningly cold, wrapped up against his chest. "What did you do to Hafny to make him bring you here?" the King said.

There was no point saying they had caught Halla. She would be in trouble, too, and the King would still ask why Hafny had not gone back for help. "Nothing," Gerald said.

"We talked," said Gair.

"What kind of talk would that be that turns my son into a traitor?" asked the King.

That was a nasty question. Neither of them had seen Hafny's behavior in this light before, but it was clear that the six Dorig in the room had done so all along. "It was a Thought," Gair said. "We stopped him shifting shape while we talked to him. It wasn't his fault."

"How like Lymen!" said the King. "What did you expect to gain by it?"

Gair knew that, for some reason, his answer had made the King savagely angry, though his calm Dorig features did not show it much. Gerald did not quite see. Or perhaps he did, but despairingly seized the only chance he had yet had to say what he had come to say.

"I wanted to come and ask you where the Halls of the Kings are, sir," he said. "If there's enough water there—" He tailed off a little as he saw he was making no impression on the King, but pulled himself together and went on. "My people could pump it out to use, you see, sir, and your people could go and live there again. Then the Moor—"

"Be quiet, Giant!" said one of the old men. He sounded so truly shocked that Gerald muttered, "Well, it's for the good of both of us," and fell into rebellious silence.

"Sir, now, am I?" the King said mockingly, and looked at Gair.

Gair, though his stomach was sinking and he knew nothing was any good, felt, like Gerald, that he had nothing to lose in saying why he had come. "I came to ask you to make peace with my people."

"Haven't you anything useful to say?" the King asked crushingly.

"Yes," said Gair, fighting against a sense of doom and failure worse than he had felt in Garholt. He dragged the cold bundle with the collar in it out of his jacket. He did not want to. But he felt that the one good he might do was to get the Songmen to lift the curse. And he knew a curse made you want to keep the thing that was cursed. In fact, at that moment, the curse and his Gift were in such raging conflict that he had no idea which was telling him to do what. He held the damp bundle out toward the three Songmen. "I wanted to ask you about this. There's a curse on it, and it may be lying on you, too."

"What is it?" asked the one who seemed chief Songman.

"A collar—one of your kind," Gair explained. "My father gave it to"—he did not like to give Gerald's name—"his father, years ago, to move the stone on top of the Haunted Mound."

Before the Songman could move, the King held out

his long pale hand. "Let me see."

Gair went up to him and reluctantly put the bundle in his hand. He did not want to give it to the King at all. And the King shivered as he took it and looked up into Gair's face in a very odd way. Gair looked down into the golden-brown eyes, which were curious even for a Dorig, and wondered why the King was staring at him like that. Since collars were in his mind, he also wondered why the King's collar, instead of being rich and elaborate like the others in the room, should be a plain twist of gold, of very ordinary workmanship. Perhaps it was some back-to-front custom.

"Where's your collar?" said the King. "You had one yesterday."

"I gave it to him," Gair said, nodding at Gerald.

The King shrugged and delicately unwrapped the wet bundle of sacking. The paper bags underneath were sodden. The King's white fingers peeled them away. And there lay the collar, a rich poisonous gleam under the plastic. The King's face went gray-white. The five other Dorig drifted away from it, muttering uneasily. Waves of evil poured from the green gold, as if the bag was no barrier at all. Gair had to back away and hang onto Gerald for support, and he could feel Gerald shivering in spite of the warmth.

"Tell me about this," the King said to the chief Songman.

The Songman's face looked deathly. "I hardly like to," he said.

"Then I'll tell you," said the King. "It was a very strong curse, a dying curse, and it was uttered in the name of all three Powers." At that, the five other Dorig made the same small, frightened sign. "But the curse is weaker now than it was," said the King. "This collar gave itself as a reward, fifteen years ago, to those who dared weaken it by moving the stone from the Mound of Sorrow. By that, the dead men there were set free and the Old Power was appeased. In its absence, the curse could be lifted." Dimly, through the flood of evil, Gair saw the King was looking at him. "What would you give to have this curse lifted?" he asked, and his soft voice seemed to come and go on the pulses from the collar.

Gair hardly knew what to say. The collar and the Gift he was still barely used to clashed in his head, a wild mingling of hope and despair, and one of them made him say, "I'd give a great deal. Anything."

"Me, too," said Gerald.

Quickly, the King sat up straight and wrapped the sacking back over the collar. "You heard that, all of you. We need a willing sacrifice for each Power remaining, and here they are. Take these two away and prepare them for sacrificing."

At least ten silver warriors were in the room before Gair understood what was happening. "Look here,"

Gerald was saying loudly. "You can't do this! We're ambassadors."

"It was lucky Hafny forgot to promise you should go back," the King said calmly. Then, not at all calmly, he said to Gair, "And I've never made a sacrifice so gladly!" Gair wondered what he had done to make the King hate him so.

They were hustled helplessly away among staring Dorig, down a long hall and into a small place with a thick door. The warriors thrust them inside it so hard that they both stumbled right to the far end and, before they could turn round, the thick door slammed behind them. Gair's first act was to whirl round and say the words for opening that door. But it remained fast shut. Vary the words as he would, Gair made no impression on it. Just as Gair's people knew how to make water safe from Dorig, so Dorig knew how to make doors safe from Lymen.

Chapter

14

CERI AND AYNA SAID GOOD-BY TO BRENDA AND set off to find their father as soon as the moat had ceased to swirl and they were sure no more bubbles were rising to the surface. Brenda was doleful at their going, but they could not help that. They waved and walked briskly away across the tufty field.

Gest and the hunt were not as far away as Ayna had supposed. Ceri said he thought they must be on their way back. He took Ayna to a bushy wood, just on the edge of the marshes. There, Ayna had that usual queer moment when she thought there was nobody there at all. Then a dog roused and stood wagging its tail at them. Ayna's eyes cleared and she saw the shapes of people sleeping under blankets everywhere she looked, blankets so much the color of the ground and the grass that they were as hard to see as a speckled moth on a tree trunk.

"Father!" called Ceri.

When Gest sat up sleepily, brushing dead leaves from

his golden beard, he seemed for a moment unnaturally small. After a day among Giants, even Gest's open ruddy face seemed little and delicate. He blinked bright blue eyes at them, startled and a little cross to be woken in the middle of the day after a hard night's hunting. Ayna found she had never realized before how much she loved him. She flung herself on him and burst into tears.

"Oh, Father! The most awful things have happened!"

She and Ceri shouted one another down to tell him. People sat up all round, dismayed and sleepy. Ondo's teeth chattered. Orban kept saying, "Ban's bones! This won't do!" And Banot got up on one knee to give Gest a meaning look.

"Said he wouldn't attack *you*."

"Yes," said Gest. "Someone we know being too clever by half. Where's Gair? I don't understand where Gair's got to."

"He's hiding behind a Giant somewhere, I bet," said Ondo.

Ayna and Ceri explained that Gair had gone with Gerald to the halls of the Dorig, taking the collar with him. "And Gair has Sight Unasked, Father. He knew there was a curse on it."

Gest got to his feet, looking thoroughly alarmed. "I know that!" he said tetchily. "He warned me. Why didn't you stop him going? It's the worst thing he could have done."

Ondo, who had not a word to say, had to content himself with looking superior. Orban said, "It never does any good to talk to Dorig. The only good Dorig are dead ones. But I always did think the boy was odd, Gest."

"*Oh be quiet!*" Gest bellowed, rounding on Orban. "None of this would have happened if you hadn't murdered the King of the Dorig's brother!"

There were shocked, angry murmurs from most of the Otmounders.

"For the sake of a collar with a curse on it," said Gest.

The murmurs died away as everyone saw the curious yellow color of Orban's face. "Who told you that?" he said. "Adara swore—"

"Adara kept her word. The King told me himself," said Gest. "Pack, everyone. Strike camp and leave the catch here." He whipped up his own blanket and folded it. "Hurry. We must get to Garholt."

"That's right," Orban said, making an unconvincing effort to be natural. "Let's kill all the damn Dorig we can!"

"Oh no, we will not!" said Gest. "Unless you *want* Kasta's throat cut, of course." Everyone was now feverishly folding blankets and strapping up bags. Gest called out so that they should all hear, "If any one of you raises a hand against a Dorig, I shall say words he will feel even beyond the grave. Now move. You can pack properly as you go."

Aunt Mary sat in her kitchen and read Gerald's note for the fourth time. The house felt emptier and quieter than she had known it for years. Gerald probably out for lunch, those three strange little children departed without warning and her brother still cavorting all over the Moor with that Mr. Claybury when they must know it was lunchtime. How thoughtless everyone was! Aunt Mary did not believe for an instant that those three children would come back to thank her, as Gerald's note said. And to add to her annoyance, that gross, fat child Brenda was hanging about the house, crunching around in the gravel and breathing like a sheep wth asthma. Why couldn't she go home?

Brenda, at that moment, put her head round the back door. "Is Gerald back yet, Miss Masterfield?"

"No he is not! *Will* you go home!" snapped Aunt Mary. "Dear," she added, not to sound unkind.

Brenda, without a word, shut the back door again. At the same moment, someone knocked at the front door. Sighing, Aunt Mary got up and answered it.

The thinnest child Aunt Mary had ever seen stood on the doorstep in a pool of water. It was wearing an odd kind of frogman's suit. Aunt Mary could not tell whether it was a girl or a boy—you so seldom could these days, she thought—but she nevertheless looked the child searchingly in the face in hopes of a clue. It was horribly pale, and the eyes that met hers were a deep amber yellow—just like a *goat's*, thought Aunt Mary. "Good God!" she told it weakly.

"Could I speak to Brenda, please?" the strange child asked anxiously. It had a peculiar lisping voice.

"Brenda doesn't live here," said Aunt Mary. "Dear."

The child looked so cast down that Aunt Mary was almost glad when Brenda burst round the side of the house like a stampeding carthorse, shouting, "Halla! What's the matter? Where's Gerald?"

Aunt Mary was not the most sensitive of Giantesses, but something in the manner of both girls made her pause in the middle of shutting the front door and ask, "Is something wrong?"

The strange girl looked at her blankly. "Oh no. I've just come to ask Brenda something." And Brenda, with her mouth stretched into a long, false smile, added, "Nothing's wrong at all."

Aunt Mary shut the front door, slightly uneasy. Then, because she was not the kind of Giantess to whom things happen, she went to bed with a headache, wondering why the house felt so peaceful for once.

Outside, Brenda took Halla's slippery elbow and towed her over the bridge and out onto the gravel, where they would not be overheard. "What *is* it, Halla?"

"Hafny," Halla said wretchedly. "I've got him here. I daren't tell his mother, let alone Father. So you *have* to help me." Puzzled and alarmed, Brenda watched Halla rip open her silvery jacket and take out a furry thing. She held it out toward Brenda in both long white hands. "Look." It was something the shape of a ferret. But, if it had eyes, they were tight shut, and it did not have either ears or legs. Brenda found it repellent. She shuddered.

"That's never Hafny!"

"Yes it is." There were tears in Halla's yellow eyes. "I was there when he did it. It's called *morgery*, but I've never seen it happen before. You're supposed to stop people before they do it. And I didn't. I thought he was just making a silly fuss, going on about being a traitor and saying he'd let Gair and Gerald down."

"He wasn't a traitor," Brenda said. "Was he?"

"That's what I said," said Halla. "But he was told Father called him one. Then they shut Gair and Gerald up and burned their hair —"

Brenda squawked. She made Halla jump, but the ferret-thing did not move. "Burned their *hair*!"

"They cut it off first," Halla explained impatiently. "It's what they do to dedicate sacrifices."

"*Sacrifices!*" squealed Brenda.

Halla saw Brenda was upset. "They won't feel it," she said. "And they're the first there have been for years, so it's quite an honor. And it's an honor to hang up to the Sun afterward."

Brenda knew Halla meant to be kind, but she could have smacked her all the same. "When are they going to do it—this sacrifice?" she demanded.

Halla shrugged. Brenda's hand almost went out to clout her. "It's nothing to do with me," said Halla. "The Feast of the Sun, maybe sooner. I don't know. But you *must* help me! Don't you understand, I unhooded to you! You've got to help me get Hafny back before Father finds out!"

She held the furry thing out to Brenda again. She was crying. Brenda simply could not credit that anyone could worry about a thing like that when two people were going to be killed. On the other hand, the shapeless furry creature did look pathetic, lying limply across Halla's palms—and Hafny seemed to have got that way because he, at least, minded about Gerald and Gair.

"How *do* you get them back?" Brenda asked gruffly.

"I don't know," said Halla. "I know you have to do it soon, or he'll die."

Making three of them, Brenda thought. "Well, I don't know if you don't. How could I?"

"But you could take him to Adara for me, couldn't you?" Halla said eagerly.

"Adara? You mean Gair's mother!"

Halla nodded. "Everyone says she's famous for

healing. Here." She pushed the furry thing into Brenda's hands.

Brenda recoiled. But Hafny's queer form did not feel nearly as unpleasant as it looked. It was as soft and warm and piteous as a sick rabbit. Brenda had half a mind to suggest to Halla that Adara might not feel like healing a Dorig if the Dorig were going to kill Gair. But Halla was probably too stupid to see that. And Brenda was fairly sure that Adara was the kind of person who would try to cure Hafny simply because he needed it. So all she said was, "Why can't *you* take him?"

Halla thought Brenda stupid, too. "Because Garholt is full of our people, of course! Father will find out I didn't stop Hafny and—tell them anything you like, but don't say I gave him to you."

"All right," said Brenda.

"Thanks." Halla smiled brilliantly—she might be stupid, but she was very pretty, too, Brenda thought wistfully—and slipped away into the moat almost without a ripple.

Brenda was left holding a warm furry something. She glanced at the house, wondering if she ought to tell Aunt Mary, and decided against it almost at once. If Mr. Masterfield had been there, he might have done something, but Aunt Mary was no good. Brenda clutched the furry shape to her chest and set off at a heavy trot to her own house beyond Gerald's wood. Gair's people were the only ones who could help. Besides, she very much wanted to see Adara on her own account.

She lumbered through the wood and along the track to Lower Farm as gently as she could. Every second she held the helpless Hafny she was more sorry for him. She could almost feel how miserable he was. He had hoped for great things.

In the farmyard, her mother's bicycle, large and old, with string laced over the back mudguard, was leaning against the wall. It had a basket, which would do beautifully for Hafny. Brenda popped him into it and hurried into the house for a cushion to make him comfortable. For once in her life, the smell of Sunday lunch meant nothing to her.

As Brenda dashed out again with the cushion, her mother shouted, "Brenda! Your dinner's ready."

Brenda stopped in the middle of the yard to roll her eyes at the sky. Parents! The high sun dazzled her, and she noticed, just above the trees, the white disk of the moon, too. "Do me good to slim!" Brenda bawled as she ran to the bicycle.

As soon as Hafny was safely bedded on the cushion, Brenda set off, pedaling for dear life, up the lane and along the road through the village. Ceri had talked of a wood. Brenda assumed he had meant the one near Garholt, which you could reach from the road beyond the village. While she got herself and Hafny there, she talked to Hafny between puffs and wheezes, trying to comfort them both. "You shouldn't get like this, Hafny. You don't want to believe that about traitors. You didn't join our side, did you? That's what they do—traitors. Oh, this hill! But it was lucky I didn't go down in the moat. I was a coward not to, I know that. But just think if I had! Cheer up, Hafny. Those Lymen'll do something, I know they will, if we get there quick."

There was no kind of response from Hafny. Perhaps the queer form he was in could neither hear nor feel. Brenda had to give up talking on the hill beyond the village. It was very steep. But she puffed her way up it in the end. There was the wood. With any luck, she would find Ayna and Ceri in a few minutes. She was leaning the bicycle against the bank, when a Landrover came grinding round the corner, going toward the village.

Oh bother! thought Brenda. Mr. Masterfield and Mr. Claybury going home for their dinners. Now I'll have to stop and tell them.

She waved. The Landrover stopped, and Mr. Masterfield rather grudgingly leaned out. "What is it? A puncture?"

"No," panted Brenda. "Something awful's gone and happened to Gerald. Only I can't stop now. I'll tell you later." She lifted Hafny carefully off his cushion and hurried into the wood.

"What's happened? Where *is* Gerald?" Mr. Masterfield shouted after her.

"The Dories got him!" Brenda shrieked over her shoulder. Birds flew clapping out of trees at the din. She ran, looking anxiously about for any sign of Ayna and Ceri. Though how I should expect to see them when I never have before, I can't think! she thought. "Ayna! Ceri!"

There was no answer, only more frantic birds. Three minutes later, she was at the other end of the wood, with the Moor spread into gray-green distance below. There was no trace of any Lymen, but Garholt humped into the green view fifty yards to the left.

"Then I'd better see to you first," Brenda said to Hafny, and surged toward the mound. When she reached it, it seemed easier on Hafny to go down it sitting. Brenda arrived at the foot of it with a rush, a slither and a squelch. A shimmer of movement in front of the mound abruptly stopped. There was sudden complete silence. Brenda stared at the last place where she had seen movement. It seemed daft, but it did look as if there might be a person standing against the nearest bush. "Ceri?" Brenda said doubtfully.

Half the bush came to life, and Ceri scudded toward her. "Brenda! What's gone wrong?"

"Ceri!" said Ayna's voice. Then she, too, hurried toward Brenda from the other side of the bush. "What is it?"

"They took Gerald and Gair for human sacrifices!" Brenda said.

"What?" someone else said sharply.

Upon that, the whole space in front of Garholt sprang to life. Brenda was bewildered, and more than a little alarmed, to find herself surrounded by warlike men and girls. These people were not smooth and skinny like the Dorig. Their hair was shaggy. They had bright, bold, determined faces. Most of the men had beards. They wore sheepskin and Moor-colored tweeds, and all of them carried knives and spears of some metal that did not seem to be iron. Though none of them was more than a few inches taller than Brenda herself, she had no doubt that even the boys of Ceri's size could make short work of her if they chose. Lymen gathered together were formidable. Dozens of bright eyes looked at her — eyes blue, gray or greenish, all of them more almond-shaped than Brenda was used to. To Brenda's confusion, at least eight of them wore golden collars of one sort or another, so that it was impossible to tell which one was Gair's father. When someone said, "How do you know that?" Brenda hugged Hafny protectively and replied to the whole band.

"Halla told me. And she did make me mad! All she cared about was not getting into trouble over Hafny."

"Bother, Halla! She's stupid," said Ceri. "What about Gair?"

Brenda told them what Halla had said. One man in a gold collar, a fair man with blue eyes, said soberly, "That's just what I was afraid of."

Another, a younger man, who had bees crawling over his face and clothes, asked, "And where's the other Dorig—the King's son?"

"Here," said Brenda, and held out the furry thing.

All the bright eyes turned to the misshapen small body, and a number of the people shuddered. A third man with a gold collar—he had a thin, clever face which Brenda liked the look of—pushed his way to the front and said, "May I see?"

Brenda found she trusted him. She let him take Hafny in his hands. He handled the queer creature very gently, turning it about and looking at it carefully, and finally laid it on the grass and squatted beside it. Everyone else gathered round to see. "Careful, Banot," someone said. "It could be a trick."

Banot shook his head. "The People of the Moon sometimes get like this," he said. "It's a form of despair." He looked up at Brenda. "It will take more words than Adara or I know to shift this one back."

"Oh dear!" said Brenda. "He was ten times nicer than that Halla."

A fourth man with a gold collar pushed forward, and a boy behind him. Brenda did not like either of them. The man had scraggly reddish hair and a pompous manner.

The boy's ears stuck out and he looked mean. "This is just wasting time," the man said. "Put the thing out of its misery and then let's open the mound." Upon this, the boy raised his spear, intending to drive it through the furry body on the ground.

"You dare!" said Brenda. "Just either of you dare, and see what you get!" She advanced on the pair of them, breathing through her nostrils like an angry bull.

The boy bolted. The man backed away. "I didn't mean it," he said, laughing uneasily.

To Ayna and Ceri, it was one of the best moments of their lives, seeing Orban and Ondo routed by an enraged and purple Giantess. But, as Brenda seemed likely to get herself stuck on the end of Orban's spear, Ceri said hastily, "I can shift Hafny back, Brenda. Father, may I use a Thought on him?"

"Yes, do," said Gest. He was the fair one, Brenda saw. She liked him, too.

Ceri drew a breath and prepared to concentrate. Immediately, the furry body dissolved and heaped itself into a mound of gray mist. The mist coiled and hardened and became Hafny, squatting in a miserable heap on the grass. He was without his hood, so that the first thing they saw was a curly head of hair. Then he raised his head, and they saw his face was ash-white and his yellow eyes ringed with red. He did indeed look desperately unhappy. But Brenda, Ayna and Ceri were not deceived.

Ceri knew he had not used a Thought. Brenda and Ayna remembered that Halla had not dissolved at all. She had shifted straight back and yelled as if it hurt her. Hafny saw the way they were looking at him and gave them a look which plainly implored them not to say anything.

The rest of the hunt was amazed. "Is that a Dorig?" one of the girls said.

"Look at its collar!" said Ondo.

"It looks almost as if it's a man!" said someone else.

"So they are," said Banot, "when they're unhooded." He tried to pull Hafny to his feet. Hafny slipped back onto the grass, groaning. Brenda thought he had cramp from keeping up that queer shape so long, but it worried Banot and Gest.

"What's the matter?" Gest asked kindly, bending over him.

Hafney looked up at him miserably. "It was my fault they're going to sacrifice Gair and the Giant," he said. "I brought them down to our halls, and I was a traitor to them and to my own people. Will you take me and sacrifice me?"

"We don't make that kind of sacrifice," Gest said.

"But you must!" Tears ran from Hafny's yellow eyes and down his white face. "Tell my father you're going to do it, so he'll let those two go."

"That's an idea," Orban said. "He's the best hostage we could have."

"I know I am," said Hafny. "Please use me."

"Nonsense," said Gest. "Come on, lad. You'd better go back to your own people."

"No!" said Hafny. "Don't you understand? I—"

"Come along," said Gest, and he picked Hafny up. Hafny struggled. Orban muttered. But Gest walked toward the main door of Garholt with silvery arms and legs flailing out on either side of him and started to say the words to open it.

Garholt shook to its roots. A loud voice said, "I don't know where she went. But you get a splendid view from here. Right across to the Gallows Stone. Look." Mr. Masterfield appeared on top of the mound, with Mr. Claybury beside him. Around Brenda, everyone melted out of sight, except for Ayna and Ceri and Gest, standing in the open with the struggling Hafny.

Mr. Claybury saw Gest. He pushed his glasses against his nose and stared. "Titch!" he said. "It *is* Titch, isn't it?"

Gest let Hafny slide to the ground. Hafny still could not stand properly, so Gest held him up. "Shift shape if you want to," he said to him. Then he tilted his head to look up at the two Giants. "I'm glad to see you," he called. "Come down. We're in trouble."

The two Giants exchanged buzzing mutters and began to descend the mound in their heavy, gingerly, Giant way. "Has this got anything to do with Gerald?"

Mr. Masterfield called over to Brenda.

"Yes," she called back.

When they were down, Mr. Claybury nodded cheerfully to Brenda, Ayna and Ceri, and both of them looked curiously at Hafny. Hafny shrank away from the prevailing largeness of the Giants, but he made no attempt to shift shape. "No more gold collars, then?" Mr. Claybury said jokingly to Gest.

Gest shook his head. "I'm very sorry I gave you that one," he said. "I didn't know it was the one with a curse on it. A woman called Kasta gave it to me, and in the dark I took it for another one which was very like it."

"We might have *known* it was Aunt Kasta!" Ayna whispered to Ceri.

"But what's the trouble?" said Mr. Masterfield.

Hafny leaned round Gest and caught Ceri's eye. He pointed meaningly at Garholt and then at Ceri. "What do you think?" Ceri asked Ayna.

"I think it's a good idea," said Ayna. "Those Giants won't understand for a week if you don't."

Ceri nodded and concentrated. Garholt rumbled open on a seething of silvery Dorig, noise, smells and confusion indescribable. Everyone in the mound knew the hunt was back. The Dorig were armed and ready, but, to judge by the shouts behind them, Miri was leading an attempt to break out. Dorig voices hissed urgently. Sheep bleated. Babies howled. The smell of a mound that had been sealed for nearly two days rolled out, mixed with the gluey scent of Dorig. And above the din, the loudest voice of all quacked: "I *insist* on going to that door!"

Both Giants spun round and stared. Ayna could have sworn Mr. Claybury said "Ooh-er!" just like Brenda. The first thing that he saw was the grim crowd of Dorig, braced in the opening. The first thing the Dorig saw was Gest apparently holding Hafny prisoner. They were horrified, one and all, and screamed abuse at Gest. The bees, finding their enemies at hand, left Med in a cloud and made for the Dorig. Med leaped up, followed by Banot, calling them to come back. And the rest of the hunt, seeing that Gest was unprotected in front of a band of angry Dorig, hurriedly appeared around him, alarming Mr. Claybury considerably. Brenda saw him take his glasses off and put them in his pocket, and she did not blame him.

The din grew louder still. Mr. Masterfield bawled at Gest, something with Gerald's name in it, and Gest replied with an explanation which plainly horrified Mr. Masterfield. Around them, everyone in the hunt was yelling to relatives inside the mound, and the people inside were shouting back. Kasta quacked deafeningly. The Dorig yelled at Gest and at one another, and Adara suddenly appeared among them, very pale and jostled this way and that, evidently as a hostage. She looked at

Ayna and at Ceri, and then her eyes searched and searched, looking for Gair. Finally she, too, called out to Gest, and Gest, rather reluctantly, replied. Ceri and Brenda put their hands over their ears.

The ground shook. Mr. Masterfield's voice rose above all the others. *"Shut up, the lot of you!"* There was dead silence. Even Kasta stopped. The nearest Dorig shrank, and braced themselves on the others behind. In the noiseless pause, Mr. Masterfield nodded at Gest.

"Thank you," said Gest, smiling his merriest smile. He turned to the Dorig. "This lad's not a prisoner," he said. "You can have him—but you might let Adara look at him, because I don't think he's well." He pushed Hafny toward the Dorig. Hafny limped a few steps and stood uncertainly, while the Dorig looked at him, under-standably puzzled. "And we've not come to fight," said Gest. "We've only got hunting-spears. We've come to ask you to take us to your King—quickly."

The silver people drew together indignantly. "We can't do that!" said the leader. "The King doesn't see Lymen and Giants."

"He'll see us," said Gest. "Take us to him. By the shortest way, if you don't mind."

"We'll do no such thing!" said the Dorig leader.

"Yes you will," said Gest. His merry smile died away and he looked grimmer than anyone had ever seen him. "I have your King's name in my head. If you don't take me to him at once, I shall put such words to that name that the King and all his people will suffer as long as he lives."

"I don't believe you," said the Dorig.

Gest beckoned to Hafny and when Hafny, looking awed and troubled, limped near enough, he bent and whispered to him. "Now tell those stubborn idiots what I said."

"He's got it," said Hafny. "He means it."

Chapter

15

GAIR AND GERALD SAT AGAINST OPPOSITE WALLS of their prison. They had given up talking. It did no good. The walls they leaned on were suave and soapy, and the light which came from them clear and unrelenting. Gerald found both horrible. Gair, who was used to something not unlike it, hated the wet warmth of the place most. Their clothes were still damp and beginning to smell of mildew. The prevailing gluey smell they both loathed.

They avoided looking at one another. Gair perhaps looked less odd than Gerald, because his hair had been slightly longer and he had been too frightened and shamed to move. The Songman had simply seized it in one hand and sheared it close by Gair's ears with the other. Gerald had fought, wildly and frantically. He had been so terrified and so angry that he became truly like a Giant out of Miri's stories, and hurled Dorig about the cell. It had taken six of them to hold him down, and much snipping by the Songman to collect a handful of hair. They did not like to look at one another's shorn and tufty heads. They were ashamed that they now seemed to belong to the Dorig to do as they liked with.

The Dorig had given them bowls of crumbled fish after that, but neither of them could eat much. It was then that they gave up talking and just waited and thought. After a while, Gerald busied himself cleaning Gair's collar and then with patiently forcing it into a shape which would fit his thicker neck. He seemed to find comfort in it. Gair could do nothing with the watch Gerald had given him. It had stopped ticking. He suspected it had drowned when Hafny brought him down through the water. And he wished Gerald would put his collar away. It reminded him of the other collar, which he knew now had brought them here to die.

For a while, Gair was furious with himself for the way he had let himself be led by a thing he knew was evil. Now he was away from that collar, he knew that without it he would have gone with Ayna and Ceri to find Gest. But it had filled his head with fine nonsense about saving his people and hopes of reasoning with the King and coming back triumphant, saving the Moor, doing what nobody could hope to do. He had thought more noble nonsense about keeping Ceri safe to be Chief after Gest, when the fact was he had confidently expected to come back. His Gift had told him otherwise, and he had ignored it. It had also told him not to give the collar to the King, but the collar had whispered that he could do some good that way, and he had believed it. Throughout, it had blurred his mind and confused his Sight. And he had *known* it had!

Now Gair was alone with his Gift, it told him coldly and quietly he was going to be a sacrifice. And his end was only the start of the end for all his people. They would be drowned, slaughtered, driven away and crushed by the huge numbers of Giants and Dorig. Gerald was sighing deeply at his own gloomy thoughts. Gair wished he had not brought this on Gerald, too. And here the rather ignoble thought struck him that he minded far more about Gerald than about nobly saving his people. Who in their senses would want to save Ondo or Aunt Kasta? He began to suspect that the collar had worked on something in him that lay very deep and was not at all noble—since even the most powerful curse could not force a person to act entirely against his nature.

Gerald carefully put Gair's collar to his neck. It was still not quite wide enough. He took it away, sighing. "I say," he said, from the midst of his own troubles, "do you find you get on with your father?"

"No," said Gair, and he thought, You, too? And Hafny as well, probably. Perhaps that was what they all had in common. Certainly Gair knew he had always stopped short of real friendship with Brad, the only other person he liked half as much, simply because he could not understand the free and easy relationship Brad had with Banot. Which was rather a waste, Gair thought, since he and Gest were chalk and cheese and probably never would have understood one another.

Then everything turned over in his head and he knew why the collar had been able to lead him on. He had thought he was the only ordinary one in his family and that Gest was disappointed in him, when, in fact, they had simply not understood one another. Gair had thought Gest a hero, then he had thought he was a cheat. And once he thought Gest a cheat, Gair knew he had set out after Giants and Dorig to cheat his way to being a hero, too. He may have saved Ayna's and Ceri's life by doing it, but that had not been his real motive. The funny thing was, now that he knew what Giants and Dorig were really like, Gair suspected that Gest *was* a hero after all. No one but a hero could have come out of those adventures unharmed, with Adara in the bargain. But Gest had done it all in an ordinary way and must feel quite ordinary to himself. The giveaway had been when Gair had sat on the bridge as bait to catch Dorig, and felt just as ordinary as before, even though he had found he had a Gift, too. All he had really wanted was to do something so blazingly heroic that Gest would have been forced to pat him on the back and praise him. And so the collar had been able to lead him on.

It was all so simple and so pitiful once he got down to

it that Gair had to laugh. He was glad it was no worse. But it had been stupid. Gerald looked at Gair in surprise. "What's so funny?"

Next second, they were both on their feet, not laughing at all, and Gerald was ramming the collar onto his neck in order to have his hands free. The thick door was open and the Dorig guards were coming for them. Six of them pounced on Gerald before he had a chance to fight, and two more seized Gair. They were hustled at speed along the shining passages to a great hall they had not seen before. It was crowded with loose-robed Dorig. There was a gallery round the three sides, also crowded. Golden collars flashed up there. Gair had a glimpse of Halla, watching with interest. He supposed Hafny must be up there somewhere, too.

Gair and Gerald were hurried out into the open space at one end of the hall where the King stood, supporting himself on the youngest-seeming Songman, with important Dorig and the other Songmen gathered about him. Gair did not like the way they looked. They were serious, awed and rather tight-faced, as people are when they have nerved themselves up for something unpleasant. In front of the King was a raised stone, like an eating-square, with dark stains on it. There were a number of bowls arranged beside this stone. Gair did not like the look of those either. When he saw the bright curved knife one of the Songmen was holding, his knees gave, and he was glad the guards were holding him. Gerald's mouth started to tremble.

The collar was lying in a strange, star-shaped hole in front of the stone table. Gair felt it pulsing before he saw it. There was something different about the emana- tions—they were weaker, but more sickening. When Gair brought his scared, blurred eyes to look at it, he saw there had been a change in it. It was no longer covered, and the edges, the outlines, the cunningly woven words, were all faintly, tremblingly black. The only parts still bright and clear were the two owls' heads at either end. By that, Gair knew the Powers must have accepted the sacrifice.

"Take them the lot-jar," said the King.

A hissing hush fell on the crowded hall. The chief Songman took up an old leather jar, which rattled heavily, and came slowly over to Gerald. He held the jar out.

Gerald's mouth twitched. "What's this?" he said.

"You draw to see which of you goes now and which waits till the Feast of the Sun," the Songman said.

"Can't you do us both together?" Gerald exclaimed. "Think of waiting alone all that time!" His mouth twitched so violently that, when the guards let his hand go so that he could draw from the jar, Gerald clapped the back of it to his mouth and kept it there. "What if we won't?" he said, muffled by his hand.

The Songman said nothing. He waited, holding out the jar, considerately pretending that Gerald was not making an undignified fuss. He looked as if he understood. In fact, Gair thought that, in his strange Dorig way, this Songman was a little like Banot.

Gair understood Gerald, well enough. Giants might be strong and could be violent, but they lived a life at a remove from fierce facts. Gerald's sister might be dead, but Gair would have taken his oath that Gerald had not seen her die. Dying was a distant, horrible idea to Gerald. He could not take it calmly when someone came and tried to make him die. Gair could not take it as a matter of course himself, exactly. But he had seen enough people die in Garholt to make it not quite so unbelievable as it was to Gerald. And since he knew quite clearly he was bound to be sacrificed, Gair tried to spare Gerald a little by reaching out and saying, "Shall I draw then?"

The Songman ignored him. Gerald said from under the back of his hand, "They're rigged, can't you see? They want me first." Gair saw he was probably right, and he was sorry, because that meant there was no hope for Gerald either.

The crowd began to grow restive, to hiss and move about, and Gerald still stood there with the back of his hand pressed to his mouth. The murmur from the crowd grew. It became a choppy roar. The King and the Dorig round him looked irritably toward the noise. The Songman holding the jar turned to look, too. His face showed surprise—no, relief—no, welcome! Gair turned to see a crowd of silver warriors forcing a way through the crowd and Banot emerge from it, dripping wet. From the look on the Songman's face, it was clear he knew Banot quite well.

"Gerald!" said Gair. Gerald, on whom the shadow of death still hung, turned and stared as if he were in a dream. Gerald's father followed Banot, like a tall iron bar, and Mr. Claybury came behind, a breathless, sagging pear-shape, trying to put his glasses back on. Then came a large group of Garholt hunters, with Adara, Ayna and Hafny, to Gair's surprise, in their midst. Hafny, because he had no hood, looked as draggled as anyone there, and as worried as Adara. Ayna, who looked much more like Adara wet, seemed to be looking after Hafny. And Ceri suddenly appeared, looking like Adara, too, with his hair straight and dripping, trying to make a purple, puffing, miserable Brenda breathe steadily and deeply.

Last of all came Gest, with his hair and beard flattened and darkened by water, looking stranger to Gair than anyone. The Songman glanced quickly from Gair to Gest, as if he was comparing them, and Gair thought he knew Gest, too. And it was clear from the expression on the King's face that he knew Gest also and was not at all sure what to do about it.

Banot stood in front of the King and bowed. Then he spoke, loudly and formally, in a way Gair had hitherto thought people only spoke in stories. "The People of the Sun have come, with two Chiefs of the People of the Earth, to have speech with the People of the Moon."

The King looked a trifle irritated, but also slightly amused, as if he, too, had last heard this kind of thing in a story. But he gave the proper answer. "The People of the Moon greet the People of the Sun and the Chiefs of the People of the Earth, and ask what they would say."

Banot said, "Their first head concerns the sacrifice of the sons of two Chiefs of these Peoples, and touches on the return of the son of the King of the People of the Moon, delivered to them in exchange—"

"What?" said the King. "Who—?"

But Banot, who was clearly in his element, continued briskly, "Their second head concerns the filling of the Moor with water, and touches on a prophecy spoken by the daughter of the Chief of Garholt, one known to have the Gift of Sight. And their third head concerns the wars between the People of the Moon and the People of the Sun, wherein the Chiefs of the People of the Earth have offered themselves arbiters." This sounded splendid. Gerald took his hand away from his mouth, and the shadow of death seemed to recede from him. Perhaps he would not have felt so hopeful had he known what a very hasty conference Banot had had with the rest, or just how few plans they had made. "Will the King speak on these heads?" said Banot.

The King looked at Banot and shrugged, Dorig fashion. His brown eyes searched the dripping crowd until they came to Hafny, between Ayna and Adara. He seemed relieved to find him. "How did you get hold of him?" he said.

Brenda cleared the last of the dike-water from her throat and said, "That was me. Halla gave him to me, and I gave him to them."

There was a hissing groan of amazement from the assembled Dorig. The King levered himself round on the young Songman's supporting shoulder to look up at the gallery. Halla's voice rang down from it. "I *didn't*! I—You—!"

"Yes, you did," Hafny called up at her. "You know you did."

The King levered himself back, cold and angry. "You," he said to Gest. "You had no business to take him prisoner!"

"I didn't," said Gest. "I gave him back to your people in Garholt. Ask your Captain here. And come to that, you had no business to take Adara prisoner, and you've certainly no business to be sacrificing my son." He pointed to Gair, standing shorn and damp among the silvery guards.

It was quite clear that every Dorig except the chief Songman had not known who Gair was. The King was astounded. He looked from Gest to Gair several times to convince himself it was true, and so did the Dorig around him, and the guards. From their expressions, Gair gathered that he with his hair shorn and Gest with his hair wet and dark must be far more alike than he had known. Maybe that was why Gest had looked so strange to him.

"Then you lied to me," the King said to Gair. "You told me your father gave this collar to the Giants."

"I thought he did," said Gair.

"And so I did," said Gest.

The King seemed unable to credit it. "The collar," he said, "belonged to Orban of Otmound, who killed my brother for it. How did you get hold of it? Were you trying to raise the curse?"

Gest shook his wet head. "I never learned how to raise a curse. I'm no Chanter. The fact was, I needed a collar in a hurry, and when Orban's wife gave me that one, I took it for yours. I don't know how Gair knew, but he certainly wasn't lying."

"Then I'm sorry," the King said regretfully, "that I didn't know this before the hair was burned. Your son looks so unlike your other two children that I thought he must be Orban's son."

Gair was appalled to think he had been mistaken for

Ondo. He did not think he had deserved that, however foolish he had been. He was not the only one. Ceri uttered an indignant squeak, and Ayna met Gair's eye, fulminating. Gest almost shouted with rage. *"Orban's son!* That cowardly lump with sheep's ears! You look at a promising lad like Gair, and you take him for Orban's! Well, look at him again, and I'll tell you he has more worth in his little finger than all the boys in Garholt together. He's already famous for his wisdom. If you doubt his courage, think of the way he and the Giant came here alone. And he has the Gift of Sight Unasked."

Gair thought he had never been so surprised, or so pleased, in his life. He knew Gest was speaking for effect. He knew the effect had been made. Every Dorig near avoided looking at Gair, and the King contrived to put the Songman he was leaning on between himself and Gair, so there was no chance of his seeing him. But Gair knew Gest. He would not have said such things unless he meant them. And he could see his father was truly proud of him. It was in the set of his head and the tones of his voice. Maybe Gest never would understand Gair, but that did not prevent him thinking Gair remarkable. Gair's heart ached. His Gift told him, cold and clear, that he was still bound to be a sacrifice, and the way the King had blocked him from sight confirmed it. And Gair had never thought life so well worth living. It seemed so cruel that Gest should go on trying to save him.

Gest dropped his anger and spoke to the King almost cajolingly, almost as Ceri might. "There was a time," he said, "when I took the old road to Otmound with a Chanter who was my friend, and we fell in with three Songmen and a fire-eating Prince, who were lying in wait for people from Otmound. I remember that there was a certain amount of fighting, until the Chanter and one of the Songmen, who were neither of them anxious to see their leader killed, both struck up a tune on their harps. It happened to be the same tune, and both claimed that it was the custom to fight to music. Whereupon, those who were fighting had to leave off to laugh, and after that, it did not seem worth starting again, so the Chanter and I went on to Otmound. It was no doubt the Chanter's own affair if, when he came back later on his own, he spent the day playing and singing by the road-side with the Prince and his Songmen. But it was more than that when I came in great need the day after and found only the Prince awake. I told him I had to have a gold collar from the neck of a Dorig. And he may have been a little sarcastic about my reason, but he agreed to change collars willingly enough. He knew as well as I did what it meant. I've not forgotten. Nor can you have done. I can see my collar on you from here, Hathil."

A gasp went round the crowded hall when Gest used the King's name. The King shrugged, half amused, half embarrassed, rather as Mr. Masterfield had been when Mr. Claybury told his story. "But," he said, "I didn't unhood to you, Gest. And I didn't say words on my collar."

"I know. You thought the collar was going to Og. I don't blame you," said Gest. "But I said words on my collar, and you wear it. And you seem to be unhood to me now, whether you like it or not. If that means anything, you've no business to kill Gair, any more than I had to hurt Hafny. And I'm told Gair changed collars with the Giant beside him, which puts him under our protection, too."

There was a pause. Gest watched the King intently. He had now done everything he could, including throwing Gair on the King's mercy by telling him his name. But it seemed it was not enough. The King's shoulders humped unhappily. "I told you," he said. "Their hair has been burned. The Powers have accepted the sacrifice. Look." He pointed to the collar, with its blackened outlines. Gest looked at it and then, helplessly, at Adara. "There really is nothing I can do," said Hathil, and it was clear he meant it.

Before Gest could say any more, Banot stepped forward again. "Let us now leave this first matter and pass to our second," he said. "This concerns the flooding of the Moor, and to speak on this comes this Chief of the People of the Earth." He beckoned Mr. Claybury forward.

At this sudden change of subject, Gerald's mouth began twitching again. "Are they going to let us go, or not?" he whispered to Gair. Brenda was whispering much the same to Ceri, and Mr. Masterfield to Med.

Gair trusted Banot. He knew what he was doing. He thought that there was every chance Banot would get Gerald off—though he knew there was no hope for himself. "You'll be all right," he whispered. "Banot's the cleverest Chanter on the Moor."

"If you ask me, he's just enjoying himself," Gerald whispered back.

Banot was not the only one. Mr. Claybury, in spite of being soaked to the skin, with useless sweat clustering on his bald patch, bustled forward as happily as Banot and made a speech. Though he spoke mainly to the King, he turned his face amiably round the hall from time to time, to make it clear he was talking to everyone there. When Gair caught up with what he was saying, he recognized the same speech Mr. Claybury had made the night before.

". . . over Southern England with a fine-tooth comb," he heard Mr. Claybury say, "and the Moor was the only place which seemed to fulfill all our requirements. Now we come to you people." Mr. Claybury's glasses twinkled round the assembled Dorig. "I gather that, for you, water is somewhere safe to live. Am I right to assume you intend to build living-halls on the floor of the Moor, once it is in use as a reservoir?"

"You are," said the King.

"Then we seem to have the same interests," said Mr. Claybury. "Though, just in passing, I do wonder how you got to know of our plans—"

He was interrupted by a wave of amusement. Every Dorig there shared it, even Hafny. Mr. Claybury's eyebrows went up, questioningly. "We find it pays to keep an eye on you Giants," the chief Songman explained. "We watched your people measure and listened to them talk."

"The advantage of being shape-shifters," added the King.

"Oh, I see," said Mr. Claybury. "Silly of me—though it's a thing I find it hard to get used to. Anyway, you'll build these halls, even though it's going to take a lot of hard work?"

"We shall have to," said one of the white-haired Dorig behind the King. "We have no room here at all now."

"I saw that, as we came," said Mr. Claybury. "You have my hearty sympathy. I've seldom seen such shocking over-crowding. But suppose I were to offer you another solution? Would you be interested?"

"Perhaps," the King said cautiously. But, though he took care not to sound very interested, there were mutters of "Yes!" from behind him, and eager whispering all over the hall.

"Good. Well, with this in mind," said Mr. Claybury, "I've been talking to this lad over here — Ceri, isn't it? — who seems to be a kind of water-diviner."

"It's called Finding Sight," said Ceri. Gerald and Gair looked at one another, exasperated to think that neither of them had thought of asking Ceri.

"Quite," said Mr. Claybury. "Now he tells me there *is* water, in quite the quantities we need, somewhere — from his description — in the area we call the Berkshire Downs. So then I had a chat with this other lad — Hafny, is that right? — and *he* seems to think that this water is probably filling a place where large numbers of you used to live. The Halls of the Kings, he called it. Do I carry you with me?"

He did. The King, and all those round him, began to talk eagerly. "Yes, but the rock faulted." "It's too deep for our pumps." "We couldn't break through the crust overhead." "The locks were useless. Water came pouring through them."

Mr. Claybury held up his hand. "Just a moment. May I remind you that we — er — People of the Earth have pumps which are possibly more powerful than yours. We need water. You need somewhere to live. So, if you could tell me the exact location of your Halls of the Kings, my office will set about investigating them immediately."

The King looked dubious. "But suppose your pumps

do no better than ours?"

Mr. Claybury chuckled. "Now this young lady doesn't seem to think so. She really seems to be able to see into the future. Why don't you ask her for yourself?" He beckoned to Ayna. "Come over here, my dear."

Ayna came as far as the star-shaped hole where the collar lay. There she shook her wet hair back and told the King daringly, "You have to ask me the right question."

"I realize," said Hathil and, not at all offended, he considered what to ask. Ayna, looking up into his narrow Dorig face, realized that here was someone who actually understood about Sight—though whether this was because Dorig had it, too, or because the King had a subtle mind, she did not know. She waited confidently, until Hathil said, "Will the People of the Earth have pumped the water from the Halls of the Kings a year from now?"

"No," said Ayna. There was a murmur of disappointment.

"In three years, then?" said the King.

"In three years," said Ayna, "the small hall at the top will be empty."

"In ten?" said the King.

"In ten years, the New Halls will be dry," said Ayna.

"And in twenty?"

"The same."

"You see?" said Mr. Claybury. "To judge from the size of the halls here, that makes an awful lot of water. We wouldn't need the Moor at all."

"Am I supposed to rejoice?" said the King. "The New Halls are rather smaller than these. To have them dry in ten years won't help us much."

"You mean you won't tell me where they are?" said Mr. Claybury. "Well, I daresay we can find them for ourselves."

"Oh, I'll tell you," said the King. He gestured to Ayna. "It's certain you'll find them anyway, and we've no quarrel with Giants. But the People of the Sun must leave the Moor whether you flood it or not. We need it to live in, and we are the elder people."

Before Mr. Claybury could reply, Banot was forward again, and Gest with him. "So we come to our third head," said Banot, "which is the wars between the Peoples of the Sun and the Moon. And herein I must begin, since I know somewhat of the customs of both. The nature that lies at the heart of the ways of the People of the Sun is that they are a warlike people, but they do not shed blood except for a reason. The nature of the People of the Moon is different: they shed blood freely, but they are at heart a gentle people, given to peace. Is this not true?"

All the Dorig in the hall seemed, to Gair's surprise, to be pleased with this description of themselves. There was a murmur of approval from the crowd and the gallery. Those round the King nodded, pleased that Banot understood. Gair thought of Halla, unfeelingly ready to pull him underwater when she got the chance, and of Hafny doing no more than trying to frighten himself and Ceri away where one of Gair's own people would have fought lustily. And he saw Banot was right. The queer cruelty of the Dorig was due to the fact that they preferred not to fight. The only Dorig who did not seem to agree with Banot was the King himself.

Gest laughed at the expression on the King's face. "That won't do for Hathil," he said. "He was born a fire-eater among the wrong people. And even he would rather use cunning than violence. Now see, Hathil, you've made a proper tangle over Garholt. You may have waited until I was out of it, but you had no business to attack it at all. You swore not to hurt Adara. You can't fight me. And you know I can't fight you. But you killed a number of my people and you hunted my children through the Moor. Why?"

From Banot's expression, he was afraid Gest's forth-rightness would make the King angry. Hathil did indeed look at Gest haughtily, but the pale Dorig flush came into his face at the same time. Banot relaxed when he saw it. Gair looked from him and Gest to the King's face and had a sudden vision of Hathil as a stag, hunted this way, pushed that, running in bewilderment to the one spot from which he could not escape. It seemed an unlikely idea, when the hall was crowded with Dorig and the King had only to snap his fingers to put an end to the hunt for good and all. But Gair knew he had seen correctly. His people were huntsmen and they hunted in crowds. Dorig were like deer, and they ran when they could. Banot and Gest were both brave men and they knew what they were doing. With Ayna, Ceri and the rest of the Garholters to back them up, they had coolly separated Hathil from the rest of the herd and were busy running him down. Gair wondered if this was the way his people had first driven the Dorig underwater.

"It was a trick, if you like," the King confessed. "I had to have the words off your wells, and I wanted to persuade you to leave the Moor. I was going to use your children as hostages and give Orban's son to the Powers. After all, my brother was only a child when Orban killed him."

"So was Orban," said Gest remorselessly. "And it seems to me that your brother has revenged himself amply over the years, both on us and on the Giants, who never harmed him. We came to talk peace, Hathil."

The King made an effort to run in a different direction. "Then you'll leave the Moor peacefully, maybe?" he said.

Banot's answer to this was to beckon Mr. Masterfield forward. "I doubt if they could leave the Moor and be safe from my people," Mr. Masterfield said.

It was as if he had stood, tall and grim, blocking the King's escape. Giants knew all about hunting, too, Gair saw. And Mr. Claybury had joined in the hunt earlier and genially helped divide the King from the herd. Gair, out hunting, had often felt a queer sympathy for the animal they hounded—it was supposed to be good to feel it: it helped you know where the creature would turn next—and he felt it so strongly now for the King that he almost cheered when Hathil showed that he understood what was going on, though being a Dorig he put it in different terms.

"I'm not a fool," he said. "Banot's playing a tune here with living strings, and now he brings in his low note. Have you come to tell me this collar's yours? Or did you know your son shot me in the leg yesterday?"

For a moment it looked as if the hunt was diverted. Mr. Masterfield turned and glared at Gerald. Gerald swallowed.

"He did quite right!" Brenda put in shrilly. "You ought to be ashamed of yourself, Mr. King! There were nine of you, all bigger than I am, all on to those three kids. They had to ask us for help. And Gerald only shot him because he kept on coming after them. He warned them. But they didn't listen."

Mr. Masterfield looked at Gerald, and Gerald nodded, very red in the face. "Well done, then," said Mr.

Masterfield. To Gair, this seemed very cool praise, but Gerald seemed to take it as the warmest congratulation. Mr. Masterfield turned to the King. "I'll pay you any compensation you ask, sir," he said.

The Songman the King was leaning on said warningly, "Our customs put it very high."

"As high as providing you with somewhere else to live?" Mr. Masterfield asked. "Until the Halls of the Kings are fit to live in again?"

The hall was immediately agog with interest. It hummed. The King looked round it as if he felt his own people had now joined in to hunt him, too. "Where?" he said.

"I still own a good deal of the land round here," said Mr. Masterfield. "By our law, that means under the ground as well. Now Banot and Gest tell me that there are quite a string of empty mounds on my land. I could agree to let you live there and make sure that no one disturbs you."

The King shrugged. "Very handsome. But I never heard of any empty mounds."

"There are hundreds," said Gest, and this surprised not only the Dorig, but a number of Garholters, too. Gest explained, "Most of the hills round the Moor are hollow— Banot and I explored some as children. Our people used to live in them, long ago, when there were more of us. They're all locked with words, but I can easily open any number you want."

The hall filled with wistful mutterings. "What would the rest of your Chiefs say to that?" the King asked. "Could you answer for Islaw and Beckhill?"

"Yes," said Gest. "All of them."

The King dashed for the last path to freedom. "Even Otmound?" he said incredulously.

"Even Otmound," answered Gest. "It'll be a pleasure. But we must agree to live and let live. You answer for your people, I'll answer for mine, and the People of the Earth will see that peace is kept."

"But not if you're going to slaughter Gerald," Mr. Masterfield said. "I might remind you that these halls are technically on my property and a number of my people would welcome the chance to explore them."

"Very true," said Mr. Claybury. "If you're still thinking of making this sacrifice, remember that if the Moor becomes a reservoir—though I only say *if*, mind you—I shall probably be obliged to make life pretty unpleasant for you and your people. I'm not making threats—I wouldn't dream of doing that—"

"Nor am I," Mr. Masterfield said jovially. "But I do go out with a gun a good deal."

That was it, Gair thought. The King had been driven to a corner from which he could not escape, because his own people would not let him. The Dorig wanted to live in those empty mounds. He was not surprised that Hathil looked so bitterly at the two Giants. "Spoken like true Giants," he said. "You don't threaten. You only show your strength. You were the most fitting owners that collar could have had."

"Hathil," said Gest, "I'm not making threats. I could say I wouldn't open those mounds, but I shall say the words because your people need them. All I'm doing is asking you to let Gair go."

Gair knew it was hopeless even before the King spoke or the Songmen looked his way. "I'm sorry," said the King. "Those two are as good as dead already. You should have come before the Powers accepted the sacrifice. If I agree to peace and let them go, the Powers will double the curse and make nonsense of anything we agreed."

Everyone looked at the collar lying in the star-shaped hole, black-edged and with such an air of corruption about it that Gair was not the only one who looked away. Mr. Claybury took his glasses off and polished them, so that he need not look. Hafny went ashy white and Gerald shivered. But Banot went on looking at it thoughtfully, long after everyone else had looked away.

"So we come back to our first head," he said. "And I have three things to say. A curse obeys the same laws as everything else. It contains the seeds of its own decay. When I look at this collar, it seems to me that it might be working to its own destruction as fast as it works to destroy its possessors. It seems to me that it did work against itself when the stone was lifted from the Haunted Mound. Because the Old Power was appeased by that, wasn't it? Might not the other two be satisfied with less than a life apiece? Could you try if they would accept a drop of blood instead?"

All the Songmen shook their heads. The chief Songman said, "No, Banot. This was a very strong dying curse. Nobody dare fob the Powers off, not once it turned black like that."

"When did it turn black?" asked Banot.

"About an hour after the hair was burned," said the Songman.

"Then may I speak?" said Adara, and she came up beside the star-shaped hole. Gair felt proud at the way the Dorig looked at her, respectfully, because of her wisdom. "I've studied to learn about the Powers for many years," she said. "And in the last few years, I have found out a little. You must stop me if I'm wrong, Songmen, but it seems to me now that, just as the Powers of the Moon, the Sun and the Earth lie behind the three people met here in these halls, so the Three Powers lie behind that again." Adara looked to see if any of the Songmen thought she was wrong, but they said nothing, so she went on. "The Old Power lies behind the Moon and is the Power of death, darkness and secrets. To it belong sufferings and old wrongs, and for that reason the moving of the stone from an old grave of murdered men appeased it, though it was still joined in the curse. Had it been loosed from the curse entirely, the collar would have turned black a little as you see it now. By what you say, I am sure that it has now been loosed from the curse, but not by the burning of hair. I think Hafny loosed it, when he put himself in our hands and might have been killed with a hunting-spear."

"Put himself in your hands?" said the King. "I thought Halla gave him to you."

Adara looked at Hafny and gave a little chuckle. Hafny was very embarrassed and made gestures to her not to say any more. "No, why?" said Adara. "It was a very clever trick, and a brave one. What is it called— *morgery*?"

The King seemed unable to help laughing. *"Morgery? Hafny—never!"*

"Halla believed me," Hafny said uncomfortably, but he was clearly glad his father was amused and not angry.

"Now the Middle Power," said Adara, serious again, "lies behind the Sun, and so it is the Power I understand best. It is a fierce Power, of light and life and the Present time. And that is the Power which asks most for blood, as all living things need to feed. But it is not unappeasable. It is Life, and I do not think it asks for death. As to the New Power, which lies behind the Earth, that is the most mysterious. I know it is the Power of birth, growth and Future time, and I think the nature of the sacrifice it asks might be different from the others."

"New things spring from the decay of life," the chief Songman said. "It asks life."

"Allow me, dear lady," said Mr. Claybury, putting his glasses on again and seeming rather happier. "As a representative of the—the People of the Earth, I think I understand this so-called New Power a little. Believe me, Your Majesty, it may be a very vigorous Power, but it is also a gentler one than you might think. It could well ask for life renewed, as it were."

Hathil looked from him to Adara. "The two of you are just twisting words," he said. "I thought only Lymen did that."

"Don't you understand?" asked Adara.

"I do!" Hathil said bitterly. So did Gair. It was truly the kill. The stag had been driven into a position from which it could not escape and now the huntsmen gathered round with spears. Gair was ashamed that Adara should be chief among them. For it was clear that the only thing they had left for Hathil to do was to take the curse upon himself—and through himself, on the rest of the Dorig. And that was neither fair nor right. The Dorig had injured his people, but the injuries had been on both sides. Now Gair knew why his Gift had been telling him so clearly that he would be a sacrifice.

He knew he had to stop the hunt.

He did not give himself time to think how much pleasanter it would be to go on living. He suspected he would have endless seconds to do that anyway. He slipped free from the guards and went to the edge of the star-shaped hole. "If the Powers need a life," he said to Hathil, "will you take mine?"

Gair tried not to look at Adara's face, nor to listen to the gasps and mutters around. But the gasps became a sort of groan. Gair looked into the hole at his feet and saw the collar blackening further, shriveling and crumbling. Under his eyes, the intricate patterns fell to earth, until only a thin gold line was left, where three words joined together two bright owls' heads. For a moment, Gair hoped that last hoop was going to crumble, too. But it did not, and he knew he would have to go through with it.

"Why did you do that?" the King said to him.

Gair looked up at him and wondered how he could express it. But it was too difficult. He shrugged, almost as if he were a Dorig, and made a horseshoe-shaped gesture to show the King that it had worked. The Middle Power was loose now. "My people are hunters," he said lamely. "And I was sorry."

He could see that Hathil understood. The King's brown eyes moved to Gerald, who was white as a sheet and had his hand pressed against his mouth again, and back to Gair standing awkwardly by the star-shaped hole. And for the first time, he looked truly sorry. "This is absurd!" he said. "The Powers can do what they like, but I'm not going to touch either of you!"

And, at his feet, the thin hoop of gold dissolved to earth again, too, writhing like a worm and crumbling away like dark ash. There was nothing left but a horseshoe-shape of darkness.

"That's what I meant," said Mr. Claybury.

As he spoke, Gair felt a wave of happiness flood over him. Everyone felt it. The hall was suddenly full of people laughing, shaking hands and shouting greetings. The King smiled at Gair. Halla leaned from the gallery and waved. Banot and the Songmen raced together and began to talk music, and the other Garholt Chanters very soon joined in. Mr. Claybury kissed Adara's hand. Then he joined Gest and Mr. Masterfield round the King and helped the King stand, while Adara turned to talk to Brenda.

"You do grant wishes, don't you?" Brenda said.

Adara, overflowing as she was with happiness, did not want to disappoint Brenda. But she was forced to shake her head.

"Oh well," said Brenda.

It did not take great gifts of divination to see what wish Brenda had wanted. "Tell me," Adara said kindly. "What do your parents look like?"

"Thin as rakes, both of them," said Brenda. "Why do you think I'm made so fat?"

Adara laughed. Everyone was so happy. "I can promise you, then," she said, "that in a very few years, you'll be thin, too. And very pretty. Would you like me to ask Ayna?"

"No," said Brenda happily. "I'll take your word." And she went bouncing off like a jovial elephant to join Hafny, Gerald, Ceri and Gair. They were in an excited group, jostled by laughing Dorig on all sides. Soon after Brenda joined them, Gair got used to the idea that he was alive after all and began to wonder why this happiness went on and on so. He understood as soon as he looked at Ceri. Ceri's was the only sober face in the hall. Gair turned to him, outraged, to tell him what he thought of people who put Thoughts on their elder brothers. Ceri winked at him and shook his head warningly. And Gair said nothing. After all, it was a very good idea.

Some of the rest of this story was in the Giant newspapers. The Moor is not going to be flooded — or not yet. If you know where to look in Berkshire, you will find Mr. Claybury's pumps and pipes, though nobody but he suspects that they are pumping the water from the Halls of the Kings. Meanwhile, the empty mounds on the Moor are opened and more Dorig move into them daily. All the Chiefs agreed to it, except Orban. Orban could not abide Dorig near. And Kasta quacked so unendingly about Ondo growing up under their influence, that, in the end, Orban brought himself to move his entire people, sheep, gold and all, out of Otmound and away from the Moor altogether. It is called flitting, and it had not been done for centuries. As Adara said sourly—it was almost the sourest thing Gair ever heard her say—if Orban and Kasta could not become famous any other way, at least they were famous for going away.

Gair is famous. He is known throughout the Moor for his magnificent triple collar, of the finest Dorig work. The words in it are Wisdom, Sight and Courage. But Giants who visit the Moor are unlikely to see him, or Dorig either. And I do not advise anyone to try. Mr. Masterfield would warn you off for trespassing—it is part of his agreement with the Dorig—and if you did happen to stumble across Garholt, the bees would give you a very unpleasant time.